Novels by Richard Helms

Geary's Year
Geary's Gold
The Valentine Profile
The Amadeus Legacy
Joker Poker
Voodoo That You Do
Juicy Watusi
Wet Debt
Naked Came the Flamingo (contributor)
Paid In Spades
Bobby J.
Grass Sandal
Cordite Wine
The Daedalus Deception
The Unresolved Seventh
The Mojito Coast
Six Mile Creek
Thunder Moon
Older Than Goodbye
Brittle Karma
Doctor Hate
A Kind and Savage Place
Vicar Brekonridge

RICHARD HELMS

PAPER WALLS/ GLASS HOUSES

The Award-Winning and Award-Nominated Short Mystery Fiction of Richard Helms

BLACK ARCH BOOKS

BLACK ARCH BOOKS

an imprint of

Barbadoes Hall Communications

Paper Walls/Glass Houses first published in *The Back Alley Webzine*, April 2007.
The Gospel According to Gordon Black first published at *The Thrilling Detective Website*, May 2007.
Silicon Kings first published in *The Back Alley Webzine*, October 2010.
The Gods for Vengeance Cry first published in *Ellery Queen Mystery Magazine*, November 2010.
Busting Red Heads first published in *Ellery Queen Mystery Magazine*, March/April 2014.
Shooting Stars first published in *Ellery Queen Mystery Magazine*, September/October 2015.
The King of Gonna first published in Ellery Queen Mystery Magazine, May/June 2018
See Humble and Die first published in **The Eyes of Texas**, Down and Out Books 2019
The Cripplegate Apprehension first published in *Ellery Queen Mystery Magazine*, July/August 2019
Sweeps Week first published in *Ellery Queen Mystery Magazine*, July/August 2021

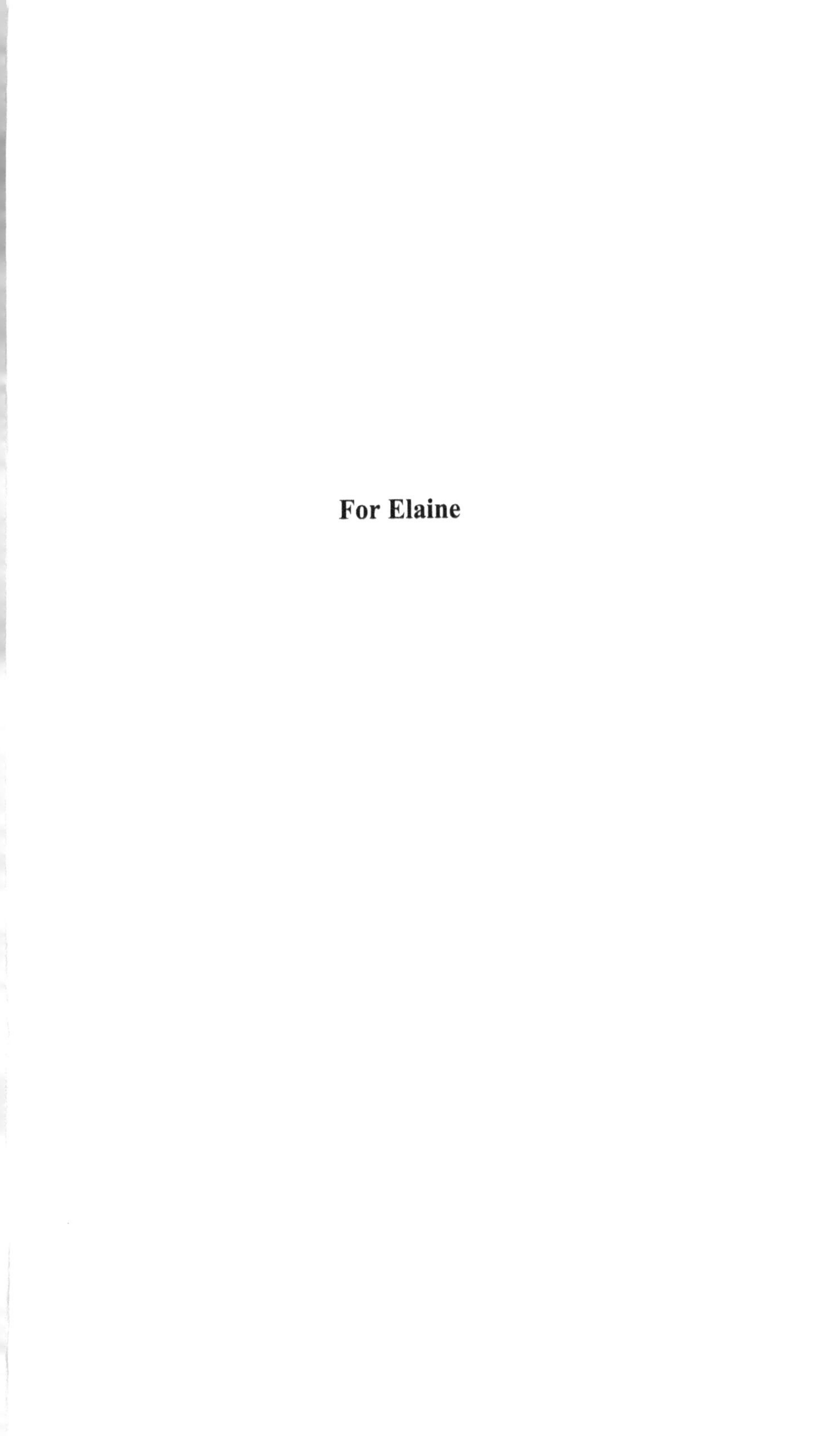

For Elaine

PAPER WALLS/GLASS HOUSES

by

Richard Helms (writing as Eric Shane)

Author's Note: This is the only short story ever published under my pseudonym Eric Shane. I established The Back Alley Webzine *in the spring of 2007. In the first issue, a writer did not return their edited story in time for publication, which left an empty slot in the webzine and no story to plug into it. I had this story lying around in my files, having recently finished it, and had nowhere to send it, so I just changed the byline to Eric Shane and published it in the first issue. It went on to win the SMFS Derringer Award for Best Novelette in 2008.*

R

I was bucks up. A script that had taken me two long weekends to write had been sold to an obscure production company in the San Fernando Valley for an obscene amount of money.

I knew exactly how to celebrate.

I dropped by a liquor store on Figueroa, grabbed a couple of bottles of Cuervo Gold and a bottle of margarita mixer, and headed over to a cheap chain motel on the beach north of Zuma.

As soon as I checked into the room, I dropped the bottles on the dresser, made a quick trip to the ice machine, and settled in for an extended pseudo-Mexican vacation.

I dialed a Spanish language channel on the television, dumped a handful of ice into a twenty-cent hotel glass, filled it halfway up with Cuervo, and the rest of the way with the mixer.

About fifteen seconds later, I did it again.

It took me right at two minutes to go through three glasses. I liked to call this 'laying the base', the way a ski resort puts down ten or twenty inches of powder before freezing the place up for the winter suckers. I had gone from zero to zonked in no time flat, and my only task now consisted of keeping the buzz alive.

I can assure you—at this I was very well-practiced.

I probably could have gone on my bender at home, but my mother had always drilled into me the axiom that you don't shit in your own nest.

I sipped the afternoon away, watched an old John Barrymore movie on TCM, and then a *Magnum PI* episode that was almost—but not quite—the worst piece of writing I had ever encountered. By then it was getting dark outside. I called a local delivery joint to have a pizza sent over.

The pizza wasn't half bad; or maybe I was just incapable of telling the difference anymore. In any case, I snarfed that bad boy down and assembled another drink.

That was pretty much the way the evening went.

I woke around one in the morning. Ten years earlier, I probably would have yanked myself out of bed and rushed to the bathroom to bury my dinner at sea. That was all in the past, though. I had developed a tolerance for the fruit of the agave that made me as impervious to its devils as Superman was to bullets. When I awakened, I felt only a dull buzzing ache at the base of my skull. I knew that I could send it packing with just a sip of Jose, but I didn't want to spoil my breakfast.

I was in a corner unit, on the fourth floor. I had splurged for the ocean-view room, even though I had no intention of spending much time staring at the sea. I sometimes liked to crack my window and listen to it, though, and I liked the salt air. It tasted like the rim of a perfectly blended margarita.

I lay in bed, listening to the beating of my forty-year-old heart, and tried to recall a time when I hadn't been cynical or jaded.

I heard a sound behind my headboard. Then came a slam as the door to the room next to mine shut with a thud. I heard locks click and a deadbolt thrown. There was the soft murmuring of voices, quiet at first, and then louder as I began to focus on them.

"Will this do?" he said.

"That's enough. Put it on the dresser," she replied.

"What now?"

"What do you think, lover?"

There was a second of silence.

"I want to turn the lights out," he said.

"On, off. Whatever trips your trigger honey."

I heard a click, and the sliver of light that crept under the connecting door to our rooms disappeared.

"What do I call you?" he asked.

"Make it easy for yourself. Call me whatever you like."

"Can I call you Esther?"

"What the hell kind of name is that?"

"It's what I want to call you."

"Your nickel, man. Lie on the bed. Esther's about to do a number on you."

I heard the rustle of sheets, a creak of worn bed springs. Then, a low moan. An expletive.

"May I touch you there?"

"You bought the whole package, sweetheart. It's all yours. It's all good. You like this?"

He moaned again. I heard the box springs protest. I became vaguely aware of my own excitement.

"What's this?" he asked.

"What do you think it is?"

"I've never… I mean, I've never worn one before."

"You start payin' for it, you better get used to wearin' one."

"How do you…"

"Hold on. Let me do it for you. I got a special way of puttin' it on."

He moaned again.

"Would you be on top?" he asked.

"Top, bottom, on the floor, in the chair, on the ceiling, it's all the same to me. Here I come."

There was a frantic creaking of the springs, and a chorus of groans, gasps, and overtures to the Almighty. It was poignant and brief. Mercifully, I heard the man almost yelp in what sounded like unexpected pleasure, and then I thought I heard a sob.

"You okay, man?" she asked.

"I'm fine. It's been… a long time."

"You feel good?"

"Yes."

"Your Esther, she did you all right?"

"You were fine."

"I'm so happy to hear it. Tell your friends. Listen, baby, I got to jet…"

"Already?"

"It's late. You're the end of my night, sweetness. Momma got to call herself a cab."

"How much…" he started to ask.

"What?"

"Could you… stay?"

"Oh, hell, man, that's gonna cost you. I got places to be."

"I can afford it. It's been such a long time since I … slept next to a woman."

"Shit. You are hard up, you know that?"

"Yes."

He sounded pitiful in a way I had never heard from anyone but a scolded child.

"How much?"

She told him.

"Yes," he said. "I can do that."

"Roll over, sugar."

I heard the springs creak again. Minutes later, all I heard was snoring.

I awoke at eight with the reflected sunlight from the Pacific streaming in my window like scalpels aimed at my retinas. I pulled the covers over my head and resolved to sleep for another hour before venturing down to the Denny's in the lobby for a Grand Slam and a Bloody Mary.

There was a thump next door.

"I left the shower running," she said.

I realized she really had stayed the entire night.

"Did you use all the shampoo?" he asked.

"I left a little. The little bottle of mouthwash wouldn't hurt you much either."

"Bitch."

"Bastard."

"I love it when you talk tough."

I heard him roll off the bed and hit the floor. Seconds later, I heard her on the telephone.

"Hi. Any messages for me… Yes. Give me the number. I'll call him from here… How did the kids do? Did Jeffrey give you any trouble going to bed?… Mother, if you let him watch one extra show, he'll stay up all night… Okay…Yes, we should be home by middle afternoon…Thanks again…Love you too…'Bye."

I heard a metallic creak as the faucet in the bathroom was shut off, and I heard a man humming.

"I hate hotel soap," he said, moments later.

"Beats bringing your own."

"Did you call your mom?"

"Yes. Jeffrey talked her into letting him stay up until almost midnight to watch a movie on HBO."

"The little con man."

"What time is checkout?"

"Eleven."

"We have time for breakfast? It's a six-hour drive back to San Francisco."

"We could stop somewhere on the way."

"No. Let's go ahead and eat here."

"Let me get dressed."

"Wait."

They didn't say anything for a few seconds.

"Damn," he said. "That's good."

"A little reward for playing along last night."

"Did you get turned on?"

"Couldn't you tell? I haven't been that wet since before the baby."

"How would I know? You made me wear that damn…"

"You loved it. Admit it."

"We must do this again. Soon."

"Get dressed. I'm hungry, and we have to get on the road. We promised to take Jeffrey to that new Disney flick tonight."

They didn't say anything else, until I heard the door to the next room open and close.

I thought I heard them giggling on the way down the hall.

I lay back in bed and thought for a while about how strange people can be.

———

"So they were playing a game!" my agent said.

"Yeah," I told him. "You see, this couple likes to take it on the road once in a while, and pretend like they aren't married. He picks her up in a bar, they go to a motel, she plays the pro and he pretends to be this helpless Sad Sack. Somehow, it gets their rocks off."

"Recharges their marriage."

"Beats wife-swapping, I guess."

"You've never met my wife," he said. "This is great. Not like your usual stuff. Don't get me wrong, you're a fine writer, but this is special. I think I can peddle it to one of the glossies."

"No shit?"

"What could it hurt to try? I don't suppose you have any more of this arty shit bouncing around inside that head of yours?"

"I'll see what I can do."

———

He sold the story to a major magazine, for more money per word than I'd seen outside of screenplays in my entire life.

I started hanging at the Zuma Beach motel more often. My liver took a beating, but the stories that floated through the wall behind my bed kept me from complaining.

Somehow, despite the fact that I was – more or less – the poster boy for wasted life, I discovered that the motel room next to mine was a sort of Pathos Central. It was like a Harry Chapin song come to life, each night more heart-wrenching than the last, and I sat in bed with my laptop and took down every word.

There was the guy who checked in, climbed on the telephone, and racked up a week's pay calling phone sex lines while he abused himself into a lather, and then spent the rest of the night whimpering and telling some absent specter how ashamed he was and how he would never do it again.

I sold that one to *The Cimarron Review*, and bought myself a used Miata with the proceeds.

Then there was the threesome who visited the room once every several weeks – two guys and a woman. I figured out after a while that the guys were the couple, and the woman their guest. Apparently it was a concession they'd made to satisfy one of the guys' occasional butch curiosity. He would test the bed springs with the woman, while the other guy would sit in a chair across the room and direct, like he was shooting a movie. For all I knew, maybe he was.

My agent passed that story along to *Mandate*, and I got my house painted.

One night a group of bikers rented the room, and ran a meth supermarket throughout the evening. Every ten minutes or so I'd hear a knock at the door, another guy ready to hand over a slice of his soul to get his weekend load on. Around two in the morning, they had to deal with a dissatisfied customer, and the whole scene nearly erupted in gunfire, while I cringed on the floor behind my bed waiting for the bullets to fly.

In my story, they actually shifted up into the heavy metal rock and roll, automatic weapons and everything, and *High Times* lapped it up like mother's milk.

All in all, my occasional lost weekend in the corner unit off Zuma had turned into something of a cash cow. My agent thought I was the second coming of Ernest Hemingway and John Steinbeck rolled into one. I found myself actually drinking less and listening more.

I was nominated for a couple of the lesser-known literary prizes.

Life was good.

I was sitting on the motel bed, nursing a Cuervo and limeade, watching an old Bogie flick on the tube, when I heard the rasp of a key in the lock of the room next door through the air space at the bottom of the connecting door.

The hallway door to the next room opened forcefully enough to bang against the wall. It made me jump a little.

"I hate you!" a woman shouted. I could hear her heels click on the tile near the door, and then the sound disappeared as she hit the carpet. She had a thick Spanish accent.

"Not so loud," a man said. "You'll wake the whole place."

"I don't care," she said. I could hear the pout in her voice. "You insulted me."

"How?"

"You talked about your wife."

I already had the laptop warmed up and ready to transcribe. This was going to be good.

"I just mentioned her. That's all."

"You should never talk about that bitch when you are with me."

"I'm sorry. I was thoughtless. What can I do to make it up to you?"

"Come here."

I thought I heard the comforter yanked forcefully from the bed. Then I heard a long, slow zipper. I figured that was the woman, or else the man was seventeen feet tall.

"Oh…my…God," the man said.

"You will make it up to me," she said. "You will be better than you have ever been."

I think he said something at that point, but the words were muffled by flesh. After a few seconds, the woman began to whimper a little, and then came the moans.

"Oh baby oh baby oh baby oh baby, just like that," she said between gasps. He said something, but I couldn't catch it. I left a space for something clever on my screen, and kept typing.

"Stop!" she commanded.

"What?"

"You are always in too much of a hurry. You need to take your time."

"All right."

"Roll over."

This woman loved to take the reins. She was commanding the guy like she was a drill sergeant.

"Oh," he said, some surprise in his voice. "You've…never done that before."

"A special treat for you, my love."

It went on like that for a while, and then came the rhythmic thumping of the headboard against the drywall, which I could feel all the way into my room.

"Oh, *jess*!" she started to wail. "Jus' like that. Ahchi, ahchi, AHCHI, *AHCHI*!"

Now, I'm no Spanish scholar, despite the fact that it's slowly becoming the official language of Southern California, so I'd never heard the word *ahchi* before. For all I knew, there was no such word, and she was just imitating an enraptured chihuahua. There was no mistaking the context, though.

Moments later, the man made a sort of choking noise, chuffed a few times, summoned a couple of deities, and then the room went silent save for a brief period of heavy breathing.

I finished typing, and waited to see if there would be a second act.

They revved up again just after sunrise. It was quicker this time, and only slightly less noisy. Afterward, the man coughed a few times, the way I've seen smokers do after trying to take up jogging, and I heard him pad across the room to the bathroom.

I heard the rasp of the shower faucets, metal on rusted metal. A couple of minutes later, the water shut off.

"You should have left it running," she complained.

He didn't answer. Instead, I heard the faucets turned again, and the water began to beat against the empty shower stall.

Then she was in the shower, humming some obscure Tejano tune I'd heard on the radio, somewhere along the line, but couldn't identify.

She turned off the water, and seconds later returned to the room.

"Bobby," she said, a coquettish lilt in her voice.

"Yes," he said.

"Do you remember what we talked about yesterday?"

"Sure. How could I forget it?"

"When do you thin' you might do it?"

"I don't know. I have to think this out very carefully. We're not talking about boosting an apple from the local grocery here. This is a major crime."

My fingers stopped cold on the keyboard.

I'd heard criminal activity in the next room several times, of course—the biker dealers, for instance, and one weekend when a roving sports book set up shop there.

This sounded different, though.

She pressed on.

"Did you know that there are places in Mexico where you can live like a king for only ten thousand a year?"

"I've heard."

"You can have a house as big as a mansion. On the beach. With servants."

"Yes."

"How much do you thin' the insurance would pay?"

I felt a chill run down my back.

"It's a quarter-million-dollar policy," he said. "With double indemnity, a half million. The house is paid for. I could sell it for another three-quarter million. I'd get the 401k proceeds, of course. That's in her will."

I nearly choked. I couldn't believe what I was hearing.

"How much is this 401k?"

"When she quit working she had maybe another half million in it. All in all, I'd say the estate would be somewhere in the range of two million, once the entire kit and caboodle is liquidated."

"Wha' is this 'kit and caboodle'?"

"It's a saying. Once I sell everything off. It would be a lot of money."

"Woul' they not suspect you?"

"I'm sure they would. They always suspect the husband first. That's why we would have to be so incredibly careful. It would have to look exactly like an accident."

As quietly as possible, I rolled off the bed and slipped into my clothes. All the while, I tried to figure out what I should do next.

In retrospect, I guess I should have called the police. What would I tell them, though? I had no idea who the couple next door was. I'd never actually heard them use the word *murder*, but it wasn't hard to read their intent from the conversation.

I glanced at my laptop, still sitting on top of the bed.

I had a transcript of their conversation, from the moment they walked into the motel room. That had to be useful for something.

"I'm hungry," the woman said. "I want breakfast."

"Me, too," the man said. "Get dressed. We'll take my bag down to the car, and get a bite. Then I have to get you home. I'm due at work at nine-thirty."

I pulled together my belongings, and prepared to leave. Just as I had everything packed, I heard the hallway door in the next room open and slam shut.

I rushed over to my door and peered through the fisheye peephole. Too late. All I could see was their backs as they headed down the hall away from me. He was tall, maybe a little over six feet. She was lithe and athletic. Her hair was ebony and tousled, and fell halfway down her back.

They disappeared from the peephole.

I tried to figure out how to get a better look.

Then I remembered that there was only a single parking lot for the motel, and the side window of my corner room had a great view of it.

I crossed the motel room and gently pulled the drapes away from one edge of the window. After a couple of minutes, I saw the couple cross the shell and asphalt lot to a silver Toyota Avalon. The man opened the trunk lid and dropped a cloth overnight bag inside. After closing the lid, he took the woman's hand, and they turned toward the Denny's next to the motel.

I quickly wrote down the license number of the Avalon.

While they ate in Denny's, I loaded my Miata, and sat in the lot waiting for them to finish. My own stomach rumbled loudly, but I didn't dare run across to the convenience store to grab a quick bite, for fear they'd leave before I could get back to my car. Besides, how would it look if some crazy-eyed guy cut a record hundred-yard dash across the street just as they were pulling out of the lot? The idea here, I reminded myself as my stomach twisted into a half-hitch, was *not* to be noticed.

After a half hour, they walked back to the Avalon. As they pulled out of the lot, I backed from my parking space and fell in behind them. I stayed pretty close for the first mile or so, and then slowly dropped back, allowing four or five other cars to fall in between us.

They drove south on the PCH, until they reached Santa Monica. The man pulled into a side street near Venice Beach, and then into a driveway attached to a squat, pink, slightly disheveled bungalow.

I stopped half a block back, practically out of sight behind a stand of palm trees and waited. The woman stepped out of the car. She blew a kiss to the man, and then walked across the postage stamp yard to the front door. After she was inside the house, the Avalon backed slowly from the driveway, reversed, and drove directly toward me!

I turned off the Miata, and dove across the front seat. The gearshift lever pressed into my abdomen like a dull knife.

I heard the Avalon cruise by, and a slight chirp from the tires as it rounded the next corner.

I knew enough about the neighborhood to realize that he had to either get back on the PCH, or turn right somewhere on down the road, unless he planned to drive right into the ocean. So, I restarted the Miata and drove past the woman's house. I jotted down the address and the name on the mailbox – *Flores* – before turning left at the next cross street and heading out toward Pico. I stopped at the light on Pico just in time to see the Avalon cross the intersection.

It seemed an eternity before the light changed, allowing me to turn right and follow him. As I had before, I kept enough distance between us to remain effectively invisible in the typical heavy Los Angeles morning traffic but stayed close enough to keep him from disappearing himself.

After several miles, he turned left, and pulled into a parking garage near La Brea. I circled the block once or twice, and then also entered the garage.

It took me a few minutes to find the Avalon. I drove up another level, found a compact car space, and parked the Miata. Then I hiked back down the incline to the Avalon.

It had been parked in a section of reserved spaces, designated as belonging to Squire Insurance. Since they were reserved, I played a hunch and walked around to the front of the car, to the concrete stop block designed to keep the car from rolling straight into the wall of the parking deck.

Sure enough, the stop block had been stenciled with the owner's name. Robert Dickman.

Considering what I had overheard the night before, I found the name somehow amusing. I would never use it in my story, though. Nobody would believe it.

I returned to the Miata and considered my next move. I had Bobby's name, and half of his female co-conspirator's name – *Flores*.

I needed more information, though, if only to flesh out the parts of the story I didn't know. I was already outlining a new screenplay in my mind and envisioning a huge sale to Warner Brothers or Paramount, maybe even Columbia Tri-Star.

Oh, and a trip to the police.

I didn't want to forget that detail.

It was a little after nine-thirty. Dickman probably would be holed up in his office for a few hours. I decided to drive back to Venice and dig up a little bit more information on the girl.

Fifteen minutes later, I pulled to the curb about two houses down, and surveyed her house. The neighborhood was quiet. Most of the residents were either at work or at school. I quickly looked around and noted that a Chevy truck parked two houses down from Ms. Flores' house, and across the street, had the rear taillight knocked out, and what looked like baseball bat dents in the rear quarter panel. An idea occurred to me.

I rooted around behind the passenger seat until I found a clipboard. I checked my glove compartment and located some car rental forms that looked properly official. After placing them on the clipboard, I put a pencil behind my ear and pulled the Miata into the driveway of the Flores house.

The woman from the motel answered the doorbell on the first ring. She opened the front door but left the iron-barred screen locked.

"*Jess*?" she asked, as she looked me over from head to toe and back.

"Are you Ms. Flores?" I asked.

"I am. Who are you?"

I borrowed a name of one of my short story characters, and flashed her a quick look at the clipboard. "I'm an adjustor with Fidelity Mutual Insurance. We've received a claim from your neighbor up the street…" I gestured toward the damaged Chevy truck, "…alleging that someone damaged his property in the last couple of days. I'm just following up with some routine site assessment. I was wondering whether I could ask you a couple of questions."

"I didn' do nothin' to his truck," she protested.

"I'm sure you didn't. I'm sorry if I gave you that impression. I just need some information about the neighborhood. Are you aware of any problems with vandalism in the area? Teenaged kids, maybe, out for a few kicks?"

"We have teenagers here. Some are okay. Others get into trouble."

"It's the troublemakers I'm interested in, ma'am… or is it *miss*?"

"*Ms.*," she replied "Angelina Flores."

I made a note on the forms attached to the clipboard.

"And these troublemaking teenagers?"

"We have gangs in Venice Beach," she said, her voice clipped. "It is not healthy to talk about them to strangers. I would imagine tha' Mr. Cantinas, he piss them off. Tha's why they mess up his truck."

"I see. I… I don't suppose you would recall exactly when Mr. Cantinas' truck was damaged?"

She waved a hand in front of her face. "No. I am sorry, but I have no idea when tha' might have happened."

"He claims it was vandalized three nights ago. Were you around that evening, Ms. Flores?"

"Wha' is this?" she said, suddenly irritated. "Do you accuse me of damaging Cantinas' truck?"

"No," I protested.

"Because, it sound very much like you thin' I had somethin' to do with this."

"Not at all," I said, trying to calm her. The neighborhood looked deserted, but who knew how many secluded denizens might be roused if she pitched a nutty right here on her front stoop? "I'm sorry for disturbing you. I just needed to get some information about the neighborhood. Please have a nice day."

I stepped backward a couple of paces, and then turned to walk back to my car.

I got back to the parking deck around eleven. I parked the Miata, this time one level down from Dickman's Avalon, and thought through my next move.

An idea came to mind. It was so transparently elegant that it almost shocked me.

I pulled a sheet of my screen credits from my briefcase, and slipped them onto the clipboard. Then I walked into the building attached to the parking garage, and checked the directory until I found Squires Insurance, on the fifth floor.

When I got off the elevator, I found myself in the middle of a cube farm maybe sixty feet square. A woman sat at a desk just off the elevator alcove. The triangle block on her desk announced her as Shirley Hicks, Administrative Assistant. I smiled at her and walked up to her desk.

I told her my name.

"I'm looking for Robert Dickman," I said.

"Is he expecting you?"

"My secretary was supposed to phone ahead to make an appointment. I'm on something of a deadline, you see."

She checked her appointment book.

"I don't see you here," she said.

"Could you check with Mr. Dickman, see if he'll talk with me? I only really need a few moments."

She regarded me the way some people look at the stuff they dredge out of their pools, but she picked up the phone and dialed three digits. After talking with the person on the other end, she racked the receiver.

"Mr. Dickman will be up in a minute or two. Please have a seat."

I was almost too nervous to sit. At just that moment I could have used a stiff belt of my buddy Jose C. I was about to come face-to-face with a man I suspected of plotting to kill his wife. That kind of thing tends to put the old ticker into overdrive.

Presently, a tall, dark man with an aquiline nose and thin lips emerged from the cube farm. He saw me sitting in the waiting area. I quickly stood and introduced myself.

"I'm a screenwriter," I told him. "I write scripts for movies and television. I'm sorry for arriving unannounced. I thought my secretary had called ahead to set an appointment."

Dickman shook my hand but seemed puzzled.

"I'm sorry, but I don't understand. What is it I can do for you?"

"I'm writing a screenplay. It includes some plot factors revolving around the insurance industry. I don't know a thing about insurance, except that it eats a huge hole in my paycheck every month. I was hoping you could answer some questions for me."

"I don't know. How did you find my name?"

"My agent," I said, quickly. "I told him about my screenplay, and he asked a friend for the name of someone in the insurance industry who could give it just that spark of realism. The friend came up with you."

"And this friend is…"

"Damned if I know. My agent talked with him. I can find out if you want. My agent is on a vacation to Cabo, though. Very out of touch, if you catch my drift."

I winked at him, as if including him on a ribald secret.

To my relief, he seemed to buy it.

"Well, I suppose I can give you a few minutes. Why don't you step back to my desk?"

I followed him through the maze of cubicles to a glassed-in office overlooking the boulevard outside. In the distance, I could make out the central city office spires through the bluish smoggy haze.

He asked me to have a seat.

"Have I seen any of your pictures?" he asked.

I pulled the sheet of credits from the clipboard and handed it to him. He looked it over.

"I've seen a couple of these," he said. "I liked this one, *Run To Sunlight*."

"I'm particularly fond of that one myself," I told him. "It paid off my house. Again, I'm sorry to barge in. I'll only take a few moments of your time. What I need is information on life insurance."

"Life insurance," he echoed.

I noted the picture on his desk. It was the image of a pretty woman in her late thirties. She was California blonde, with bright blue eyes and a fetching smile. She looked like the kind of woman whose father gave her a nose job for her sweet sixteen birthday present.

"Your wife?" I asked, pointing to the picture.

"Yes," he said, a bit uncomfortably.

"She's lovely. She looks a little familiar. She doesn't work in the film business, does she?"

"She did, at one time. She quit when we got married. Life insurance, you say?"

"Yes. This screenplay I'm writing turns on the concept of double indemnity. You know, like the old movie."

Dickman seemed noticeably uncomfortable.

"Double indemnity," he repeated, not a question.

"What I need to know is how the term applies in the modern world. In the movie written by Billy Wilder and Raymond Chandler back in the forties, the idea was that a life insurance policy pays double if the insured dies in an accident. I was wondering whether this is still the case."

"Well," Dickman said. "I can't speak to the arrangements in the industry before I was even born. However, if you're talking about modern insurance policy, then I'd say that double indemnity works more or less the way you've described it. It has to be written into the policy as a condition of insurance, though."

"So, some policies don't provide for double indemnity?"

"No, not specifically. There are a number of conditions that have to be met in order for the policy to be doubled. For instance, the insured's death usually has to occur prior to a specific age."

"Is that age always standard?"

"Not exactly."

"Is it likely that someone over the age of, say, forty might be eligible for double indemnity?"

"Well, as the age of the insured increases, the availability of a double payment decreases. You see, the purpose of double indemnity is to compensate a younger family, in the case of accidental death, for the income that might have been earned in the working life of the deceased."

"I see. What other conditions are there?"

"In most cases, death must result from bodily injury that is related solely to external, violent, and accidental means, with no other contributing cause. Death must occur within a specified period after the injury."

"Okay," I said, writing furiously on the legal pad I'd attached to the clipboard. "So, being killed during – say – a robbery wouldn't meet the criteria."

"Not exactly. The policy would stipulate the conditions. If the policy includes murder as a qualifying condition, then double indemnity would apply."

"Terrific," I said, without looking up from the pad. "You have no idea how helpful this is. Everything you've told me fits in with my plot. This couldn't be better."

"Would you mind if I asked you what your story is about?"

"My screenplay," I corrected. "Basically, it's a murder-for-pay plot. It's about a man who's having an affair with a manipulative, controlling woman. She convinces him that if they arrange for his wife to have an accident, they can run away together on the proceeds from her insurance. The hook is that the insurance will pay double, because she dies during a robbery. What do you think?"

Dickman was clearly distressed. His neck had reddened, to match his ears. If I could have taken his blood pressure at that moment, he probably would have set some kind of Guinness record.

"It…seems somewhat…far-fetched," he stammered. "Of course, I don't see a lot of movies these days. Perhaps…perhaps because of the insurance angle I can see problems that the average viewer would miss."

"Such as?"

He waved his hand, dismissively.

"Oh, think nothing of it. Technical details, really. They would probably just bog down the movie. It sounds as if you have a very good beginning there. I wish you the very best with it. Now, if you will excuse me, I do have a pressing meeting."

I thanked him for his time and told him I could find my own way out.

I made my way back to the parking deck, to the Miata, and waited. After several minutes, I heard a tortured squeal of tires on concrete, and smiled as Dickman's Toyota Avalon rushed past me toward the exit of the deck.

Again, careful to keep a safe distance, I followed him back to Venice Beach. As I had suspected, he drove directly to Angelina Flores' house, and skidded to a halt in her driveway. He jumped from the car and ran to her front door. Apparently, he had called her on his cell phone, because she opened the front door before he got to it. He hustled inside.

Minutes later, they both left the house and climbed into the Avalon.

I followed them back toward the city. They stopped at a restaurant and went inside. I could see them through the window. First Dickman talked animatedly, waving his hands about and gesticulating wildly. After a few moments, Angelina mimicked him. Whatever they were discussing, I had a feeling that it wasn't about sports, and that it didn't spell any good tidings for the soon-to-be *late* Mrs. Dickman.

On one hand, I felt as if I should do something. Call the cops, maybe.

I realized that I still didn't have much to offer them. Eavesdropped conversations in a motel room? Clandestine meetings in a restaurant? A nervous reaction when I presented Dickman with a scenario close to the one I suspect him of plotting against his own wife? He was right. It did seem a little far-fetched.

On the other hand, I thought, what if they were planning at just that second to escalate their plans? What if they decided that the time was ripe, and that Mrs. Dickman needed to die before the sun set over the Pacific?

I'm callous, calculating, and cynical, but I didn't think I could live with myself if I sat on this story for the sake of a boffo screenplay, and allowed an innocent woman to be murdered for money.

I opened my laptop and latched onto a wireless network from the coffee house next to the restaurant. I pulled up a website that listed addresses and telephone numbers and asked it to search for Robert Dickman in the L.A. area.

I was in luck. There was only one listing. Even better, it wasn't too far away, in the Hollywood Hills. I was familiar with the area. Everyone in the film business is. It was the kind of place where houses jut out from hillsides and you can run across a wild coyote just sitting in a driveway watching the cars go by.

I jotted the address on my clipboard and headed off across the city toward that big old white sign in the sky.

Robert Dickman lived in a Spanish styled bungalow situated on the edge of a hill, with the deck cantilevered over a deep canyon. It was just a matter of time before an earthquake or a mudslide sent his home sledding down the hillside. From the looks of the place, though, it had survived forty or fifty years of Southern California weather and disasters.

I parked a short distance up the hill, hiked down to Dickman's circular drive, and walked up to the front door. Seconds after I rang the bell, a speaker next to the jamb crackled.

"Can I help you?" a woman's voice said.

"Are you Mrs. Dickman?" I asked.

"Yes."

"Your husband is Robert Dickman, who works at Squire Insurance?"

There was a pause.

"Oh, my God. What's happened?"

"Please. I'm sorry; I didn't mean to frighten you."

I stopped, realizing that, if I told her what I had come to say, I would be doing exactly that.

"What do you want?"

I told her my name.

"This is very difficult," I said. "I'm not exactly certain how to approach you with this."

"I don't like this," she said, through the speaker. "I think you should go."

"Not before I have a chance to talk with you."

"I'm calling the police."

I tried to think quickly. Maybe the police were exactly what I wanted at that moment. I could explain to them what I had learned.

What were the chances they'd believe me, though? What proof did I have besides a tryst in a neighboring hotel room and talk of insurance policies?

I slapped the screen door frame.

"I think your husband is planning to kill you!" I blurted.

There was silence for a long moment.

Then I heard the deadbolt click. The door opened.

"I think you'd better explain yourself," she said through the screen.

A half hour later, I sat in Janet Dickman's living room, sipping a Sprite as I finished my story.

"Let me get this straight," she said. "You overheard this conversation through a motel room wall?"

I nodded.

"Isn't it possible that you didn't understand what they were saying?"

"I don't think so," I said. "The wall is very thin, and there's a connecting door between the rooms with a gap under it. I could hear pretty clearly."

"What am I saying?" she asked, as she stared wistfully out the sliding doors, over the deck, and across the canyon. "I'm arguing with you, and it's obvious my husband is cheating on me. If he can do that, I suppose he could do anything."

We were interrupted by the sound of a car pulling into the drive. A car door opened and slammed shut.

"My husband!" she said. "What should we do?"

"Hide me," I said. "And act naturally."

She grabbed my hand and pulled me across the living room to the kitchen. She opened the door to a pantry and pointed inside.

"Robert never comes into the kitchen, except to get a beer from the refrigerator. Hide in here."

"What are you going to do?" I asked.

"I don't know. When it's safe, I'll let you out."

She pushed me into the narrow space and closed the door. I pushed it open just a crack, so I could see and hear what happened.

Dickman walked through the front door and draped his suit jacket over one of the bar stools.

"Darling!" Janet said, with just the slightest quaver in her voice. "What are you doing home so early?"

"I decided to take the afternoon off," he said. "Rough morning. Have you gotten any calls? Someone looking for me?"

"No."

"There was this guy at the office, said he was given my name by his agent. Probably nothing."

Just as Janet had told me, Dickman walked around the bar into the kitchen, and grabbed a beer from the refrigerator. He popped the tab and took a long swallow.

Janet stepped out to the deck through the sliding door. I could see her wrap her arms around herself. She rocked side to side a little. Robert followed her out.

"What is it?" he asked, as he placed the beer onto the deck rail.

She turned and slapped him, hard. He reeled backward. His hand raised to palm his cheek.

"What in hell!" he gasped.

"I know," she said.

"What?"

"I know about… her."

"I have no idea what you're talking about."

"The motel in Zuma Beach?"

He stepped back a foot or two. He ran one hand through his thick black hair.

"Oh, my God," he said. "You hired a detective?"

That was when Janet made her mistake. If she had said *yes*, then Dickman faced a messy divorce, a little embarrassment, and some nasty alimony, but he'd never have tried to harm her.

"No," she said, instead. "I followed you."

Through the crack between the pantry door and the jamb, I saw Dickman's face redden. His fists clenched. Even from my clumsy angle I could tell that he was furious.

"You…stupid…interfering…*bitch*!" he growled.

He reached out, grabbed her by the upper arms, and swung her around. Slowly, he started walking her toward the deck rail.

"You've ruined *everything,*" he said, his voice low and menacing. "You stuck your nose where it didn't belong. To think, I had decided not to do anything about you. I'd decided it was too dangerous. Now, you leave me no choice."

"You're hurting me!" she said.

She glanced backward, into the canyon hollow, as her backside touched the redwood rail. It was a sheer hundred-foot drop beyond the deck, with nothing but rocks and scrub below. Nobody could survive a fall from that height.

I stepped out of the pantry, dashed around the bar, and onto the deck.

"Let go of her!" I yelled, finding it hard to believe that it was my own voice shouting.

He turned and saw me.

"You!" he gasped. "What in hell are you doing in my *house?*"

Janet took the opportunity to break away from him. She ran and hid behind me. In retrospect, she could have chosen some more substantial protection.

Dickman stomped across the deck, grabbed me by the lapels of my sport coat, and tried to lift me off the ground.

"Let go!" I yelled.

"Answer me! What have you been telling my wife? Why were you really in my office today?"

I wedged my hands between his wrists, and jerked them upward rapidly, breaking his grip. Immediately, he lunged at me again, grabbing for my neck. We were only a couple of feet from the edge of the deck. I could see the dizzying abyss beyond the railing.

I planted my feet as he reached for me and shoved him backward with both hands against his chest.

He staggered back, off balance, until his butt hit the deck railing. His arms flailed helplessly as his momentum started to pivot him over the rail. Janet Dickman screamed as he rotated backward, his eyes wide with terror. He rolled over the rail into space.

At the last second, he reached out and tried to grab the rail to stop himself from launching into empty air. His fingers scraped the wood, but he couldn't gain a firm grip.

A couple of seconds later, I heard him hit the rocks. It was a sound I'll never forget.

I leaned over the railing and looked down. Dickman's broken body had hit the incline and had rolled and skidded along the desert scrub before coming to a stop. He looked like a truck had rolled over him.

I became aware of Janet at my side. Her hand covered her mouth. She turned to me.

"Did you hit him?" she asked.

I was too stunned to understand. I shook my head, trying to clear it.

"*Did you hit him?*" she asked again, more insistently this time.

"What?" I asked.

"In the face! Did you punch him?"

"I…don't understand," I said. "No. I just shoved him."

She backed away from the deck rail and began to walk in a small circle.

"Good. Okay. If you had hit him, there would be bruises. The police would ask questions about that. Why in hell did you come here, anyway? You could have ruined everything!"

"What?"

"It doesn't matter now."

She walked to the telephone, dialed three digits. Seconds later, her voice changed dramatically.

"I need help!" she choked into the receiver, between sobs. "My husband's fallen from our deck. I think he's terribly hurt. I think he might be dying!"

There was a pause.

"That's right. 4730 Holly Canyon Road. Please come quickly!"

She replaced the receiver and turned to me.

"We don't have much time. You can't be here, understand? You have to go."

"Wait," I protested. "I pushed him over the railing. The police are going to want to know what happened."

"He fell off the deck. It was an accident. That's what we're going to tell the police."

"I can't lie about this. He was attacking me. It was self-defense. I didn't do anything wrong. He was planning to kill you."

"I don't have time to argue with you," she said. "I can make it worth your while. I can give you money. A lot of money. Between his insurance and his savings and investments, there will be several million. I can give you a hundred thousand to just disappear. You could take the money and go to Mexico. You could live like a king there for ten thousand a year or so. You could have a house overlooking the beach. You could even have servants. Just take the money and go, before the police arrive!"

I stared at her, unable to speak.

I had heard those exact words once before, earlier that day.

The front door opened. Angelina Flores rushed into the house.

"Wha' happened?" she asked. "I heard a scream."

She rushed over to the rail and peered over.

"Honey," she said, as she embraced Janet. "You did it!"

"No," Janet said, nodding toward me. "He did."

Angelina turned to me.

"Wha' are you doing here?" she asked. "You were jus' supposed to be a witness!"

"What?" I asked, as the truth slowly began to dawn on me.

"She's right," Janet said. "Your agent really shouldn't drink so much. I met him at a party a few months ago. He told me all about this author he represented, who listened to people in the next motel room and wrote stories about them. That's what gave Angel and me the idea."

"You…set me up?" I stammered.

"You were just supposed to be a witness. You weren't supposed to get involved, not directly. Angel was supposed to get Robert to try to kill me. I've been taking martial arts training during the day while he's at work. I could have tossed him over the rail without even thinking about it. All I had to do was get him to attack me out here."

Angelina picked up the story from there.

"We wanted you to hear me plotting with that jerk to keel her," she said. "Afterward, you could testify about wha' you had heard. It would' have convinced the police that it was self-defense."

"But…" I said, trying to catch up. "But that would implicate *you*!"

Even in my shock, I was trying to clean up the plot lines, as if I were doing the punch on a screenplay.

"I called the police," she said. "From the car. I tol' them that Robert was out of his mind. I tol' them that he had threatened to kill Janet, and that I had not been able to talk him out of it."

"You have to leave!" Janet said, grabbing my arm. "The police are on their way. The ambulance will be here any second. You can't be here when they arrive. A quarter million! I'll give you that much if you'll just go!"

The girls were right. You can live like a king in Mexico for very little. Sure, it costs more than ten grand a year, but not a *lot* more.

I live in a pretty little house overlooking the Sea of Cortez now. It has a couple of nice-sized bedrooms, a lovely terrace where I write as I watch the boats sail on the crystal waters, and an incredible living room where I sometimes entertain friends. The sea breezes waft through the house day and night, sort of like nature's air conditioning.

Through the miracle of satellite Internet, I can still write my stories and screenplays, and send them to my agent in Los Angeles. I hardly ever get to the United States anymore.

I discovered you can get really great tequila cheap down here.

On clear days, all I have to do is pull out my binoculars, and I can see Janet and Angelina lounging on the deck of their own villa a half mile away.

I took the money, of course. I figured I had earned it, for playing the unwitting role of the patsy in Janet's murder plot. After moving to Mexico, I hired a former Mexican prize fighter to work as my bodyguard. He also cooks like a French chef and makes a mean margarita. His girlfriend keeps the place clean.

I keep a close eye on the girls. We have an uneasy truce. Even though it would be tough for the American officials to touch us down here, we all know what we did. It's kind of like what that old boy Sun Tzu said: *Keep your friends close, but keep your enemies closer.*

I think, though, that our tenuous relationship will eventually be more closely defined by another ancient axiom, something Ben Franklin once said.

Three can keep a secret, if two of them are dead.

You do the math.

THE GOSPEL ACCORDING TO GORDON BLACK

by

Richard Helms

Author's Note: This Eamon Gold story was first published at Kevin Burton Smith's Thrilling Detective Website *in 2007. It was edited by Gerald So. By 2007, my character Eamon Gold had already appeared in two novels, including* ***Cordite Wine****, which was a finalist for the PWA Shamus Award in 2006. An Eamon Gold novel (****Brittle Karma****) won the Shamus Award in 2021.* The Gospel According to Gordon Black *won the SMFS Derringer Award in the Short Story category in 2008.*

R

Gordon Black was a short man with an intimidating stare. His hair and beard were completely white. He liked to accentuate his points by drawing circles in the air with his index fingers.

"We are nothing but organic flotsam, bobbing in the infinite sea of life. Don't you agree, Mr. Gold?"

"Sure," I said.

At eighty dollars an hour, plus expenses, I could agree with all sorts of garbage.

"I don't hear much conviction in your voice," Gordon Black said.

"Conviction costs extra."

"A cynic, huh?"

"If I had a nickel for every time someone's called me that, I wouldn't need to charge eighty dollars an hour."

"So, you're like the psychiatrists, who nod and agree with their patients so long as the clock is ticking?"

I made a note on the legal pad I had brought to Gordon Black's office.

Has had experience with psychiatrists.

"I am for hire," I said. "I don't do this for fun."

"How do I know you can help me?"

"Beats me. I don't know yet what you want me to do."

He thought for a moment.

"I've founded a new religion. Perhaps you've heard of it."

"Sorry. I let my subscription to *New Religions Magazine* lapse a couple of years ago."

He smiled.

I smiled back.

We had shared a secret joke.

I could do this all day.

"My philosophy is simple. We are nothing but temporal flesh. There is nothing before us, and nothing after we die. Our entire existence is encompassed by the time between our births and our deaths."

"Okay."

"My religion doesn't require a supreme being meting out rewards and punishments to regulate our behavior. What we do with—or *to*—one another is and should be regulated by the concepts of civility and mutual respect."

"What's the payoff?" I asked.

Black rubbed the side of his nose and seemed to take my moral measurements with his onyx-colored eyes.

"The...*payoff*, as you refer to it, is social order and peace. The reward for being a good person is being a good person. That leads to a sense of peace and contentment, feelings of good will, and behavior regulated by internal values rather than external judgment."

"And, in the interest of social order, what kind of behavior would you *not* condone?" I asked.

"Any behavior that is hurtful, damaging, or coerced."

"So, whatever two or more people want to do together—as long as they agree to it and nobody forces anybody else—you're fine with that?"

"Of course."

"And," I said, "This is different from hedonism...*how*?"

"Hedonism?"

"An existential philosophy based on the concept of shifting moral constants and the pursuit of pleasure."

Black leaned his plush button-and-tuck leather office chair back and surveyed me again. His opinion of me was changing by the moment.

Or maybe I just saw it that way.

"An educated man? In your profession?"

"I'm only a part-time thug. I played college football. One of the few requirements of my scholarship was that I attend classes. A lot of my teammates took this as an opportunity to nap during the day. I decided I might as well pay attention and learn something."

"Like hedonism?"

"There were plenty of opportunities in college to study hedonism."

"I see," he said. "Well, there may be more than a little bit of the hedonistic philosophy in my religious manifesto. I also borrowed some parts of Zen Buddhism, the Kabballah, and some of the more naturalistic pantheistic traditions."

I had a feeling he was playing a tape in his head and transcribing it for me. I stifled a yawn.

"What about hope?" I said.

"What about it?"

"I'm no expert, but it seems to me that one of the foundations of most religions is the aspect of hope. People adhere to a system of beliefs because it offers them some relief from their personal fears."

"Fears of what, exactly?" Black asked.

"Well…death, mostly. People gravitate toward the promise of salvation. They like to think that there's something to look forward to beyond the grave. You don't offer them that."

"Self-delusion," he said, making a dismissive circle with his hand. "Fairy tales. Isn't it better to admit that we are temporal beings, and savor every second of our brief moment in the sun? Isn't it better to sample the entire buffet of experience, to delight in the wholeness of life?"

"But with respect," I said.

"Of course. Pleasure without respect is exploitation. We don't exploit others."

I made a couple more notes and looked back up at him.

"Well, this is fun," I said. "But how, exactly, can I help you?"

"I'm being defamed," he said. "People are spreading lies about me."

"What kind of lies?"

"They're saying that I engage in pederasty, and drug use, and the vilest things."

"Who are these people? Do you have some idea of their identities?"

"Oh, you know. The usual voices of the religious establishment. The Christian Right, all the established and entrenched faiths. They attack that which threatens them."

"That's a lot of suspects. Could you narrow it down a bit?"

"The loudest of my critics are on the Internet. I have a number of screen names I can give you."

I stopped writing and thought about it for a second.

"This sounds more like a legal problem. If you think you are being slandered, perhaps you need an attorney, not a private investigator."

"I can deal with the criticisms from the established religious camps. Now, though, I think I'm being blackmailed."

He picked up the telephone and dialed three numbers.

"Could you bring in the envelope?" he said, and then hung up the phone. A moment later, a woman walked into the office.

She was tall and redheaded. Her conservative business suit struggled to conceal a very well-tended and genetically prosperous body. I could see the outline of her bra through the sheer white blouse under her tweed jacket. Her eyes were like emeralds.

"This is Emma Rhodden," Black announced. "If I am the head of my church, Emma is its heart. She is my closest confidant. This is Mr. Gold, Emma. We talked about him earlier."

She slipped her hand into mine and squeezed. Her eyes locked onto my eyes.

"Mr. Gold. How nice to meet you. Thank you for helping Gordon and the Church."

She handed me the envelope, then turned and left the office. She closed the door behind her.

"I bet you just respect the hell out of her," I said.

"The envelope, Mr. Gold."

I broke the seal on the manila envelope and fished inside. It contained a computer printout.

"Emma found that slid under the front door when she came into the office the other day," he said.

It was a photograph of Black. With or without respect, the act in which he was engaged was illegal in every state.

"It's faked, of course," he said.

"Of course."

"Very cleverly done, though. The computer programs for manipulating images become more sophisticated every year."

The attached message was straightforward. *Stop spreading your Godless beliefs, or this will be delivered to the authorities.*

"I could prove in court that the image was manufactured," Black said. "But it would be expensive, and once something like this is reported in the papers it hardly ever matters whether you're later exonerated. People will believe what they will believe. I don't mind criticism. This, however, begs for intervention. I want you to find the people who sent this threat and stop them."

"And you think these people who have attacked you on the Internet are the best candidates?"

"They're a place to start."

I considered the implications. Starting out with a list of screen names wasn't promising. I had dealt with online companies in the past and had found them to be about as cooperative with their records as Swiss banks. Attaching names to the people who had openly criticized Gordon Black and his new religion would take some doing. I could envision hours and hours of inquiries.

At eighty dollars an hour plus expenses.

"Sure," I said. "I'll look into it."

The list Gordon Black had provided wasn't exactly a smoking gun. The Internet is full to the brim with wacky types who luxuriate in anonymity, and who believe that their firewalls shield them from every aspect of the real world.

That kind of presumption just bugs the hell out of me.

On the other hand, these people do know a thing or two about their medium, and one of the Prime Directives of the ether world is that one can expect complete protection of one's true identity by the ISP.

So, I decided that the only way to catch a little fish was to use a larger phish.

The idea came to me halfway through my second Anchor Porter of the day, as I sat on the deck at my Montara Beach house, resting after working for three straight hours on a copy of a Hauser classical guitar I'd promised to build for a friend in Seattle. I build musical instruments as a hobby. It helps clear my mind and gives me something to do with my hands when my girlfriend Heidi is at work.

All of the screen names provided by Gordon Black shared a common factor. They all hated Gordon Black. In effect, they had become a sort of loosely connected club which practically begged for organization. It also occurred to me that, since they had so openly expressed their opinions with Mr. Black, they might also be open to sharing their thoughts with each other.

I allowed my plan to gestate a bit as I finished the bottle of Anchor, and then I went inside to fire up my computer.

It took me a half hour to compose the phishing letter. In effect, it was a warning about the dangers of Black's New

Existence Revelations Ministries, and an invitation to join an email list so that the recipients could pool their resentment and the power of their voices. When it was finished, I read it over twice and had to admit that it was more than a little convincing. For a couple of moments, I wondered whether I was playing for the right team.

I saved the letter, and then went to a website that hosts mail lists. It took me ten minutes to set up one called '*Bogus Faiths*'. I also toggled the little box that said I had to approve each new member. That way, I could be certain that I wouldn't be jammed with applicants who might stumble on a link to my private little club. I wanted to concentrate on the names from Black's list.

Finally, I sent my phishing email to each of the people from the list.

The next morning, I booted my computer and dropped by the mail list site, to see if I'd had any nibbles from my phishing expedition.

I had expected two or three responses right away. There are people out there who will join a chain gang if they're properly invited. I found that eight of the nine names on the list Gordon Black had given me had requested to join the list. Apparently, I had underestimated the zeal among my little mob of zealots.

Now, here's the beautiful part about my plan. In order to join a list with this particular server, you had to become a member. Membership was free, because eventually the server would flood your email in-box with dozens of commercial messages a day.

When you joined the server, you had to provide your name, your address, and other vital demographic data such as your age, income, buying habits, etc. Then, before the server passed along your response to the list owner, they'd vet you by sending an email to you, and you'd have to respond directly before you were approved to play with the rest of the kids.

Finally—and this is the beautiful part I mentioned—the server provided me with all of this information when my little phishies applied to join my list.

Within minutes, I had a printout on my desk which outlined the names, addresses, genders, ages, and buying habits of almost every screen name Black had given me. Only one name on the list, *RodOfGod@---.net,* had failed to take the bait.

Not too surprisingly, almost all of the people on the list lived in the Bay area. Gordon Black's church was relatively new, and accordingly small. It was a safe bet that its reputation had not had time to spread near and far. One suspect, a fellow named Hiram Darles, lived in Sacramento. The rest of the addresses were in places like Sausalito, San Jose, Daly City, and in San Francisco proper.

I made a list of the members arranged by farthest distance from the city inward and decided to visit as many as possible. I doubted that any would admit to sending the picture to Gordon Black, but I've also found that most extortionists prefer to operate from behind a screen. Most of them, when exposed, wilt in the light of day, especially if that light comes in the form of a six-foot guy with malice in his eyes.

I decided to skip Hiram Darles for this round. Sacramento was nowhere near the longest distance I'd driven to interview someone, but it would take the better part of a day, and I decided it made more sense to see as many people in as short a time as possible.

The first person on the list lived in San Jose. Her name was Cynthia Raab. She lived in a one-bedroom apartment over a drugstore. Her bookshelves were lined with every known edition of the Bible, multiple volumes of Concordances and religious commentaries, and several lazy cats. The apartment smelled like urine. She didn't own a computer. She used the one down at the local library. She thought Photoshop was a camera store. I scratched her off my list.

The next prospect was much more promising. He was actually a minister in Pacifica. I caught him coming out the front door.

I flashed him my ID and asked for a few minutes of his time. He was tall, but lean and sort of sickly. His skin was translucent, his eyes watery. I had a hard time imagining him railing from the pulpit. His name was Avery Sipe.

"What do you want?" he asked.

"You've been sending threatening emails to Gordon Black," I said. His mouth started to form an argument, but I wasn't in the mood to listen. "Don't bother. I have the evidence."

"I wouldn't say they were threatening," Sipe said.

"We can let the courts deal with that," I said.

"The . . . the courts?"

I had never seen an Adam's apple bob four full inches before. I was so impressed that I almost forgot what I wanted to say.

"Mr. Black has received threats accompanied by pictures. If you sent them, now would be a good time to tell me. I'm a trained professional. If you lie, I'll know."

I gave him my menacing look, the one I save for bill collectors and yappy dogs.

He swallowed twice, shook his head.

"I didn't do it," he pleaded.

"No more contact with Black," I said. "Not a peep. I know who you are, and I can come back when you least expect me. Is there anything you don't understand about that?"

He shook his head again. I nodded, turned, and walked back to my car. I didn't look back. It's impolite to stare when a man soils his pants.

Heidi Fluhr and I had dinner at my Montara Beach house. I grilled ribeye steaks and winter vegetables, and we were enjoying it with a bottle of Corona Farms cabernet.

Heidi is an art dealer, a big healthy northern European blonde with prodigious appetites, and my current squeeze—not necessarily in that order of importance. We had been seeing each other for almost two years. I liked it. She liked it. Beyond that, we weren't into making plans.

As we ate, I told her about my phishing scheme.

"Devious," she said.

"I was shooting for ingenious and elegant."

"Have you had any responses?"

"I haven't checked yet."

"Oooh, let's go take a look. I love to watch you play detective."

I allowed Heidi to look over my shoulder as I played with my suspects' heads. I opened my computer and accessed the email list. As she kneaded my shoulders, I typed the following message:

> *Has anyone else been hassled by some glandular case in the last day or so? I'd love to know if any of you were accosted by this character, and what he told you. I find it highly suspicious that right after I start this list I get boosted by a private investigator. I'm all for putting a stop to the sacrilege that Gordon Black calls a church, but I sure don't want to get in trouble with the cops.*

I toggled the SEND key and sat back to let the issue cook for a while.

"What now?" Heidi asked.

"Good question," I said. "Sometimes you just have to stir the stew and wait to see what comes to the surface."

"You're fucking with their heads, you mean."

"More or less. I scared a lot of people today. They're going to want to talk about that with people they think they can trust. If I'm lucky, I can make one of them slip and tell me what I want to know."

"In your own unique and effective way, I'd imagine."

"If you want thuggery done," I said, "you go to the Head Thug."

I was interrupted by a little gong sound, and a small dialogue box popped up on my screen.

InHisName: RU online?

"One of my little phishes," I explained to Heidi. "That was quick."

I quickly typed a response.

InHisName: That guy visited me 2.

"Did he threaten you?" I mouthed as I typed.

Told me stop hassling Black.

"He scared me," I keyed.

How he find us?

"Don't know."

Satan has great powers.

"Tell me about it," I keyed. "Wish I had some way to get Black to back off."

What u mean?

"Something embarrassing or incriminating," I wrote.

Me 2. GTG.

The dialogue box disappeared.

"*GTG*?" Heidi asked.

"*Got to go,*" I said, translating. "IM-speak. Something the kids came up with."

"What do you think about this guy?"

"InHisName?"

"Yeah."

"I think that *guy* is a sixty-year-old woman who lives in San Bruno. Her name is Kate, and she's an ex-hippie who spent most of the 1960s in Haight-Ashbury, grooving with the Jerry and the Dead. She's not the blackmailer."

"So why did you bait her?"

"Excuse me?"

"That last bit about wanting something to make Black back off? You were trying to get her to admit that she had something on him."

"Not exactly."

"What, then?"

"I was planting seeds. She's part of my email list. It might look suspicious if I—as the list owner—came right out and asked if any of the members has a picture of Black with a goat, but if one of the other members brings it up, it won't look so hinky."

"And when someone comes forward?"

"Then I have my extortionist. Now, what can we do while we wait?"

"What did you have in mind?"

"We could always canoodle."

"You expect me to canoodle just because you cooked dinner?"

"Of course not. I expect you to canoodle because I am irresistibly handsome, and because I make your toes curl."

"And because you're so devious," she said.

"Yes," I added. "Devious helps."

I spent most of the night monitoring the email list. Nobody else tried to IM me, but the list was busy until after one in the morning. Sometime around midnight, my buddy Kate InHisName uploaded a message to the list.

> *We should fight fire with fire*, she wrote. *Gordon Black and his blasphemers think they can scare us off with threats and intimidation. I'd bet he'd back off in a New York minute if he knew we could threaten him back. Maybe we could hire some kind of private investigator to get some dirt on Black...*

I laughed out loud when I read that one. For a second, I considered playing both sides of the street.

Well, maybe it was only half a second. I have scruples, after all.

Heidi got up before I did, dressed, and left for her apartment. I awoke just after nine-thirty. I hit the shower, got dressed and shaved, and settled down in my kitchen for some toaster waffles and a lot of hot coffee.

As I waited for the coffee to brew, I logged on to my laptop and checked the list.

Around two in the morning, one of my phishes had uploaded a message. It was short, sweet, and succinct.

> *I have something we could use on Black, it said. I have pictures. Bad pictures. I don't want to share them with you, because they*

> *are evil, but he sure wouldn't want to see them made public.*

Bingo.

I checked the screen name. *PiusXIX.* I checked it against my list.

Hiram Darles. My guy in Sacramento. The only suspect from Gordon Black's list whom I hadn't personally visited yet. That was probably why he was so bold on the list.

I finished my breakfast, loaded his address into my GPS, and climbed into my car to make the trip to the state capitol.

Hiram Darles lived in a small California bungalow in a neighborhood of similar houses constructed in the Roaring Twenties. The yard was well-tended, the flower beds weeded to distraction, and someone had brazed an ornate wrought-iron cross to the screen door on the shady front porch.

From the street, I could see a car parked in the single garage at the back end of the gravel driveway. I hoped that the car belonged to Darles and not his wife.

I banged on the front door and waited. After several seconds, I heard heavy footsteps nearing the door.

I waited as the person inside released three different deadbolt locks. Hiram Darles opened the door. He was about my age but had allowed himself to go to suet. His most prominent features were cheeks that puffed out like *fugu*, and his ruddy flopping jowls. His eyes seemed set back in folds of skin. He wore a pair of jeans and a WWJD sweatshirt.

"Hiram Darles?" I said, as he unlatched the screen.

I could see the color drain from his face. His cheeks went from rosy to ashen in seconds.

"Oh, my God, it's you!" he said.

He tried to slam the door, but I already had my size thirteen wedged in the jamb. I pulled the picture Gordon Black had given me from my back pocket, unfolded it, and held it up to him.

"Look familiar, Hiram?" I asked.

"Oh my God oh my God oh my God oh my God..." he chanted. "You go away. I didn't give you permission to come in this house. You're trespassing."

"You're supposedly devout," I said. "I think you're supposed to forgive trespasses, aren't you? Tell me about the picture, Hiram."

"I don't know what you're talking about."

"Extortion is a crime," I said. "Right now, it's just you and me talking. Just a couple of guys. I have the Sacramento Police on my cell phone speed dial. You decide not to be friendly, and I can have them here in about five minutes. What's it going to be?"

He glanced back into the house, as if looking for some place to hide. Looking at him, I concluded that it would have to be a really big place. Finally, he stepped out onto the porch, and closed the door behind him.

"You can't come inside," he said.

"The hell I can't," I told him. "If I want to, I'll come inside, toss the place, reprogram your VCR, and neuter your cat. Do we understand each other?"

"You are a tool of Satan!" he said, indignantly.

I leaned in very close to his face. His breath smelled like cheese.

I held out the photo again.

"You put this under Gordon Black's door," I said. I didn't phrase it as a question.

He nodded. I could see tears welling at the corners of his eyes.

"Mr. Black is very upset about this," I said.

"Gordon Black is a demon. He was sent by Satan to lead the unwary astray from the true path. Someone had to stop him."

"And you decided to be that person."

"No. I was chosen. I received that picture as an attachment to an email from a fellow believer. He—or she, it's hard to tell online—said I should give it to Gordon Black as an example of the power of the Lord, and the damnation that awaits Black if he doesn't repent."

"Who sent it to you?"

"I can't recall. It doesn't matter. I wrote the demand at the bottom. I delivered the message. I'd do it again."

I nodded and looked away, out at the street, as I mulled my options.

Being a private cop has advantages and disadvantages. Among the disadvantages is the relative paucity of things you can do to miscreants once you track them down. I could have danced around the porch with Hiram for a couple of rounds, left him bruised and wiser, but all that would have proven was that I was bigger and meaner, and would probably just fuel his righteous anger, and justify future misbehavior.

"Here's the deal," I said, as I turned back to him. "You got lazy, and you got caught. Now I know who you are, and I know what you did, and you could go to jail for a long time for it."

"I just wanted him to stop," Hiram whined.

"I know. And I don't care. I work for Gordon Black, and Gordon Black wants this foolishness to end. So, no more messages. Save someone in your own neighborhood. If there are any more threats, I'm coming after you first. Is there anything I need to repeat?"

He shook his head. A weighty tear plopped from his cheek onto the painted deck of the porch.

I folded the picture, stuffed it in my jacket pocket, and left Darles to his own private recriminations.

I met with Gordon Black later that afternoon. I handed him the list of suspects I'd culled from my phishing expedition and told him that Hiram Darles was the person who had tried to blackmail him. I urged him to go light on Darles who, after all, was only doing what he thought was right, no matter how illegally he went about it.

To his credit, Black accepted the advice.

"You're probably right," he said. "And I'd be a hypocrite if I didn't at least try to respect his beliefs."

"Yes," I said. "We do want to avoid accusations of hypocrisy."

"What is that supposed to mean?" Black asked.

"Nothing. I'll send you a bill."

———

Six months later, I was bucks up. I had been hired by a couple of Silicon Valley geeks to unravel an industrial espionage case, and they had been very grateful for my results. Since I had time to kill and money to blow, I took Heidi on an impromptu trip to Lake Tahoe.

We had been back for a couple of days. It was Sunday. We were lounging in Heidi's Russian Hill apartment. She read the *Chronicle* local section as I nibbled on some toast, perused the sports pages, and considered hiring a sailboat to play on the bay that afternoon.

"Eamon?" Heidi asked, looking up from the paper.

"Hmmm?"

"What was the name of that guy in Sacramento you nabbed for extortion last Christmas?"

I had to think hard to recall. I don't store a lot of the perps I run down in long-term memory.

"Darles," I said, after a moment. "Hymie, Horace, something like that."

"*Hiram*?"

"Yeah, that's it. What about him?"

She handed me the paper. It was turned to the obits.

"He's dead," she said.

I scanned the notice. Age forty-three. I thought he had looked a lot older, actually. Died suddenly. No cause listed. No survivors.

Not a lot to say for a life. Services were that afternoon at a funeral home in Sacramento.

"Probably a heart attack," I said. "The guy was a walking advertisement for statins. Hand me the funnies?"

"No."

"I can't have the funnies?"

"No, not that. I mean, *'No, it wasn't a heart attack.'* Look on page three."

It took me a moment to find the fifteen-line blurb near the bottom of the page, recounting a hit-and-run two nights before. The details were sketchy, partly because Darles was a nobody, and probably partly because the police didn't have much to tell the beat reporter who wrote the piece.

"Victim was Hiram Darles, age forty-three," I read. "Police are looking for a black SUV, make unknown."

"What do you think?"

"I think the SUV should be easy to find. A guy Darles' size would put a hefty dent in a Hummer."

"I mean, do you think it was intentional?"

"Why would you say that?"

"Well, he was an extortionist."

"Not a very good one. And I put him out of business. Darles was big and slow, and not very bright to boot. He probably just stepped off the wrong curb at the right time and couldn't get out of the way fast enough. You want to go sailing this afternoon?"

We did go sailing, but as we tacked around on the chop out in the Golden Gate, I couldn't get my mind off Hiram Darles.

I might not have recalled his name right off the bat, but I hadn't forgotten the fear in his eyes. Intimidation is one of the tools of my trade, but sometimes it carries a nasty personal freight charge.

When we got back to my house, I booted my computer and checked out the *Bogus Faiths* email list I had set up to phish for Gordon Black-haters. I hadn't taken the list down after closing Black's case, because I wanted to make sure Darles didn't grow a pair after my visit and decide to tempt fate.

After a month with no posts from him, I had finally lost interest and gone on to other projects. Somehow, though, I had never gotten around to taking down the list.

To my surprise, there were no recent posts. The last one had been about three months earlier, from the nice lady with the cats in San Jose—what was her name? *Raab.* After that—nothing. It was possible, of course, that with such a small membership the list had simply petered out. I'd seen it happen before on a couple of guitar-making sites I had joined.

On the other hand, the list had been bustling when I abandoned it. My little group of suspects hadn't seemed the kind of folk to cut and run on a subject so close to their hearts. These people had been not only devout, but vocal about it. It was more than a little curious that they had gone silent.

I thought about it that evening in the shop I had set up in the living room at my house in Montara as I worked on a banjo I'd agreed to build for a friend in Ukiah. Heidi lounged on the sofa in an extra-large Forty-Niners tee shirt and little else, reading a Jonathan Santlofer novel. She liked Santlofer because he was an artist as well as an author, and she had carried one or two of his pieces in her gallery over the years.

"Where are they?" I said, mostly to myself.

"Probably where you last left them," she said, without looking up.

"I was thinking about my little phishes."

"The holy rollers you conned on that email list?"

"Yeah. No messages in almost three months. Where did they go?"

"You're a detective. Why don't you . . . what's that thing you do?"

"Look into it?"

"Yeah. You should do that."

"You know," I said. "I think I will."

I put aside the banjo and booted the computer in the spare bedroom. It took me a moment to access my case records, and to print out the list of suspects I had developed during the Gordon Black case.

I sat on the sofa. Heidi curled up against my side. I picked up the telephone and dialed Kate *InHisName* in San Bruno.

Annoying three tone signal. An electronic voice advised me that the number was no longer in service.

More questions.

The old lady with the cats in San Jose—Cynthia Raab—same *no longer in service* message. I could see a free spirit like Kate pulling up stakes, but Raab seemed to have hunkered down for the remainder of her breathing time. I dialed Avery Sipe's number in Pacifica, just a couple of miles to the north of my Montara house.

Someone picked up the phone on the third ring.

"Hello?"

Female voice. Sounded like she was in her late teens or early twenties.

"Could I speak with Mr. Sipe, please?"

"Sure. Hold on."

I heard her put down the receiver. Moments later, someone picked it up again.

"This is Curtis Sipe," a man said.

"Excuse me. I was trying to reach Avery Sipe."

"I'm sorry. I'm afraid that . . .who's calling please?"

"My name is Eamon Gold."

"Did you have some business with my father?"

It was time for a little fancy stepping. I didn't like the way he was referring to Avery in the past tense.

"We met about six months ago. I was just following up on our conversation."

"I see. I'm very sorry to have to tell you this, Mr. Gold, but my father… passed away."

"My goodness. When?"

"In February. It was very sudden."

I apologized for bothering him and racked the receiver.

Heidi had heard enough to distract her from Santlofer.

"Two of them are dead?" she asked.

"Maybe four. I need to do some research."

Every detective worth his license subscribes to one kind of database or another. Unlike the online search engines, these databases can provide you with information very few people want posted on their websites. With little more than a name, a date of birth, or a Social Security number, I could find out how much money you make, what kind of car you drive, and how much you paid in taxes in the last year.

I could also find out whether you were still walking the Earth, or simply permanently occcupying a hundred cubic feet of it.

I knew that Darles and Sipe were dead. I pulled up a news story on Sipe whom, it appeared, had fallen from a cliff at the beach in Pacifica in February. No biggie there. The coastline of California is pocked with literally hundreds of dangerous cliffs, and hardly a day goes by that you don't read about someone falling off of one.

I checked on Cynthia Raab next. Asphyxiated in April when her pilot light went out while she was asleep.

Kate Corrigan, the hippie in San Bruno? Electrocuted by her hair dryer.

The list went on and on. Every member of my list had died in the six months since I had recruited them. Each death an apparent accident.

Sitting next to me at the computer, Heidi shivered.

"Damn, Gold. What's going on here?"

"I don't know," I said, reaching for the telephone. "But I think it's time I went back to church."

Gordon Black wasted no time escorting me into his office.

"Mr. Gold," he said, as I sat across the desk from him. "I must say, I didn't expect to see you again. I trust my check cleared?"

"Yes. This isn't a collection call."

I placed a printed summary of the fates of my phishes on his desk and watched as he read over it.

"Oh, my," he said, placing the paper down on the desk calendar. "I know how this must look…"

"Really?"

"Of course. I'm an intelligent man. I hired you to find these people and make them stop harassing me. Now they're all dead. It makes me look . . .well, vengeful."

"And it makes me look like an accomplice," I said. "I hope you haven't compromised me, Gordon."

"Not at all. I'm shocked at this news."

"Here's the deal," I told him. "Two people had access to this list. Obviously, I did. I gave you a report of my investigation after I shook Hiram Darles' tree. That report contained the names and addresses of every person I contacted. Now they're dead. I know I didn't do it. That leaves you."

"Not . . . necessarily," he said. "I discussed this case with several members of my staff—informally, that is—in a meeting several days after you met with Darles."

"How many members?"

"Three. These are good people, Mr. Gold. They're my closest advisors. Almost apostles, you might say. They revere me."

"Would they kill for you?"

"Now you're being melodramatic.

"Give me their names."

"Is that really necessary?"

"Nine people are dead, Mr. Black. That implies a certain necessity. One accident, I can buy. Two, a coincidence perhaps. Nine seems excessively improbable. Give me the names of the people you told, or I call the cops right now."

"I don't think so," said a woman behind me.

I turned to face Emma Rhodden, the 'heart' of Gordon Black's church. She held a nasty-looking .32 caliber automatic.

"Emma?" Black said. "Put that down."

"No," she said. "I'm afraid I've already underestimated Mr. Gold one too many times."

With my back half turned to her, Emma couldn't see my right hand snake across my belly toward the shoulder holster, where I kept my Browning nine-mike.

Or maybe she could.

"Don't do that," she said. "My father taught me how to shoot when I was just a child. I would kill you before you turn halfway around. Pull out your gun, by the handle, with two fingers, and place it on the floor."

"Rhodden," I said, as I followed her directions. "*RodofGod.* You were the name on Black's list who never joined my email group. You live in Sausalito, don't you?"

"What are you saying?" Black demanded. "Emma is completely loyal to me."

"Hiram Darles told me someone he didn't know sent the picture he used to blackmail you. Since he admitted sliding it under your door, my job was done. I didn't bother to find out who actually manufactured the picture. It wasn't part of the job I agreed to do."

"You're so smart, aren't you?" Emma said.

"Smart enough to know you gave Darles that picture, Emma. What I can't quite figure out is *why*?"

"Neither can I," Black said. "Why did you do this horrible thing, Emma?"

"There is no such thing as bad publicity, Gordon. A church--*any* church—runs on money. Money comes from contributions. I figured if Darles released that picture, we'd get publicity, lots of it. Most people, people who can't understand what we're doing, would disregard us as a bunch of kooks and sex addicts. The *right* people, though, would flock to us in droves. Collections would skyrocket. We'd have the money to grow the way you had always dreamed of growing."

"I never would have agreed to such a scheme."

"Why do you think I never *told* you?" Emma said. "I know how proud you are, Gordon. I knew you'd never give in to Darles' extortion. I figured the picture would be distributed, one way or the other."

"My God," Black said, shaking his head. "You don't know what you've done. Why kill all those people?"

"Darles again. Somehow, he found his way to me. He was a computer geek. He figured out a way to get my name from the email address. When he found out I was with the church, he threatened to expose me, beginning with the people he'd gotten to know on Gold's email list."

"Did he do it?" Black asked.

"I don't know. Because of the protocols Gold placed on the list, I couldn't find out what Darles had told them. So, I had to get rid of each of the people on the list, one by one."

"It was important to make them look like accidents," I said, never taking my eyes off Emma's gun. "Murders make the front page of the newspaper. People who die in accidents barely make the obits."

"We have to get rid of him, Gordon," Emma said.

"What on Earth are you talking about?" Black said.

"I'm a liability," I said. "Emma believes you'll forgive her. She's the heart of your ministry, after all. The head can never separate itself from the heart. I, on the other hand, can ruin everything. Emma expects that you'll overlook just one more *accident*."

"It's out of the question," Black said. "Emma, I love you as much as I've loved anyone. What you've done, though, is monstrous. You have acted without respect or tolerance for others. I'm afraid I have no alternative other than to excommunicate you from the church. Please put down the gun."

"What?" she asked. Her face looked puzzled.

"The gun. I must insist that you put it down."

"I did it all for you!"

"I regret that. I really do. I'll say it again. You must put the gun down."

"I . . . I can't," she whimpered.

"I imagine that the policeman behind you would insist," Gordon said.

She gave him one look of incredulity, for only a second, before the uniformed cop who had crept up behind her leveled his own automatic and barked at her to drop her weapon. Shocked, she let go of the pistol almost instantly. It fell to the floor like a neglected stone.

As soon as she was cuffed, a plainclothes detective entered the room.

"Detective Crymes," I said, "this is Gordon Black."

"I wish I could say it's a pleasure, Mr. Black," Crymes said.

"Detective Crymes is with the Robbery-Homicide Division, Pacifica Police," I explained. "Once I figured out that you or one of your people had to have killed my phishes, I contacted him. Avery Sipe, one of Emma's victims, lived in Pacifica. That made it Detective Crymes' case."

I pulled my cell phone from my jacket pocket and held it up.

"Did you hear the entire conversation?" I asked.

"Every word," Crymes said. "Seems Ms. Rhodden here has a lot of explaining to do. I'll still need some information from you, Eamon. Can I reach you at the Montara house?"

"Or at my office in San Francisco."

"I'll call you."

He and the uniformed cop helped Emma to her feet and escorted her out of the office to the waiting patrol car.

———

A week or so later, Heidi and I were at the Montara house, preparing to grill Alaskan salmon and silver queen corn. The mail truck drove up and left something in my mailbox.

I retrieved it, and opened the envelope as I walked back to the deck.

"What's that?" she asked.

"A check," I said. "From Gordon Black. The note says he wants to reward me for saving his church."

"Is it a nice check?"

"Very nice. Feel like a trip? Someplace warm, with lots of sand and fruity drinks?"

"I could go someplace warm. I'm still not certain I understand this church of Black's."

"Maybe I'm just old and stuffy," I said, "but it seems more like a cover for Black and his followers to indulge adolescent fantasies."

"Different strokes for different folks."

"I do believe that you've just quoted the California state motto," I said.

"How long is it going to take the charcoal to be ready to grill?"

"A half hour or so. Why?"

She grinned at me, her eyes twinkling.

"Thought we might head to the back of the house for a while. Maybe get in a little . . . you know. Worship."

I took her hand and led her through the sliding glass doors into the house.

"Let us pray," I said.

SILICON KINGS

by

Richard Helms

Author's Note:This was the third Eamon Gold story to garner an award nomination, this time in 2011 for the SMFS Derringer Award. I recall the moment this story came to me, sometime in 2009. I was cutting the grass and thinking about what story I'd write next, and this one popped into my head. By the time I finished the front yard, I had most of the first act complete in my head. Wrote this one in about a week, and published it in The Back Alley Webzine.
R

Wally Bean was almost twenty years younger than I was.

He was worth about thirty million more.

He had my rapt attention.

"Do you know much about computers, Mr. Gold?" he asked.

"I know how to turn one on," I said. "I can make it go *beep*."

"I own a computer company. Specifically, we write software."

"I hear there's a lot of money in that these days."

"Yes, you could say. Last year my company netted about two hundred million."

"Dollars?" I asked.

"And change."

"You can buy a lot of help for just the change," I noted.

He ignored me.

"We have a problem. Someone has been stealing our code."

"How does someone do that?"

"That's the problem. Code writing is a fairly high-tech operation. You'd be surprised how many people don't even know what it is."

"Including myself. I failed COBOL in high school."

He regarded me with something that I took for pity. Apparently, I had just flunked my human race test. I checked to make sure my opposable thumbs were still attached.

"Well, we're way beyond COBOL now," he said.

His inference was clear. I was not only extinct, I was fossilized.

"There are some people, though, who actually think in code. They live and breathe it. We look for those people. We scour colleges looking for the right candidates and snap them up."

"*We* being?"

"My company is called Dynogix. What do you know about it?"

"A little."

"We've been working on a new type of Web browser. It will be thirty percent faster than the competition."

"And someone is stealing the code for your browser?"

"Yes."

"How do you know?"

"One of our technicians cracked into a sample of a beta version of a new browser being developed by another company. Like I said, these guys live their lives in code. He recognized several specific strings, because he had written them."

"It's not possible that someone else just stumbled on the same strings? I heard once that an infinite number of monkeys typing on an infinite number of typewriters…"

"Not in this case," Wally said, interrupting me. "This was part of our development code, the stuff that actually speeds up the new browser. It's revolutionary stuff."

"What was the name of the company developing the other program?"

"SymSystems. Their owner was one of my old coworkers, when I started at IntelliPro."

"Are any of you Silicon Valley companies just named after a person, or are you all neologisms?"

He stared at me for a few moments.

I think he blinked once or twice.

Rebooting, I guess.

He reached into his jacket pocket and slipped a folded piece of paper across my desk. I opened it.

"That's Jeff Lopiano," he said.

It was a high-quality graphic of a man in his late twenties, with thinning hair and a cheesy little moustache. His eyes were a watery blue. I could have stirred a highball with his neck.

"This guy owns SymSystems?" I said.

He nodded.

"I've included all the information we could put together—address, license tag numbers, telephone numbers. There's also some information about SymSystems there."

"So you think this guy Lopiano's behind the code theft?"

"We found it in his program."

"But he didn't actually write the program, correct?"

"Well, if it's his program and our code, he would have had to authorize the theft. I'd like you to find out how he stole it, and close up the leak."

"Excuse me, but that sounds like an internal security problem. That's not exactly my line of work. How did you find me, anyway?"

"I was referred to you."

"Who referred you?"

"Aubrey Innes."

I nodded and turned my swivel desk chair to face the window of my office. It was a crisp day in San Francisco, and my window faced Mount Tam across the bay. There were ten or twelve sailboats on the water between the Golden Gate Bridge and Alcatraz.

I wished I were on one of them.

"Aubrey Innes manufactures cell phones," I said.

"Yes."

"There's a big difference between finding out who's spiriting away cases of cell phones, and who's stealing what amounts to intellectual property, Mr. Bean."

"I don't see your point."

"Did you tell Aubrey all about your problem?"

"Yes."

"I wonder why he sent you to me, then."

"I don't know."

"Let's find out," I said.

I turned the chair back to face Wally Bean and picked up the receiver to my telephone.

Several moments later, I had Aubrey Innes on the line.

"Aubrey, I'm sitting in my office with a fellow you referred to me."

"Do tell?"

"Wally Bean?"

"Yes, I did," he said.

"I'm not certain what he wants, and I was hoping you could help me out a little."

"Wally has a problem, Eamon," Aubrey said.

"Code theft," I said.

"He has a much bigger problem than the simple theft of code."

"I think you'd better explain that."

"I can't, not without betraying a confidence. Let's just say you'll find out about it very soon."

"You're not being much help, here," I noted.

"You don't need my help. It will all become clear within a day or so."

We exchanged pleasantries for a moment or so, and then I hung up.

"Aubrey says your problem is bigger than code theft," I told Wally Bean.

"I don't know what he means."

"He said I would, in a day or so."

Wally pulled out a checkbook and a Mont Blanc pen. I liked the pen. I wasn't crazy about the checkbook.

"What are you doing?" I asked.

"Writing you a check," he said, without looking up.

"Don't do that."

That made him look up.

"I haven't decided whether to take your case," I told him.

"You're otherwise employed?"

"No. Actually I'm between cases."

"Then what's the problem?"

"No problem. It's just the way I am. I take the cases I want to take."

He continued to stare.

"It's a *me* thing." I said. "You wouldn't understand."

He nodded and turned back to writing his check.

"I understand a lot more than you think," he said. "The high-tech data business was built on the backs of rugged individualists. We don't spend a lot of time worrying about things like vertical lines of communication or getting permission."

He tore the check from his wallet and placed it on the desk. I didn't touch it, but I could see it from where I was sitting.

It was too big to miss.

"That's a retainer," he said. "This situation is very important to me. If Aubrey Innes says you're the guy for the job, I want you on it. Think it over. If you want the job, deposit the check and give me a call. If you don't want it, tear it up and give me a call so I can find someone else."

He stood and leaned over my desk to shake my hand.

"I'm betting you cash the check," he said.

I listened as he walked down the stairs to Jefferson Street.

I looked down at the check on my desk. Then I swiveled back to watch the sailboats on the bay.

I was still watching the sailboats when Heidi Fluhr walked up the steps to my office. We had a lunch date. She didn't knock. She doesn't have to.

Heidi is like the Swedish farmer's daughter on steroids. She's six feet of all girl and bunches of it. Sleeping with her is like running a triathlon.

Three times in one night.

She had cut her hair a few weeks before. It fell in short blonde wisps around her perfectly complected face and her cool blue eyes.

We had dated for a couple of years. It wasn't serious, but neither was I interested in breaking it off anytime soon. Playing night games with Heidi is like driving a Formula 1 car. Afterward, nothing else seems to stack up.

"Ready?" she asked.

"Sure," I said. I picked up the check and placed it in my desk drawer.

"New job?"

"I don't know yet. I'm thinking it over."

"What's the deal?"

"Computer gig. Industrial espionage. James Bond stuff."

"Sounds like fun."

"Sounds like a headache, on top of a toothache. Where do you want to eat?"

We walked down Jefferson past the Hyde Pier to Fisherman's Wharf and took a booth at a place that had iced bins full of shellfish out front. I wasn't very hungry, so I ordered clam chowder in a sourdough loaf bowl. Heidi ordered half the appetizer menu.

And a salad.

"I finished the dreadnaught last night," I said, as we sipped our tea.

"Oh," she said. "That explains why you're so distant today. Every time you finish an instrument you get the thousand-yard stare."

"Do not," I said.

But I knew she was right. I build guitars and other stringed instruments as a hobby. Sometimes I think I'd rather do it for a living, but then it wouldn't be fun anymore.

"What will you build next?" she asked.

"I haven't decided yet."

"Kind of like the job."

"Yeah. Kind of like the job."

"Maybe a Selmer Maccaferri," I said, a couple of minutes later, between bites of the chowder.

"Say again?"

"It's a jazz guitar from the thirties. I have the plans for it at the Montara house. I might make it next."

"Good for you," she said.

I looked up.

She smiled.

"It's important to clarify your options."

I walked her back to her store. Heidi owns the art gallery just underneath my office. I don't understand a lot of the stuff she sells, but that's okay. She doesn't understand a lot of my work.

It keeps us from getting too involved in each other's lives.

Heidi went back to work, and I walked up the steps to my office.

There was a man sitting in my waiting room.

"Come into my office, Mr. Lopiano," I said.

He stood as I opened the door to my inner office.

"You know who I am?"

"I'm a detective," I said. "I know all kinds of things."

I took my seat behind the desk, and he sat in the same seat where Wally Bean had that morning.

"Let me guess," I said, "You have a problem at SymSystems."

His head bobbed around on his pencil neck like a dashboard chihuahua.

"Amazing," he said.

"Did Aubrey Innes send you?" I asked.

"Yes. Did he tell you I was coming?"

"No. Educated guess."

I made a note to slap Aubrey around a little the next time I saw him.

"Want to make a bet?" I said.

"I'm not sure."

I pulled a twenty from my pocket and slapped it down on my desk.

"That twenty says you're working on a new Web browser, and someone's been stealing your code."

"Aubrey *did* talk with you."

"Yes, but not about you."

I opened my desk drawer and pulled out Wally Bean's check and a pen. It wasn't a Mont Blanc, but it wrote just fine. I turned the check over and endorsed it, then stuffed it in my shirt pocket.

"What's that?" Lopiano asked.

"A decision I just made. Let's talk about your problem."

"I've come to kick your ass," I said, as I settled into the leather chair next to Aubrey Innes' sofa. He was on the sofa. In front of him was a fine sterling tea service. I recalled that Aubrey didn't drink coffee.

"Tea?" he asked.

"No thanks. What's the big idea, sending those kids to me?"

"Bean and Lopiano?"

"Yeah."

"The situation amused me. I thought it would interest you."

"Did they come to you individually too?"

"They telephoned. I knew both of them when we were grunts at DiaCom. Actually, Jeff Lopiano called me first. Wanted to know what Wally was up to. Like I knew."

"Why would he call you?"

"I put the word out, anyone needed an investigator, I could set them up. You did a good job closing a hole in my distribution system last year. I was impressed."

"Not that I can't use the work…" I said.

"Feeling a little manipulated?"

"No more than your average pretzel."

"So, what do you think?"

"I should discuss my clients' business with you?"

"I see," Innes said, pouring tea into a Wedgwood china cup.

"Ethics," I said. "Confidentiality. You understand."

"Of course. On the other hand, I'm not bound by any such constraints. Do you mind if I think out loud for a moment?"

"Not at all."

"We have two very bright, but very introverted guys. Despite their obvious physical dissimilarities, they are intellectual and emotional twins, which is to say they are at an intellectual age somewhere around a thousand, and an emotional age of five or six. At one time, they were very close friends."

"But competitive?"

"Of course. It's a competitive business. Breakthroughs come every thirty-seven seconds. You need to stay on top of things. Some of these guys work three, four years without taking a vacation."

"But there are rewards."

"It's not coincidental that Bill Gates is the richest man in the world, Eamon."

"Interesting that they would branch off into individual companies working on the same stuff."

"You mean, why didn't they combine their talents? Form a single company and shoot for some kind of synergistic energy?"

"Yeah. That thing you just said."

"Ah, well...." Innes said, sipping his tea. "Now we enter the realm of gossip."

"Oh, goody."

"There was a girl."

"There always is," I said.

Heidi and I had spent the night at my house in Montara.

I had converted the living room into a workshop, where I built my instruments. I am a messy luthier. I had spent the afternoon the day before cleaning the shop and sharpening my hand tools, while Heidi trotted across the Pacific Coast Highway to Montara Beach to shed her clothes, read a book, and arouse the marine wildlife.

We grilled steaks that evening and ate on my deck overlooking the beach. We drank a lot of California merlot. The rest of the evening was a fleshy blur.

I awoke around eight-thirty with my mind working on the problem of Wally Bean and Jeff Lopiano. I dressed in jeans and a cutoff sweatshirt, made some coffee, and started puttering around the shop.

While I worked on joining the two halves of a Sitka spruce soundboard, I reviewed what Aubrey Innes had told me.

Wally Bean and Jeff Lopiano were fast buddies at DiaCom, after graduating from Cal Tech. It was their first job in the computer industry. Their primary interest was seeing how much more information they could stuff onto a silicon chip, even as they explored how much smaller they could make the chip.

Their secondary interest was Linda Pickett.

According to Aubrey, Jeff Lopiano claimed to have seen her first, as if that counted for anything. Maybe, for eggheads like my clients, it did.

DiaCom had a "work hard–play hard" philosophy. Its owner, a hoary old veteran of the high-tech business (whom, I might add, was younger than I) was a little hyperactive, and expected that his younger talent would keep up with him. Besides putting in hundred-hour weeks, there were lots of company "activities" that involved things like water skiing and hang-gliding. In the evenings, the entire crew tended to congregate at local watering holes to lubricate the next day's brainworks.

It was at one of those bars that Jeff Lopiano first spotted Linda Pickett. As Aubrey Innes told it, Wally Bean may have seen her one or two seconds later, but in Silicon Valley a second or two might as well be a lifetime.

The door to my bedroom opened. Heidi stumbled out, naked, and plopped down on the sofa that ran the length of the fourth wall of the living room. Not many women can lounge around in the buff and look natural. Heidi looked like she was posing for Titian.

"There's coffee," I said.

"Oh, thank God," she moaned, rising from the couch. She padded into the kitchen.

While she poured, I laid the bookmatched spruce on top of some pipe clamps, ran a bead of wood glue down the joined edges, and then pulled them together with the clamps. In a few hours I would take the joined top plate out and plane it to its final thickness.

Or not.

The nice thing about instrument building was that nobody made me account for my time.

Heidi walked back into the living room and looked at me drowsily over the steam rising from her morning brew.

"What in hell did we do last night?" she asked.

"Pretty much all of it," I said.

"Uh huh," she said, nodding. "That explains it. What are you working on?"

"Maccaferri guitar. The kind Django Reinhardt played."

"If you say so. You have to work today?"

"I'm planning to meet with a couple of clients around one."

"It's just nine now."

"Yes."

"I have a shower running."

"I thought I heard the water."

"We could get clean."

"That would be nice."

"And then we could get dirty again."

"That would be nicer," I said, as I set the guitar top aside to dry.

Jeff Lopiano sat nervously across from me, tapping on a small digital device in his hand with a stylus. I sat calmly and watched him. The window behind me was open, and a cool breeze wafted in off the bay.

The door to my office opened, and Wally Bean walked in.

"What's he doing here?" Lopiano asked.

"What's he doing here?" Bean asked.

"When you think of it, in the larger sense, what are any of us doing here?" I reflected. "In this case, though, I think you two have some things in common. At the moment, that includes having hired me to investigate each other."

"That's a conflict of interest," Bean protested.

"I don't think so," I said. "Please, have a seat."

Bean sat, reluctantly, in the seat next to Lopiano.

"Hey, Wally," Lopiano said.

"Hi, Jeff."

"Now, to business," I said. "Both of you were referred here by Aubrey Innes. Each of you took him into your confidence and told him essentially the same story. Each of you thinks the other has stolen your work. Follow me so far?"

They both nodded. Intellectual and emotional animated twin bookends.

"Detecting 101 says that this falls under the category of the impossible. A couple of ideas have occurred to me. One says that one or both of you are lying."

"Now just a minute!" Lopiano protested.

I held up a hand to silence him.

"That was just one idea. Another idea says that both of you are telling the truth but blaming the wrong person. I could bounce back and forth between you like a ping-pong ball, but that would just waste a lot of time and make me dizzy, so I decided to get you both in the same room and try to hash this out."

I waited for some kind of response.

When none came, I continued.

"Mr. Bean, when did you first notice that your code had been used by Mr. Lopiano?"

"Stolen, you mean…" Bean said.

"Like hell," Lopiano argued.

"Can we focus?" I said. "Mr. Bean, when did you discover the same code in both programs?"

"About a week ago. Like I said, one of my engineers obtained a beta test version of SymSystems' new browser."

"Where did he get this version?" I asked.

"I didn't ask."

"Of course not," Lopiano chirped. "You didn't want to be implicated."

I ignored him.

"What was this engineer's name?"

"Lionel Stukes."

I turned to Lopiano.

"And when did you notice your code in Mr. Bean's software?"

"About a week ago, also," Lopiano said. "It was brought to my attention by the director of my development crew, Les Crampley."

I wrote *Lionel Stukes* and *Les Crampley* on a legal pad next to my phone.

"How did Crampley obtain it?"

Lopiano mumbled something.

"Come again?" I asked.

"I didn't ask," Lopiano said, a little too loud and little too petulantly.

"For people with so much on the line, you guys sure don't ask many questions," I said.

Neither of them replied. They just sat there like a couple of school kids called up on the principal's carpet for smoking in the boys' room.

"Okay," I said. "I'm going to need whatever information you can give me on Stukes and Crampley."

Lionel Stukes had been dead for about twelve hours when I arrived at his house in Daly City. The front door was festooned with yellow crime tape, and a Pacifica Police detective named Crymes stood on the front walk talking with a uniformed cop.

"Crymes," I said, as I walked up to him.

"Wait a minute, Gold," he said. He told the uniformed cop to go back on patrol, and then turned to me.

"I hope you dropped by to confess," he said.

"To what?"

"Making such a mess of the guy owns this place."

"What happened?"

"Looks like he got into an awful fight. The living room is a wreck, and not just the parts he bled all over. Someone went after him with a blunt object and an agenda. Want to look?"

"Pass. Did he have a roommate or a live-in girlfriend?"

"Not that we can tell. What mail we found was addressed to him. What's your involvement?"

"He worked for one of my clients. Software engineer. I needed to ask him a couple of questions."

"I might want to talk with your client," he said.

"Trust me," I said. "You don't."

"What was he, bangin' your client's wife?"

"You wish it were that easy. Stukes had acquired some software for my client. I wanted to find out where and how."

"Industrial espionage case?"

"I'm not sure, yet. Maybe."

"Keep me posted?"

"Got you on speed dial," I said, as I headed back to my car.

A car was backing out of Les Crampley's driveway just as I drove up his street in Palo Alto. I had a couple of options. I could have blocked his path, jerked him through the keyhole, and beat some answers out of him, but I had generally found that an unproductive approach.

So, I decided to follow him.

I let him get a couple of hundred yards ahead of me, then fell into a loose tail. When we got onto Interstate 280, I let a couple of cars separate us, while I watched his license plate through the windows. Unless he had X-ray vision, he couldn't know I was back there.

He pulled off at an exit near Redwood City, and I went with him. He drove to an office park, where he parked in a lot outside a squat complex of single-story buildings.

I parked one lot over, with a good view of the car.

The door opened, and I realized I hadn't been following Les Crampley at all. The woman who got out was dressed in black jeans and a black tank top. Her inky hair was cut at indiscriminate lengths on top and back, with a long fringe running down the back of her neck, like a rock musician. Even from a distance I could make out her kohl-rimmed eyes and the glittery accumulata of jewelry punched through the skin of her face, nose, lips, and ears. She wasn't all that tall, but she was lanky and loose-limbed as she strode from the car to the front door of the building.

I pulled my binoculars out and scanned the front door, where I found a sign that said Core Logic.

I stepped out of the car and walked casually over to the next lot to memorize her license tag. I kept walking and pulled out my cell phone.

Shirley Jones is a pal who works for the DMV at the San Francisco Civic Center. We have a past, but that was over before I met Heidi.

"This is Gold," I said.

"Yes, sir. What can I do for you?"

"Your boss is hovering?"

"That's correct, sir."

"I need a license tag traced." I gave her the number.

"Please hold, sir."

I suffered through an elevator music rendition of some Andrew Lloyd Webber tune, until she came back on the line.

"Is there lunch in this for me?"

"Not today. I'll owe you."

"You already owe me, skinflint."

"I'm in kind of a hurry, Shirl."

"The owner's name is Linda Pickett."

"Thanks, gotta boogie."

"Wait a min…"

But I had punched the END button. Linda Pickett had walked out of Core Logic and was headed back to her car.

I returned to my car and backed it out of the lot just as she hit the stop sign at the highway. I noted which way she turned and made the same turn when I got there. I could make out her car about a quarter mile ahead, so I hammered down for a mile or so to cut the distance a little, and then throttled back when I had reached at a comfortable gap.

It didn't take an Einstein to figure out that Linda Pickett was probably the conduit for the beta versions of the software that Les Crampley and Lionel Stukes had received. What I couldn't figure out was why she was playing both sides against the middle. Somehow, I thought, Core Logic had to fit in to the picture, unless she was also stringing along some poor programmer sap there.

Since Lionel Stukes had been murdered, I also figured that this put Les Crampley either at risk, or directly in the limelight as a suspect. I thumbed Crymes' number on my cell speed dial.

"Crymes."

"This is Gold. I'm tailing a chick named Linda Pickett. I saw her leave a house belonging to another guy named Les Crampley about a half hour ago. Crampley found some of his code in a program that your dead guy was writing for a company called SymSystems."

"Silicon Valley outfit?"

"Yeah. The dead guy, Stukes, worked for Dynogix. I thought you might want to check in on Crampley. If he isn't dead, he might have a lot of explaining to do."

I gave him Crampley's address and signed off. I dialed Kevin Krantz at the Business desk of the *Chronicle.* Kevin and I go back a long way.

"Kevin, this is Eamon Gold."

"Who do you want me to check on this time?"

"So young. So cynical."

"Yeah, yeah. What's up?"

"Company called Core Logic. It's in Redwood."

"You on your cell?"

"Yeah."

"I'll get back to you."

I followed Linda Pickett through San Mateo and Daly City. She was headed back into San Francisco. As long as we were on the freeway, I could lay back a quarter mile or so, keep a few cars between us. If I was lucky, and hadn't lost my touch, she'd never know I was there.

My cell beeped. I answered it.

"This is Kevin."

"What did you find?"

"Core Logic. Founded three years ago by Hack German, a former IBM techno-geek."

"What do they do?"

"What does anyone do down in Silicon Valley? He writes software."

"What kind of software?"

"In his case, he's been developing a search engine. He saw how Google and Yahoo had made their founders very rich men, and he wants to slice off a piece of that pie."

"Search engine," I said.

"Does that mean something?"

"I don't know. What do you know about ongoing projects at Dynogix and SymSystems?"

"Not much. I'd have to get back to you."

"The quicker the better, Kev."

Linda Pickett pulled off the highway at the Bayshore Expressway, and then took the off ramp at Van Ness. I followed her through SoMa until she hung a left at Bush and parked in the driveway of a house between Bush and Pine in the Fillmore district.

Just as I pulled over to the curb, my cell phone rang.

"This is Kevin," he told me when I answered. "There's a lot of talk about both Dynogix and SymSystems, but it's all back-channel stuff. It seems their legal eagles have been preparing some patent submissions."

"Browsers," I said. "I already know about that."

"No. Well, sort of, but not exactly. What do you know about the Grid, Eamon?"

"You mean like the old Firesign Theater stuff? *Grid Willing*, that kind of thing?"

"Hardly. The Grid is the next big thing. It's going to make the World Wide Web look like a rural party line. Super high-speed information access, ungodly bandwidth, real high-tech whizbang stuff."

"So?"

"So, forward-thinking techies are already preparing to get onboard with this Grid thingie. It seems the patents being sought by Dynogix and SymSystems revolve around super-spiders."

"You've lost me."

"Spiders are part of the browsing software used by search engines to acquire and catalog webpage information. They prowl around the Web in the background, reading pages and links, and indexing what they find. That way, when you type 'wombats' into a search engine, all it has to do is find that word in the index, and it lists all the pages containing the word."

"And these super-spiders will do the same thing on this Grid?"

"Exactly. The first company to patent a Grid-compatible search engine using hyperspeed super-spiders is going to make a buttload of money."

"Define *buttload.*"

"Billions, Eamon. If I were a savvy investor, which I am, I'd start buying both Dynogix and SymSystems, just to hedge my bets."

"What about Core Logic?"

"What about them?"

"You said earlier that they were into search engines also."

"Yeah. I did, didn't I? What are you up to, anyway?"

"I'm not sure. I'd hold off buying stock, though, if I were you. Some of the players might get benched."

I sat in my car, watching the front of the house Linda Pickett had entered, and tried to figure out what was going on. Linda had left Les Crampley's house and had driven all the way to Redwood City, and then spent a grand total of five minutes inside Core Logic. Then she had driven all the way back to the city. My guess was that she had gone to

Core Logic just to drop off something. She really hadn't been there long enough to get into any lengthy conversations.

I pulled out the cell phone and called Heidi at the art gallery.

"I could use a favor," I said.

"Okay."

"Check your phone book. I need to know if there's a listing for Linda Pickett on Bush Street."

"Give me a sec…No. I don't see one. There's an L. Pickett on Figueroa in San Jose. A lot of women list themselves by their first initials."

"Yeah. They do. Give me the Figueroa address and phone number."

She recited them from the phone book, and I wrote them on the pad suspended from the dash of my car. I thanked her, with a promise of more attention later in the evening and signed off.

My next call was to Kevin Krantz at the paper.

"Got your criss-cross phone directory handy?" I asked.

"Sure."

"I need a listing for a house on Bush Street."

I gave him the house number.

"According to the directory, it's a residence. Fellow named Kerry Clapp. You want the phone number?"

"Sure."

I sat in the car for a few more minutes, ruminating over what I knew, and what I didn't. Then I pulled out the cell phone on a hunch, got the number for Core Logic, and had information connect me.

"Core Logic," a woman answered.

"Kerry Clapp, please?"

"I'm sorry, sir. Mr. Clapp isn't in today. Can I take a message?"

"Um, I need to speak with someone directly. Is his supervisor available?"

"Certainly sir. I'll connect you."

There was a brief interlude, and then someone picked up the phone.

"This is Hack German," he said. "Can I help you?"

"Actually, I was trying to get in touch with Kerry Clapp," I said.

"Yes. Kerry's out today. Is there anything I can do for you, Mr…"

"I don't know," I said, evading his probe. "This is a little convoluted. I was hoping Mr. Clapp could put me in touch with Linda Pickett."

There was a moment of silence on the other end.

"Who is this?" he asked. His voice had taken on a cold, edgy tone.

I ended the call and turned off the telephone. Maybe German could trace me and maybe he couldn't. I didn't have a voicemail system on my cell, so he couldn't find me that way. If he tried to call me back, he'd just get an out-of-service message.

Nobody had entered or left the Bush Street house since Linda Pickett had gone inside. I waited about five minutes, just long enough for German to get tired of trying to ring me back, and then I called Crymes.

"Did you find Les Crampley?" I asked.

"Yeah. He was at home."

"What was his story?"

"About what, Gold? He was safe and sound, not a scratch on him. He also said he'd never heard of a woman named Linda Pickett."

"He's lying. I saw her leave his house not two hours ago."

"You didn't see him with her, though."

"No, but..."

"You want to fill me in on what's going on?"

"I'm still putting it together. I think it involves theft of intellectual property, and an attempt by a company called Core Logic to keep two other companies—Dynogix and SymSystems—from filing a patent application for a computer browsing system they're both developing."

"Industrial espionage shit."

"It has the smell of it."

"Not the kind of thing that usually leads to murder."

"According to one of my sources, there are billions of dollars at stake. Makes a hell of a motive."

"I agree. I need what you've got."

"I'm staking out a house owned by a guy named Kerry Clapp. He works for this Core Logic company. He isn't at work today. I saw Linda Pickett go inside the house about ten minutes ago. When I called Core Logic, the owner, fellow named Hack German, lost all his warmth when I told him I was looking for Linda Pickett. Linda Pickett was involved in a lust triangle with the owners of Dynogix and SymSystems three or four years ago, which led them to split up and go their separate ways."

"This Linda Pickett gets around."

"I think she may be the conduit between your dead guy and Les Crampley. I think she's been stealing code from both of them and shuttling it back and forth. Probably told them it was coming from Core Logic, since they're working on the same kind of programs."

"You're losing me."

"The first company to file a patent application for this new kind of search engine will make Microsoft look like a corner Mom and Pop operation. By pitting Dynogix against SymSystems, Core Logic buys time to perfect its product and file first."

"It still doesn't explain why Stukes was murdered."

"I know. Maybe he figured out what was going on."

The front door of the Bush Street house opened, and two people walked out. One was Linda Pickett. The other was a tall, sinewy man in his thirties. His hair was pulled back in a blond ponytail.

"Looks like my guys are on the move," I said. "I'll have to call you back, Crymes."

"Gold, wait…"

I turned off the phone and dropped my car into gear just as Linda Pickett and her fellow pulled out of the driveway and headed east on Bush, toward Van Ness.

As I had expected, they drove straight to Core Logic. I had a feeling when I saw them that the rangy guy with the ponytail was Clapp. I also was willing to bet that when Hack German couldn't get me back on the phone he called Clapp, who just happened to be with Linda Pickett, and summoned them to Core Logic for a strategic planning pow-wow.

I parked nearby, in the same lot I had used earlier that day, and watched as Linda Pickett and the guy I thought was Clapp got out of the car and walked inside.

Recalling that at least one person had already been killed, I grabbed my Browning automatic from the glove compartment and stowed it on my belt, underneath my jacket.

I strolled casually into the Core Logic office. Like a lot of Silicon Valley companies, it was little more than a shell housing a cube farm with a few standalone offices for the top brass. There was a girl sitting at the front desk who looked as if she should have been in high school.

"Is Hack in?" I asked.

"I'm sorry. He's in a meeting."

She nodded toward on end of the hall, at a closed door next to a warren of cubicles.

"Any idea how long he's going to be?" I asked. "I'm on kind of a tight schedule."

"Do you have an appointment, Mr…."

"No. Just blowing through town. Thought I'd look ol' Hack up, maybe drag him out to bend an elbow and reminisce about the college days."

"If you'd like to take a seat," she said, nodding toward the waiting area. Her arms, by all appearances, must have been paralyzed, because she pointed toward everything with her chin. "He should be available shortly."

"Sure. Just one thing. Do you have a bathroom around here somewhere? I just drove in from the airport, and I had to sit in traffic for a while."

She directed me back along the hallway toward the cube farm. Perfect.

I walked back along the hall, almost all the way to the closed office door, then turned left toward the bathroom. When I peeked back around the corner, the receptionist had left her desk.

There was an open door across the hall. It appeared to be some kind of small conference room. I walked through the open door and closed it behind me.

A dry erase whiteboard had been installed on the wall next to the closed office the girl had shown me. I picked up one of the drinking glasses from the water station and held it up to the board. It made a terrific sound conductor.

People in the next room sounded agitated.

"Why in hell did you have to kill him?" a man said.

"He'd figured out where the code originated. He was going to rat us out to Bean."

"I thought you were going to handle Stukes."

"I did, up to a point," a female voice said. Must have been Linda Pickett. "When he discovered the code came from Core Logic instead of SymSystems, he felt betrayed. He called me over specifically to tell me he was going to turn us in. He'd figured out the entire scheme. He was even going to call Lopiano over at SymSystems."

"We didn't have a choice," the other male voice said. I decided he must be Clapp.

"What about the other one? Crampley?"

"He's on board," Linda said. "I offered to let him in on the take once the Core Logic super-spider gets patented and goes into production. I also told him we could keep getting together for sex. I tried it with Stukes, but he apparently had more scruples."

The telephone in the next room buzzed, and I heard someone pick it up.

"Yes, Brenda…Okay, thanks."

A second later, a connecting door to my right opened, and Clapp dashed into the room. He grabbed me by the collar and dragged me toward German's office. I elbowed him stiffly just under the ribs and heard the air blast out of his lungs just before he fell to his knees.

By that time, though, German was all over me. He was a big guy, maybe six-two, and he worked out. He tried to put me in a full nelson. I quickly dropped and broke his grip, but he kneed me in the kidneys as I went down. A wave of heat and nausea flooded through my torso. I felt a hand snake under my jacket. Before I could stop him, German had my gun.

"Just stay down!" he ordered. "Who in hell are you?"

I tried to make some words come out, but the pain in my lower back kept me from getting enough air to produce anything more audible than a croak.

At that moment, my cell phone jangled in my jacket pocket.

German jacked me up against the wall, held me there with his forearm against my windpipe, and grabbed the cell phone with his free hand. He held it in front of my eyes.

"Who is it?" he demanded.

I looked at the number.

"A cop. His name is Crymes. Pacifica PD."

He let it ring. After a few moments, it stopped.

"The cops!" he said to Linda Pickett, who had joined us in the meeting room. "Look what you've brought down on our heads, you stupid bitch!"

He went through my pockets and found my leather card folder.

"He's a PI," German said. "Name's Eamon Gold."

"Never heard of him," Clapp said. He had finally gotten his breath back and was standing next to German.

"What are you doing here, Gold?" German asked. He accented his question with a sharp fist to the short ribs on my right side. I winced and made a silent promise to clean his clock the first chance I got.

"Working a case," I said.

"Who hired you?"

"Bean and Lopiano. I've already told Crymes, that cop who was on the phone, the entire scheme. I told him that Linda Pickett was feeding Core Logic code to Stukes and Crampley. I know about the super-spider patent application, and how you're trying to divert Dynogix and SymSystems by making them each think the other is stealing their code, until you can snipe them. Crymes knows everything."

"Don't shit me, man. If the cops knew everything, they'd be here already."

"This is fucked," Clapp said. "I didn't sign on for this kind of shitstorm. I'm leaving."

With his arm still pinned against my windpipe, German swung my Browning around and leveled it at Clapp.

"Nobody leaves!" he said.

"Now you've got balls?" Clapp said. "I beat the living shit out of Stukes last night because you didn't have the guts to stop him."

"That was different," German said. "I can't let you leave until we know how much Gold here has passed on to the cops."

"Christ!" Clapp said. "We are going *down*, man."

"No, we aren't," German argued. "Worst case, we have to leave the country. I have millions stashed away in the offshore accounts. We'll be just fine."

"What about her?" Clapp said, pointing at Linda. "She's the connection with Dynogix and SymSystems."

"Man," I rasped. "You guys aren't even good enough to be lousy criminals. What made you think you could get away with this?"

"It was *her* idea!" Clapp said.

"Shut up!" German said. "Let me think!"

"She came to us," Clapp said, ignoring him. "She said she had a way to keep Lopiano and Bean off balance long enough for us to get the jump on the super-spider program."

"I said shut up!" German said, just before I pivoted and sank my teeth into his forearm.

He screamed at the instant pain, and his other hand jerked. I heard the Browning explode in the crowded room, and a little scarlet flower erupted on the front of Clapp's shirt. He clawed at the hole, as the flower grew into a splotch, and then a cascade. Slowly, he sat down on the floor, unable to take his eyes off the life that flooded out of him one heartbeat at a time.

I rammed my knee up into German's balls and took great delight in the way his eyes widened as his mouth formed this silent round circle, just before he dropped the Browning, doubled over, and clutched his arms to his midsection.

Linda Pickett grabbed the Browning as German went down and had me cold before I could stop her. Her hands trembled as she tried to keep the barrel pointed at my chest. She didn't say anything. Her eyes were dilated to the point that all I could see were pupils. She was running on pure adrenalin, and any second her fist was going to spasm and park a nine-mike round right into my heart.

Just when I thought she was about to go ballistic, she cut to her right and dashed back into German's office. I heard her run down the hall, and I took off after her.

She ran right into Crymes and a couple of uniformed Redwood City patrol cops as they walked in the front door. They instinctively drew down on her.

"Drop the fucking weapon!" Crymes yelled, using the command voice they teach in the academy.

She froze and dropped the Browning to the floor. I stood behind her, my hands already in the air.

"The others are in the back," I said. "German killed Clapp, I think."

Crymes directed the patrolmen to the back, as he started to cuff Linda.

"You must have called from the parking lot," I said.

"I was going to check Core Logic out based on your call a little while ago. I got here and saw that piece of shit car of yours. Figured you beat me to the punch. Looks like I missed the party."

"I overheard them talking about killing Stukes," I said.

"All in good time, Eamon. Let's figure out what happened here first."

"So Clapp killed Lionel Stukes," I told Heidi over dinner that night at my Montara house. "It seems Linda Pickett was screwing about everyone except German, and she must have been top shelf, because these guys would do just about anything for her. She told Clapp that Stukes was going to turn them all in for conspiracy, and Clapp paid Stukes a visit."

"What happens next?" Heidi asked.

"Linda's no idiot. As soon as she dropped the gun she started talking deal with Crymes. She'll give up Hack German for both the conspiracy and for killing Clapp. He'll get minimal time on the conspiracy, since it's basically a white-collar beef. He didn't really mean to kill Clapp, either, so he'll probably get off with involuntary manslaughter. Linda Pickett will probably get off with probation. Same for Crampley."

"Hardly seems fair," she said. "Two guys are dead over all this."

"That's not all. Once they realized they'd both been royally dicked by Linda Pickett, Lopiano and Bean buried the hatchet. They're talking merger, and they're planning to launch their super-spider as a joint venture. Want to hear the best part? The hot shit code that makes the whole thing run really did belong to Core Logic to begin with, for all the good it does German now."

She finished her wine and placed the glass back on the table.

"And the silicon kings were very grateful to their savior," she noted.

"It's a good thing, too. I lost the Browning. It's a murder weapon, so the police confiscated it. I'll never get it back."

"Yeah, but you do get the consolation prize," she said.

"What's that?"

She stood and started unbuttoning her blouse.

"Me," she said.

It was a fair trade.

THE GODS FOR VENGEANCE CRY

by

Richard Helms

Author's Note:

*Failed seminarian, retired forensic psychologist, disgraced college professor, and slacker New Orleans jazz cornet player Pat Gallegher has been my franchise series character for almost thirty years. By the time this story was published in 2010, two Pat Gallegher novels (**Juicy Watusi; Wet Debt**) had already been finalists for the PWA Shamus Award. This story also introduces Judd Wheeler, the protagonist in three of my novels.* The Gods for Vengeance Cry *was published in* Ellery Queen Mystery Magazine *in 2010. In 2011, it was a finalist for the SMFS Derringer Award, the MRI Macavity Award, and the ITW Thriller Award. It won the Thriller Award for Best Short Story in 2011.*
R

There are sixteen bones in the human hand. I had managed to break five of mine retrieving a poodle, the object of a messy custody dispute. I had also learned an important lesson: Owning a poodle doesn't mean you aren't a tough guy.

Fortunately, I'm also a tough guy. The poodle was returned to its rightful owner, who was so insanely happy that she paid my fee and the medical bills to have my hand set.

The money was dwindling quickly, though. At six-six and two-eighty, I go through a lot of food. I can't cook anything more substantial than a pop tart, so I take all my meals in restaurants.

I was quickly joining the ranks of the bucks-down.

I sat in Holliday's, nursing a Dixie Beer, when Shorty—Holliday's owner and my boss—wandered in from the alleyway. Shorty is a human fireplug, square as a checkers board, and ugly as roadkill.

"Gallegher," he said "I might have some work for you."

Besides being a recently handicapped cornet player, I make a few bucks on the side looking for—and usually finding—things that have disappeared. Poodles, for instance. Sometimes people don't like it when I show up to recover things. Sometimes they try to resist. They seldom resist for long.

"Remember Katie Costner?" he asked.

"Blonde kid. Worked here as a waitress about a year ago."

"She's dead."

I nodded. I think I might have furrowed my brow a bit.

Thousands of young people gravitate to the French Quarter each year. Some adapt. Some don't.

Some die.

You don't like to admit it, but you get used to it.

"I'm sorry to hear that," I said. "What happened?"

"They found her in her flop, down at the far end of Decatur, near Esplanade. She'd been strangled."

"Boyfriend?"

"Word has it she wasn't involved."

"You kept up with her after she quit?"

"I checked in on her once or twice. Brought her some food from time to time."

I nodded. Sometimes, Shorty dumps a boatload of surprise on you.

"The police officers working the case say she was from some flyspeck town in North Carolina. Place called Prosperity. Cops can't locate her parents. There's five hundred in it for you if you can track them down."

Shorty pulled a Dixie from the ice bin and twisted off the cap.

"People ought to hear about it when their kids die," he said.

A check on the Internet revealed that nobody named Costner owned a telephone in Prosperity. That didn't mean much. The number could have been unlisted, or maybe they used cell phones. Listed land lines are going the way of the passenger pigeon.

I also checked with a friend of mine in the Robbery-Homicide Division at NOPD, a scrawny, scarecrow-looking guy named Farley Nuckolls. Farley and I had butted heads a bunch of times over the years, but he gave me a reasonably wide berth since I passed along information when I fell across it.

Most of the time.

"She was strangled," he said.

"Harder than it sounds," I noted.

"Do tell. Personal experience?"

"I've never been strangled, if that's what you meant. As a retired psychologist I know a thing or two about the way the brain works. To do a strangling right, you have to cut off a person's oxygen supply for four minutes, minimum, unless you squeeze hard enough to fracture the hyoid bone in the larynx. Killing someone that way means you really have to go in committed."

"The forensic boys concur."

"No clues, then?"

"Not much to go on. The murder weapon was a twisted scarf. The killer apparently wore gloves. No epithelials on the scarf. No prints in the apartment. She was probably killed by a man."

"Or a female wrestler," I added.

"Don't complicate my life."

When Shorty referred to Prosperity as a flyspeck town, he had inadvertently given it a promotion. The main commercial district was confined to a five-acre area at the intersection of a couple of two-lane highways, and consisted of a strip shopping center, a doctor and a dentist, an attorney, and the town hall. At least the strip had a pizza parlor.

I ordered a garbage pie and sat at a booth facing out the picture window as I ate. It was already dusk, the end of a long day on the road. I hadn't seen a motel in town, and I was a little hazy as to where I was going to bunk down for the night.

The parking lot of the strip center seemed to be a gathering place for the disenchanted youth of Prosperity. They hung in clusters and stood around trying to look surly and threatening.

I finished my dinner, dropped a tip on the table, and slipped my Saints hat on.

I was halfway to my car when one of the kids stepped in front of me.

"Got a smoke?" he asked. A stray lock of limp hair fell across his left eye.

"No. I don't smoke, and you shouldn't either," I said.

"I don't like being told what to do," he said.

"Imagine that."

"If you don't have a cigarette, maybe you can spare a few bucks so I can buy my own."

Several of the kids had circled around and were now at my six. I was slowly being surrounded. I didn't think they meant to rob me, not in a place this public. They did, however, expect to intimidate me.

I don't intimidate easily.

I pulled a five from my pocket.

The kid reached for it. I jerked it back. Something like a mix of confusion and anger crossed his features.

"Tell you what," I said. "This five goes to the first guy who can tell me where a family named Costner lives in this area."

The kid opened his jacket and showed me a knife in his belt.

"I'll tell *you* what," he said. "You let me have the five, and I'll let you get in your car and get lost."

I palmed the bill and placed it back in my pocket.

Without saying a word, I turned toward my car.

As I expected, I felt a hand grip my shoulder.

"I'm talkin' to you, man," the kid said, with a fearlessness born of the pack mentality. He was certain that his numbers made him invincible.

He was wrong.

With my good hand, I reached up and grabbed his wrist. Several seconds later, the kid who'd touched me sat on the ground howling over the greenstick break in his radius bone, and the kid who'd tried to help him sat next to my car trying to hold back a scarlet torrent from his broken nose. The other two seemed to vacillate between taking up the attack and running like thieves.

We were interrupted by the *whoop* of a siren, and flashing lights. I knew what that meant. I stepped back and raised both hands to make it clear that I was unarmed.

"What's going on?" a man said behind me. I turned to face the cop who had stepped out of his cruiser. He was tall and skinny, with rawhide skin and sad eyes. He had augmented his uniform with snakeskin boots.

"I was going to my car when these punks tried to shake me down."

"He broke my nose, Slim!" one of the youths said.

"And he snapped my arm like it was a twig!" the leader whined.

"Just defending myself," I said to the cop. "The kid with the broken arm has a knife in his belt. He threatened me with it."

The cop leaned down, opened the leader's jacket, and pulled the knife from his belt. Then turned to me.

"Are you hurt?" he asked.

"No."

"Didn't reckon so. You come with me. I need to file a report. Rooster, you and Sonny head on home, get your folks to take you to the emergency room. You come by the station tomorrow if you want to file a complaint."

"A complaint!" I said.

"That's enough out of you, mister!" Slim said. "Come have a seat in the cruiser. I need to get some information from you."

Half an hour later, I sat in the Prosperity Police Station. The cop, Slim Tackett, hadn't cuffed me, but neither did he seem interested in letting me go.

The front door to the station opened, and another officer stepped inside. He was tall and barrel-chested and athletic. He wore a gray Stetson over close-cropped dark hair going slowly silver at the temples. His eyes were blue and penetrating.

"This him?" he asked Tackett.

"Name's Gallegher, Chief. Roy Patrick Gallegher. He's from New Orleans."

"New Orleans?" the chief said, as he glanced over the report. "You're a long way from home."

"I can't wait to get back," I said.

"You can go on," the chief told Tackett.

"Thanks, Chief," Tackett said. He left without saluting.

The chief told me to sit tight. He walked to the back of the station and returned with two cups of coffee.

"You take sugar or cream?" he asked.

"Beer," I said.

He grinned, for just a second, reached into his shirt pocket and handed me a couple of paper packets of sweetener. Then he sat behind the desk.

"Judd Wheeler," he said. "I'm the chief of police here in Prosperity. We aren't accustomed to riots in the shopping center parking lot."

"As I told the other officer, I had just finished dinner and was heading for my car when these kids decided to hit me up for cash."

"So you assaulted them."

"The kid with the broken arm threatened me with a knife. I tried to leave. He decided to press the issue."

Wheeler nodded.

"Rooster Broome. You tie fifteen Bliss County Broomes together, and you might get a triple-digit IQ. Between you and me, I've kind of hoped for some time now that someone would clean Rooster's clock."

"So we're jake?"

"No, Mr. Gallegher. We are not *jake*. I got two Prosperity kids in the ER over in Morgan, and you don't have a scratch on you. I'm not certain how to explain that. You some kind of tough guy?"

"Yes," I said.

I thought Wheeler's eyes might have widened a bit.

"Honest, too," I said.

"Are you so honest that if I send to New Orleans for your arrest record, they're gonna come up empty?"

"I've been arrested in New Orleans," I said. "Several times. All the charges were dropped. If you want, you can check with Detective Farley Nuckolls in Robbery-Homicide, at the Rampart Street Station in the French Quarter."

"Friend of yours?"

"We go back a few years. He can tell you anything you want to know."

Wheeler drew a few circles on his desktop with his index finger, and then took a sip of his coffee.

"What I want to know," he said, finally, "is what you're doing in Prosperity."

"I work in a bar in the French Quarter. There was a girl who waited tables there for a while. She was murdered several days ago. I'm trying to find her family."

"What was this girl's name?"

"Katie Costner."

Wheeler nodded and took another sip of his coffee.

"Katie Costner left Prosperity about five years ago," he said.

"You knew her?"

"We crossed paths. Gave her folks no end of grief. Broke their hearts, though, when she blew town."

"Maybe you can help me track them down. My boss in New Orleans wants me to inform them of her death, make arrangements for the funeral."

"Well," Wheeler said. "Now, that's going to be a problem."

"They've moved away?"

"No. They're still here. Will be forever, I reckon."

It took me a moment to catch his drift.

"Oh," I said.

"Katie's father died about three years ago. Cancer. Got it working in the textile dye mill over in Mica Wells. Her mother passed about a year later. Ate herself to death after her husband died. Diabetes."

"Tough deal," I said.

"The person you need to talk to is Quincy Pressley. He's the preacher at the Lutheran Church over off Ebenezer Road. The Costners are buried in his churchyard."

I glanced at my watch.

"It's a little late to call on him now. Is there a motel nearby I could flop for the night?"

"Sorry. Nearest motel is over in Morgan, about fifteen miles. Why don't you stay here?"

"In the jail?"

"Sure. The beds in the cells are plenty comfortable. We serve a first-class breakfast in the morning, from over at the Piggly Wiggly in the shopping center. It'll be nice and quiet."

"Am I under arrest, Chief?"

He shook his head.

"Let's call it protective custody. The Broomes are a clannish bunch—you know, with a capital *K*. They aren't going to be very happy that some out-of-towner maimed one of their own, no matter how much he may have deserved it. They won't come anywhere near the jail, though. They seem allergic to it. If it makes you feel any better, I'll leave the cell door unlocked."

And that's how I came to spend the night in the Prosperity jail.

———

Chief Wheeler hadn't lied. The breakfast carted in from the Piggly Wiggly was top shelf. Market cut pepper bacon, scrambled eggs, grits, and two biscuits, which I washed down with coffee from the pot in the back of the station. It wasn't Café du Monde, but as country breakfasts go it hit the spot.

Wheeler had kept his word also about unlocking the cell door.

I was just finishing my second biscuit when he walked in the front door of the station and headed straight back to the holding cells. He carried a thick sheaf of fax paper.

"Your buddy Nuckolls gets to work early," he said. "You failed to mention last night that you used to be a cop."

"I was a consultant. Nashua PD in New Hampshire. Forensic psychologist. Never wore a badge. I did their profiling."

"Says here you killed a suspect named Ed Hix."

"I don't like to talk about that," I said.

"I can imagine why."

"Read the report, Chief. Hix killed the detective working the case, and it was down to Hix or me. I decided it was a lot better for everyone in the long run if Hix didn't walk out of those woods."

"You emptied an automatic into him. Fourteen shots."

"That was all the gun held. I'm not going to apologize for what I did, and I'm not going to minimize it either. Either Hix was going to die, or I was. I can't complain about the way things worked out."

"You've led a very interesting life down in New Orleans. Detective Nuckolls seems to think that you've killed as many as six people over the last decade."

"He's entitled to his opinion."

Wheeler set the sheaf of faxes down on his desk.

"Besides the fact that you seem to be some sort of walking Angel of Death, Detective Nuckolls says you're generally dependable, probably honest, and even says you were responsible for stopping a serial murderer down there a couple of years ago."

"It could have gone the other way very easily."

"Here's my problem, Gallegher. I keep the peace here in Prosperity. This is a quiet little town. We like it that way. I would be very appreciative if you'd complete your business here and then go home, preferably without littering the landscape with bodies I'd have to bury."

We talked for a while longer, as he vetted me by way of the reports he had received from New Orleans, and then he offered to drive me over to meet Reverend Pressley.

"I have a car, over in the shopping center lot."

"The roads, once you get away from the commercial district, can get a little confusing. Let me drive you out there, then I can bring you back once you have an idea of where you're going."

I couldn't argue with logic like that. He led me out to one of the cruisers and held the passenger side door for me as I sat down.

"Have you lived in this town long?" I asked, as he pulled out of the lot onto the Morgan Highway.

"All my life," he said. "My father was a farmer. His father was a farmer. All the Wheelers back to before the Revolutionary War were farmers."

"You're not a farmer."

"Had to end sometime. I wasn't very good at it. Guess I didn't inherit the right genes. Doesn't matter. Nobody's going to be a farmer in Prosperity in a few years."

"Why's that?"

He pointed to a subdivision off to the left of the highway. It was filled with large, boxy, red brick houses of the style I had come to refer to as '*garage-mahals*.'

"Tax refugees. They think they're getting away from it all, but they insist on having all the comforts of big-city life. These neighborhoods are spreading like seventeen-year locusts. The population in Prosperity has doubled in the last five years. I expect it'll double again in the next two."

"Tough break, suburban sprawl. And you have to keep a lid on all of it."

"That's why they pay me the big bucks."

We drove past an opulent new high school, and over a bridge spanning a tributary called Six Mile Creek. Slowly, the McMansion developments faded away, the land seemed to become more fertile, and farms began to appear on each side of the highway.

"This is the Prosperity I remember from when I was a kid," Wheeler said. "I'm going to miss it. Now, to get to Quincy's church, you turn left just past this tobacco drying barn up here, onto the Ebenezer Church Road…"

A few minutes later, we pulled into the gravel parking lot of a white frame church. A plaque screwed into the siding next to the front door proclaimed that the church had stood on that spot since 1764.

As we climbed out of the cruiser, a man stepped out the front door and waved at Wheeler. He stood in the high five-foot range, with a paunchy stomach, two-and-a-half chins, and thinning hair. He wore glasses. He stepped down to the gravel lot and extended his hand to the chief.

Wheeler shook with him, and then pointed in my direction.

"This is the fellow I mentioned on the phone," he said. "Quincy Pressley, Pat Gallegher."

I grasped Quincy's hand. Despite looking out of shape, he had a surprisingly strong grip.

"I was so sorry to hear about Katie," Quincy said. "The Costners have been a tragic family over the last several years. If you'll follow me…"

He turned and started to walk around the church. We followed him. As we rounded the corner, I saw a cemetery behind the building. It stretched for almost an acre.

"We have people in our churchyard from the pre-Revolutionary times," Pressley boasted. "People come from five counties in every direction just to do gravestone rubbings. Katie's parents are buried just over here."

He wended his way between faded gravestones and depressed patches of earth to a section filled with more recent monuments. We stopped in front of a rectangle of relatively new grass.

"Katie's mother," he said, pointing to the rectangle. Above it was a flat bronze plaque set into the ground, with the word COSTNER in large, raised letters.

"There's a space on the other side prepared for Katie. I had hoped that it would be many years before I would have to use it."

"So she's going to be buried here," I said.

"Yes. John and Susan insisted on it. Despite the fact that Katie left them many years ago, they always believed that they would be reunited. And, now, I suppose they will. How did she die?" he asked.

"It was murder," I said. "She was strangled."

"How sad. I'm afraid there aren't many people here in Prosperity who will attend the funeral. So many of the young folks have gone off to the cities or have married and moved away for new jobs."

"Hold on a minute," I said, as I pulled out my cell phone.

Farley was in his office at the Rampart Station. There were no new leads in the case, but the forensic team and the M.E. had completed all their procedures.

"The family belonged to a Lutheran Church here in Prosperity," I reported. "They had arranged for a burial site for her, before they died."

"Okay. Have the preacher there fax the release papers, and we'll arrange for transport."

He gave me the numbers for Pressley to send the information.

I folded the phone and placed it back into my pocket.

"Fastest five hundred bucks I ever made," I said.

"What?" Pressley asked.

"My boss hired me to find Katie's parents. I did. I guess my job's over."

"Did you know Katie?" Pressley asked.

"A little. She waited tables in the bar where I work."

"Would you mind, in that case, staying on for a while?"

I guess my face reflected the question in my head.

"For the funeral," he clarified. "It's so sad when I hold a funeral and nobody attends. It would be nice to have someone here who knew the girl. I never really got to know her, personally. Someone should be here who did."

I know a thing or two about lonely deaths and somber, empty funerals. Next to an advertisement for an unused wedding gown, a funeral without mourners is about the saddest thing I can imagine.

"Sure," I said. "No problem. I'll need to find a place to stay until they deliver the body."

"Why not stay with me?" Quincy said. "The church provides me with a nice little house—three bedrooms, lots of space. It's just me there. You'd be welcome to stay."

I thought about it for a second.

"Sounds great," I said.

"I'll take you back to your car," Wheeler said. "And I'll draw you a map to get back here. It's trickier than it looks."

———

I awoke the next morning to the smell of frying sausage and cinnamon.

I pulled on my clothes, made my bed like a good guest, and found my way to Quincy's kitchen. He stood there in his black slacks and a short-sleeved shirt, with an apron tied around his waist.

"Thought the aroma might awaken you," he said, as he sat at the table. "I have oatmeal with brown sugar and cinnamon, sausage, and scrambled eggs. You take coffee?"

"Sure," I said, as I took a seat.

I picked up the fork with my weak hand and started to sample the sausage, when I noted that Quincy had his hands folded in front of him, and his eyes closed. One eye winked open.

I set the fork down and waited for him to finish his prayer.

"Are you a religious man?" he asked.

"I was raised Catholic," I told him. "Even went to seminary, but I didn't finish."

"Crisis of faith?"

"You know about that sort of thing?"

"Of course. Doubt is a human condition, Mr. Gallegher."

"Please, call me Pat."

"How'd you do that?" he said, pointing to my cast.

I told him the story about the poodle and the tough guy. Some of it was funny, if it hadn't happened to you. He laughed at the appropriate places, but as I finished the story his face seemed to go dark.

"I have a feeling you lead an adventurous life," he said.

"Things happen," I said.

"And then you have to fight your way out."

"It isn't something I do on purpose, at least not most of the time. You get a reputation, though. People know you can do something other people can't, and they come to you when they're in need. I have a hard time turning down people in need, no matter how badly I want to."

"So you're some kind of detective?"

"No," I said. "I'm a musician. I play a horn in a bar. The rest of it is…it just happens. I suppose being a musician doesn't really count for much."

"Nonsense," Quincy said. "You have a gift. You can speak a language in which it is impossible to say a mean or hurtful thing. You should be proud of that."

I nodded and turned my attention to the meal. As I ate, a thought occurred to me.

"Where would you suggest I go to learn more about Katie?"

He hesitated for a second.

"I'm going to be the only mourner at her graveside," I added. "I think I should know more about her. Where did she go to school?"

"Everyone in this town goes to Prosperity Glen High School."

"You think there might be people there who'd recall her?"

"There's only one way to find out," Quincy said.

———

It took me about five minutes to reach the school parking lot. I had a feeling it took about five minutes to get anywhere in Prosperity from just about anywhere else in Prosperity.

I first asked to see the principal. If things went as I expected, I would probably ask a lot of personal questions before the day was out. It would be nice to have the imprimatur of the big guy in the front office.

The principal was a sallow, bleary-eyed man in his fifties named Hart Compton. He invited me directly back to his office.

"How can I help you, Mr. Gallegher?"

I told him about Katie Costner's murder, and how I had come from New Orleans to find her family.

"Yes," he said. "Very sad. The whole affair. So the entire family's dead now."

"Yes."

"I'm not certain what you want."

"The police detective investigating her murder back in New Orleans likes to have as much information as he can get. He's there. I'm here. Maybe I can find out something about Katie's life in Prosperity that had some bearing on her murder in New Orleans."

"An…official inquiry?"

"Some friendly questions," I said. "You can check with the detective."

I gave him Farley's number. Compton asked me to wait in the outer office while he called. After ten minutes, he opened his door and gestured for me to come back in.

"Your detective friend vouches for you," he said.

"He's in a charitable mood."

"He also asked me to pass along a request, in the interest of good public relations, that you not kill anyone in the course of your inquiries."

I cleared my throat.

"Is this something you're likely to do?" Compton asked.

"I'll make a special effort."

"Yes," he said, with obvious discomfort. "I should advise you in advance. You aren't likely to find many of the faculty and staff receptive to your questions."

"Why's that?"

He took off his glasses and rubbed a spot on the bridge of his nose, as if warding off a headache. I had a feeling he did that a lot.

"Katie left town under something of a cloud. People weren't particularly sad to see her go."

"Could you tell me more?"

"Oh, I'm sure you'll hear plenty."

"Where's your library?" I asked.

"We call it a Media Center."

"Of course you do."

"It's just down the hall to the right. Why do you ask?"

"More background. Would it be all right if I peruse some of your back yearbooks?"

I asked the woman at the front desk in the library where I could find back yearbooks. She directed me to the reference center and showed me where it was.

"Are you looking for anything specific?" she asked.

"I'm trying to find anything I can on a girl who attended Prosperity Glen several years ago. Her name was Katie Costner."

It was as if someone flipped a switch on her entire personality. She stepped back half a step. The air between us chilled twenty degrees.

"I'm sorry," she said. "There's nothing I can tell you."

"You don't recall her?"

"I'm very busy," she said, which I found a very facile way of avoiding my question. "The yearbooks are in the reference center."

I shrugged and walked to the reference center. According to the papers Hart Compton had given me, Katie had graduated six years earlier. I flipped directly to the senior pictures. Each one had a quote at the bottom and a list of the student's achievements. It took me a moment to find Katie's picture. She didn't look terribly different than I remembered, except that her hair was longer. She also seemed somewhat happier in the picture than I recalled her in real life.

Her quote read '*Love looks through a telescope; envy, through a microscope.*'

She had only one achievement in four years of high school – Chorus I.

It was as if she had drifted through four years of school and scarcely made a ripple.

Katie's algebra instructor was on a planning break. I decided to stop by her classroom.

Myra Soames was in her fifties, plump, red of cheeks, and going gracefully gray. She invited me into her classroom when I knocked on the door. I introduced myself.

"I'm from New Orleans," I said. "I've been sent up here to look into some background information on a former student named Katie Costner."

Just as the librarian had, Myra Soames suddenly bristled and grew cool toward me.

"Why are you asking about Katie Costner?" she asked. "Is she in some kind of trouble?"

"Only if the theologians are right," I said. "She's dead."

I thought the news of Katie's death might soften Ms. Soames a bit. Instead, she grew even colder.

"I wish I could say I was sorry," she said. "But if you're right, and there is an eternal judgment, then Katie is in a great deal of trouble. I'm a Christian woman, Mr. Gallegher, Bible-raised and river-dunked. It's a sin to speak ill of the dead. I'll say no more on the matter. If you'll excuse me, I have papers to grade."

"Is there anyone you can think of—a former classmate maybe—who knew Katie when she was a student here?"

"I'd say there were a great number of students who knew Katie, in every sense. You should check at the Piggly Wiggly. The assistant manager there, Rob Kiser, was a friend of hers as I recall. Now, please, I am very busy…"

I visited three other teachers, and none of them would discuss Katie with me. I got the strong impression that none of them had cared for the girl, and that none of them were particularly distressed to discover that she had died.

I gave up and drove over to the Piggly Wiggly. The manager there paged Rob Kiser to come to the front office.

Kiser, like Katie, was probably in his early twenties. He had red hair and residual facial acne. His fingernails were ragged and bitten.

I introduced myself and dropped the news about Katie on him.

"That's too bad," he said, without a lot of emotion.

"I was led to believe that you were one of her friends."

"Friends," he repeated. "Yeah, I suppose you could say that. At least at one time. Katie didn't keep friends for long."

"Why was that?"

"She just didn't. It was her personality, I guess. I reckon most people in this town weren't sorry to see the back of her car when she left."

"Just what did this girl do that was so bad?"

"Sorry, Mr. Gallegher, but you come to the wrong place. I got work to do, if you don't mind."

The Prosperity Police Department was in a row of buildings on a hill overlooking the strip mall and the Piggly Wiggly. I hiked up the concrete steps and around to the front of the station.

"Chief Wheeler in?" I asked the woman at the front desk.

Before she could page him, Wheeler walked out of his office and stepped into the waiting room.

"You've been busy," he said. "Step back to my office."

I followed him into the other room. He gestured toward a couple of chairs across the desk from his seat, and we both sat facing each other for several moments.

"I've gotten three different calls about you today," he said.

"It's nice to know people care."

"Oh, they care, all right. They care a great deal about people walking in out of the blue and dredging up muck from years ago that ought to be left alone. If I'd known you were going to drive around Prosperity upsetting people, I'd have let you stay at the motel in Morgan."

I leaned back in my seat and soaked in his malicious cop gawp. People who never hang around the police tend to be intimidated by them. I had learned a long time ago that intimidation is one more coin of the realm in law enforcement.

"Nobody will talk with me," I said. "Just what did Katie do that was so terrible?"

Wheeler stood for a second, and stared out the window of his office, his thumbs hooked in his Sam Browne belt. Then he turned and took his seat behind his desk again.

"I had only been chief of police for a couple of years when Katie took off," he said. "Katie was what you'd call *wild.* I reckon the only way anyone could have contained her would have been with a whip and a chair.

"There was this boy, Roger Thoreson. Nice kid. Lived with his mother. His father was dead. Tall kid. Clear of eye. Athletic. Smart. A real winner. He was the class president at both the middle school and the high school. Three letter man at Prosperity Glen. He turned down a football scholarship to South Carolina, because Duke offered him a full ride on academics."

"A shining light."

"Like a beacon. Everyone loved him, expected great things out of Roger. Thought he was going to put Prosperity on the map. Roger took an interest in Katie Costner. Katie came with a lot of baggage, a lot of whispers behind her back. Everybody knew she was promiscuous. This is a conservative town. People who don't conform spend a lot of time fending off those who do.

"I think, maybe, Roger felt bad for Katie. He started spending time with her. One thing led to another and…well, by August that boy was just plain girl-stupid over her. Most people think she was his first, you know, in bed. Roger started talking crazy, saying maybe he'd go to the state college over in Parker County rather than Duke. He even talked about getting married.

"His mother—shoot, just about everybody—tried to talk him out of it. It was like talking to a fish. Nothing got through to him. Then, about two weeks before school was supposed to start, Katie pulled the plug."

"She broke up with Roger?" I asked.

"Told him it was over. Said she'd taken up with some boy over in Mica Wells. Roger drove over there, looked up the kid, and offered to fight him for Katie. The kid kicked Roger's butt all over half the county. Roger had to go to the ER over in Morgan, get some stitches in his scalp.

"After Roger got back from the hospital, he and Katie had a terrible fight on his front porch. Stories vary depending on who tells them, but all the neighbors agree that Katie told Roger to get out of her life. Then she stomped off the porch, got in her car, and peeled out as she left the driveway."

"Tough deal for a young guy."

"Later that night, Roger's mother went up to his room to tell him goodnight. She found him in a bathtub full of pink water, his eyes fixed on some point a billion miles away. When I got there about five minutes later, Karen Thoreson was still screaming."

"The people in this town thought Katie killed their dreams for Roger Thoreson," I said.

"That pretty much sums it up. If people didn't like Katie before that, they plain despised her afterward. She tried to stand up to it. That only made people hate her more. Finally, she gave up, packed what belongings she had, climbed in her car, and drove away."

"That's why people didn't want to talk about her," I said.

"There're people in Prosperity who still think Lee gave up too early at Appomattox. Katie Costner's affair with Roger Thoreson is still an open wound. You ran around Properity today pouring salt in it."

"You could have told me all this yesterday," I said. "Could have saved me a lot of trouble."

"You weren't looking for Katie yesterday. You were looking for her parents. If I'd thought you were planning to dig up all the bodies in town, I'd have told you. That was my mistake."

I drove back to Quincy's house. He had been cutting the grass. I found him sitting on his front steps, sipping from a bottle of beer.

"Got another one?" I asked as I walked up.

"In the fridge."

I grabbed a bottle and joined him on the steps.

"Nice little town you have here," I said.

"We like it."

"You might have mentioned that Katie Costner was the town hump."

"I'm no gossip, Pat. That kind of thing doesn't go over well with the congregation."

"I think I understand now why Katie's funeral will be so poorly attended."

"It's a sad story."

"A lot of people hated her."

"True."

"You think any of them hated her enough to kill her?"

He had been raising the bottle to his mouth but stopped halfway.

"What are you suggesting?"

"I haven't been completely open with you, Quincy. I've done a lot of bad things in my life. For the last ten years or so, I've been trying to make that right. A lot of the things I do to balance the scales of my flimsy karma involve crimes. Like murder."

"And?"

"I know a thing or two about murder. I understand some of the reasons why people kill. Revenge is one of the biggies."

"I don't know. It seems a stretch to me."

"How so?"

"You can't escape yourself. Katie might have fled Prosperity, but she had to take herself wherever she went. Her personality being what it was, she was certain to behave the same way wherever she landed."

"Meaning that she was bound to make people angry with her no matter where she lived."

"Seems reasonable. Maybe Katie pulled the same stunt she did with Roger Thoreson on some poor guy down in New Orleans, someone more inclined to kill her than he was to kill himself."

"Maybe that makes more sense."

"It's certainly a simpler explanation than somebody from Prosperity harboring a grudge for five years before driving or flying all the way to New Orleans to do Katie in. I've made the arrangements for Katie's body to be transported here. We could have her funeral the day after tomorrow, and then you can be on your way back home. Would that suit you?"

My curiosity about Katie had been satisfied. I called Farley and told him what I had learned. I also suggested he might consider the possibility that Katie had been murdered by a disappointed suitor in New Orleans.

That done, I had little to occupy myself until Katie's body arrived. Fortunately, Quincy had an excellent library. He left after breakfast the next day to make hospital visits. I foraged his bookcase until I found an interesting collection of stories. Then I settled in his living room to read.

The telephone rang around eleven o'clock. I hesitated answering it, since I was little more than a traveler using his home for shelter. Then I recalled that—as a minister—Quincy had to respond to any number of emergencies on a daily basis. The least I could do was take a message.

"Quincy Pressley's residence," I said.

"Could I speak with Reverend Pressley?" a woman asked. Her voice sounded dry and weathered.

"I'm sorry. He's out. Can I take a message?"

"Who's this?"

"I'm visiting with Reverend Pressley. He's making hospital visits this morning. Any message for him, ma'am?"

"I'd appreciate it if you'd tell him that Inez Stillman called."

I wrote her information on a pad next to the phone.

"Anything else?"

"No, just tell him that I hope his cousin is feeling much better. He hasn't said anything about her, has he?"

"Not to me, ma'am."

"And one more thing. Could you tell him I called to thank him for those delicious pralines he brought back from his trip?"

Something like an electric tingle began at the base of my skull. It was a signal that I'd long since learned not to ignore.

"Pralines, ma'am?"

"Yes, he brought them to me to apologize for canceling our dinner. He picked them up while visiting his sick cousin."

"Of course," I said. "Reverend Pressley didn't say exactly where his sick cousin lives, did he?"

"I think he mentioned someplace in Louisiana. Isn't that where they make the best pralines?"

"So I hear. Do you still have the box the pralines came in?"

"Certainly. They're so rich, I may be a month finishing them."

"As it happens, I'm from Louisiana, and I'm always on the lookout for good pralines. Could you check the box and see where he bought them?"

"Just a moment."

I tried to keep my breathing and pulse from racing, as the electric tingle became a buzz that filled my head.

At the very best, Quincy Pressley had withheld information from me.

I didn't like to think about the worst.

“Here it is,” she said, as she got back on the phone. “The box is from the Allons Praline Factory. That part is in English. Then the rest is words I don’t recognize. The first is R-U-E. Then D-E, and after that is C-H-A-R-T…”

“Rue de Chartres,” I said, in a practiced French accent. “What about the rest?”

“The next line is spelled V-I-E-U-X, and C-A…”

“That’s all right, Mrs. Stillman. I know the rest.”

“Now how on earth can you know the rest? I haven’t spelled it yet.”

“I know it anyway. I’ll be sure to pass your message on to Reverend Pressley. And you enjoy those pralines, you hear?”

I racked the receiver and stared at the wall for a few moments.

I knew the Allons Praline Factory, and I knew Rue de Chartres.

Vieux Carre was another name for the French Quarter in New Orleans.

Where I lived.

Where Katie Costner had been murdered.

And, as I had just discovered, where Quincy Pressley had been only a day or so before I came to Prosperity.

Perhaps, I tried to convince myself, it was all a coincidence. Maybe Quincy really did have a sick cousin. Maybe he had simply neglected to tell me he had just returned from New Orleans.

I had to know more.

Among the many dubious talents I have acquired over the years is the ability to toss a desk without leaving any evidence that I'd been there. I quickly went through his drawers. Quincy kept his desk in meticulous shape. It didn't take long to find his bank and credit statements.

Within minutes, I discovered a set of used air tickets indicating that he had flown to New Orleans two days before Katie Costner was murdered and had flown back the day after the killing. They were sitting on top of a manila envelope, the only two items in the top right drawer of the desk. I opened the manila envelope, looked at the contents, and knew almost everything I needed to know.

Circumstantial, maybe. On the other hand, it meant that I had to confront Quincy with what I'd found.

And I needed to make a telephone call.

Quincy returned from the hospital around lunchtime. I waited for him in the living room, with the canceled ticket stubs in my hand.

"Hi, Pat," he said. "Hope you weren't too bored."

"Not at all," I said. "You had a call."

"Oh? From whom?"

"Inez Stillman."

I thought I saw him freeze for perhaps half a second.

"Lovely woman," he said. "Pillar of the church."

"She likes you, too. She asked me to give you a message."

"What is it?"

I lowered my voice and tried to sound menacing.

"She loves the pralines."

This time he did come to a full stop, his back to me. I think I saw his shoulders rise and his chest expand in an exhausted sigh. When he turned toward me, slowly, I could see the concern in his eyes.

"You have something to say?" he asked.

"Just a question. Why?"

Quincy shrugged and sat in the wing chair that had been placed perpendicular to the sofa.

"That's a pretty big question," he said. "It implies that you think you know something."

"Let's say that I'm about ninety-five percent certain that you killed Katie Costner. Can we start with that?"

"Sure," he said. "You can't prove anything, of course. I really do have a sick cousin in Louisiana. She provided me with an excellent reason to go to New Orleans. I'd been waiting for some time for an excuse."

I held up the manila envelope I had found.

"This is a report from the private investigator you hired to find Katie."

"Yes. Her mother's request. Susan was all alone after her husband died. She knew she was sick, and she wasn't inclined to do much about it. She asked me to find her daughter. She wanted Katie to come back to Prosperity for the funeral when she died. I hired that investigator. He did a very thorough job. Doesn't prove I did anything."

I laid the envelope on the sofa.

"I'm not a cop," I said. "I'm not in the proof business. I know you did it, and you know you did it. I only want to know why."

Quincy stood, slowly.

"I think I may have a sherry. Could I interest you in one?"

"No."

He crossed to the small cabinet in the front room, opened it, and poured a bit of amber liquid in a cordial glass. He returned to his seat and took a sip.

"I came to Prosperity, oh, thirty years ago, only a few years after I was ordained. I felt a calling. I wanted to work in a small town, where I could make a real difference. I wanted my service to have meaning.

"There was a young man who came to me. He brought his wife. They were having…" he waved his free hand in the air. "…marital difficulties. The man was depressed. The woman was frustrated, and unsatisfied. They were on the verge of separation and divorce. The woman wanted a child, very badly, and it didn't appear that she was likely to have one.

"I was in this very room one day, preparing a sermon, when the wife came to my door. She was crying. She was frightened that her husband might be considering leaving her. I tried to comfort her. I offered her a sherry," he said, holding up the glass. "She accepted it.

"We talked at length. When she left, I felt that I had done a good thing. I liked that feeling. It was the reason I came here, to do good things.

"She returned several days later, again seeking comfort. I did what I could. After a few weeks, she visited every three days or so. Then she offered to volunteer in the church. I needed the help, so I accepted."

He took another sip from the cordial glass.

"I have no desire to go over the more sordid details. I'll simply say that we became much closer than we should have. I regretted it, certainly. I am a man of the cloth, after all, but I am also a man. A…very weak man, it seems. The wife came to me after a few months, almost shaking with excitement. She said there had been a miracle, and that she was going to have a baby. She believed that this child would mend the torn fabric of her marriage."

"This came as something of a surprise to her husband, I'd imagine."

"I think he ignored the improbability of it all and decided to accept the child as a gift from God—which, in an abstract and indirect sense, it certainly was. They had a boy."

"Roger Thoreson," I said.

"Yes."

"Roger was your son, and the apple of everyone's eye in this town. Everyone blamed Katie Costner for his suicide."

"Yes."

"*You* blamed Katie for his suicide."

"Well, of course I did. After his father died, I tried to act the role of a surrogate father to Roger. I tried to warn him about Katie. He wouldn't listen. She lured him in, and she drained him, and then she moved on, like the vampire she was."

I tried to pick up the story.

"Katie's father died, and she didn't attend the funeral. Her mother became ill and asked you to find her. You hired the detective. He located her and told you where she was. Katie's mother died, and you didn't bother to tell Katie."

"She wouldn't have come," Quincy said. "Katie had no intention of ever setting foot in Prosperity again, after the way she had been treated. There was no point in contacting her."

"You knew where she was, though," I said. "You waited until you had a reason to travel to Louisiana. You flew to New Orleans. You went to Katie's home. She welcomed you, of course. You're a preacher. You weren't one of those people who drove her out of town. You passed the time of day, and then you found the opportunity to strike, and you choked the life right out of her."

"And then I bought a box of pralines for Inez Stillman," he said. "It's true. Every word."

He drained the glass of sherry and examined the glint of sunlight in the cut glass cordial.

"I… think perhaps another would do nicely," he said.

He stood and went again to the cabinet. He reached in, but instead of pulling out the decanter, he withdrew a nasty looking revolver.

"It really would have been much better if you had stayed in New Orleans."

"You don't want to do that," I said.

"The gravediggers were at the church this morning. They just finished Katie's grave. The people from the funeral supply will deliver the vault for the casket in an hour or two. My plan is for you to be at the bottom of that grave, covered with a tarpaulin. The vault will be placed on top of you. It's made of concrete, and I daresay it will crush you quite badly. Nobody will ever know you are buried underneath Katie."

"That's not going to happen," I said.

"You're a stranger here. Nobody knows you. Nobody will miss you if you simply disappear. Now, I need you to go to the back of the house. I can't have blood all over my living room. Clues, you know. I watch the television crime shows. I know what to avoid."

"No," I said.

"What? This is a real gun, Pat. I know how to use it. Don't think for a second I won't just shoot you where you sit."

I should have been angry, but Quincy just saddened me.

"You aren't going to shoot me."

"Give me one good reason why I won't."

Judd Wheeler stepped into the room from the kitchen and leveled a pump shotgun at Quincy.

"Because if you do, I'll have to shoot *you*," he said. "I heard everything. Gallegher called me right after he found the evidence and explained his theory. He picked me up at the station, so my cruiser wouldn't be here when you got home. Drop your gun right now, or I will drop it for you."

Quincy was distracted, so I shot out my hand and grabbed the revolver from him. He seemed mystified. He didn't even bother to resist.

I felt a little sorry for him.

The next day, I stood at the graveside while the local Methodist minister conducted Katie Costner's burial ceremony in Quincy Pressley's stead. I had long since resolved my differences with religion and I allowed myself to focus on the reverence of the occasion.

Katie was buried next to her parents. Just two rows over lay Roger Thoreson and his mother, and the man who died thinking he was Roger's father. It felt a lot like the end of a Shakespeare tragedy—two families brought to ruin by the weaknesses and flaws of a man who believed that he was both an instrument of mercy and a sword of vengeance.

I didn't stick around to see them lower the casket into the vault. I didn't want to hear the scrape of wood on concrete, or the thud of falling earth. I had endured enough of Prosperity and its secrets to last me a lifetime.

By dinner I was three hundred miles closer to home.

SHOOTING STARS

by
Richard Helms

Author's Note: This second Bowie Crapster/Boy Boatright story first appeared in the September/October 2015 double issue of Ellery Queen Mystery Magazine. *While he was nothing like my protagonist, Bowie Crapster was a real person, a retiree from the US Chamber of Commerce who looked a little like Charlie Ruggles. He was in his late seventies when I met him in 1969, and I was just a teen. We performed in several plays together. I asked him if I could use his name in a story someday, and he said,* "Wait until I'm dead. There's only room for one Bowie Crapster on this planet at a time." *He had absolutely nothing in common with my fictional Bowie Crapster except his name, but both were genuine characters. This story was a finalist for the SMFS Derringer Award in 2016, and I think the real Bowie would have loved it.*
R

Even after the crime scene guys finished wrecking it, Nigel Bowles' trailer looked nicer than my apartment.

It wasn't a trailer, actually, but a forty-two-foot motor home with a fully equipped bedroom, kitchen, and a wet bar that nearly brought me to tears.

The marble tub in the bathroom sported a waterfall spigot and gold-plated knobs which gleamed under thirty miniature LED lamps set into the ceiling. Behind the tub was a wall of one-foot square mirrors with streaks of gold foil set into the silver behind the glass.

It was going to take more than a rag and a bottle of 409 to clean the tub after they dragged Nigel Bowles' bloody body out of it.

A crowd around the motor home stood in shocked silence as the body was wheeled away. A couple of the girls started to cry. I scanned the crowd quickly to look for any face that seemed out of place or especially self-satisfied. No such luck.

I gestured to Scotty Baggs, the other detective assigned to the case. Scotty was only four or five years out of the Academy, and he wore his youth the way a school kid wears a *Kick Me* sign.

"What do we know?" I asked.

"The dead guy is Nigel Bowles. You know who this guy is, don't you?"

"No. Fill me in."

"Jesus, Boy, don't you ever watch television?"

"I'm not really a TV kind of guy."

Baggs shook his head, as if he expected my frail, aged, desiccated body to crumble to dust any minute.

"Nigel Bowles is a judge on *Star Quest*," he said.

"Never heard of it."

"They take kids off the street, audition 'em for the show. Each kid sings a song each week, and then one of them is voted off."

"By the judges?"

"No, by the viewers. They vote on the telephone."

"What's the winner get?"

"A million dollars and a recording contract."

I nodded. "Sounds like motive enough for me."

"Not with this guy. I think half the country would like a shot at getting him in a closed room for five minutes."

"Why?"

"He's a jerk. This guy loves to cut people down to size. You really ought to look at the show."

A woman in a smart twill skirt and a silk blouse stepped up to the police line. She was followed by a guy in jeans and a Black Sabbath tee shirt, who was toting a television camera. The woman, Lila Arcenaux, called me over.

"Boy!" she shouted. "Can you give me a minute?"

I walked over, and she cued the cameraman.

"This is Lila Arcenaux, at the Convention Center, where police are investigating a death on the set of *Star Quest*. I have Morgan Police Detective Amboy Boatright, who has been assigned to the case. Detective Boatright, can you tell us who was removed from that motor home?"

"No comment."

"We have reports that it was Nigel Bowles, one of the *Star Quest* judges."

"Sorry I can't help you."

"Did the person in the motor home die of natural causes?"

"No comment," I repeated.

"Does the fact that you, a detective with the Morgan PD Robbery/Homicide Division, have been assigned to the case indicate foul play?"

"We'll make a statement as soon as we have more facts," I said. "Until then, I'm afraid I can't comment."

"Thank you, Detective Boatright."

She slashed her throat with her index finger. The cameraman flipped a couple of switches and lowered the camera.

"You're a ballbuster, Boy," she said. "The least you could do is throw me a bone on this thing."

"No, Lila, that's the most I could do. The least I could do is ignore you completely."

She batted her eyelashes at me a couple of times, trying her best to remind me of earlier times when our relationship had been on a damn better than a first name basis. I wasn't buying. That was a long time ago. Both of us had racked up a little mileage in the interim.

"C'mon," she said. "Off the record. Is it Nigel Bowles?"

"Off the record?" I asked.

She nodded, and flicked her tongue over her lips quickly.

"No comment," I said.

A couple of hours later, Scotty Baggs and I sat in a lounge off the main theater at the Bliss County Convention Center, waiting. My cell phone beeped. I saw it was a call from Billy Epps, the chief at Crime Scene Analysis. He had promised to call me as soon as the Medical Examiner did a preliminary post-mortem on Bowles.

"What'cha got, Billy?"

"COD's a bullet wound that transected the aorta. He bled out in less than a minute. He was shot four times. The other three would have been non-fatal. We pulled out four .22 slugs."

"Sounds like the killer was working through an agenda. Any idea when it happened?"

"Based on liver temp and degree of rigor, I'd say sometime before midnight last night."

"Hold on." I covered the phone and turned to Scotty. "When was he last seen alive?"

"He attended a production meeting after dinner. They broke around nine o'clock, and Bowles headed for his motor home. Nobody reported seeing him after that."

"Sometime between nine and midnight work for you?" I asked Epps.

"Sounds about right."

"Keep me posted," I said.

"What killed him?" Baggs asked.

"Pop gun. That's why nobody heard it when he was shot."

"The guy who found him says the stereo in the motor home was playing extra loud. He turned it off before calling the cops."

"Thereby screwing up our entire crime scene."

"He's a television puke, Boy. He don't know what's what."

"Sure. So, Dr. Contemporary Culture, why is this show in Morgan?"

"They're touring all the towns where the first six winners lived."

"Run that by me again?"

"This is the show's seventh season. There have been six winners before. Two years ago, the winner was Shirelle Forte, from here in Morgan."

"I've heard of her."

"I'm not surprised. She's been on every radio station in town."

"Sports Talk?"

"You know what I mean. The show's already visited Beaux Bridge, Louisiana; Indianapolis; Las Vegas; and Billings, Montana. This is the fifth city on the tour."

"Because Shirelle Forte was from here."

"Yeah."

"So the first four winners were from the other cities."

"That's right."

"What's the sixth city?"

"Atlanta. Why? Is it important?"

"It is if I don't know. Can't say for certain if it matters, now that I do. Start the murder book on this one. If this television show is as popular as you say, it's going to be a high-profile case."

My cell phone beeped again. It was the Morgan Chief of Police, Temple Mulcahey.

"Where are you?" Mulcahey asked.

"A lounge in the Convention Center. Just got the preliminary post-mort."

"You got a television there?"

"Sure."

"Check out Channel Nine."

I reached over and picked up the remote. The first thing I saw on the screen was Lila Arcenaux's faultlessly made-up face.

> *"...confirming that the man killed at the* Star Quest *set at the Bliss County Convention Center was none other than the show's most controversial judge, Nigel Bowles. This same source..."*

"Aw, hell..." I muttered.

"It was a matter of time, Boy," Mulcahey said. "Something like this isn't going to stay a secret long. You can't blame Lila for breaking it."

"Sure I can."

"There's more."

I didn't like the tone of his voice.

"What?"

"Got a telephone call from one of the other judges on the show, Aida Kennedy."

"Please tell me she confessed."

"People like us don't get that lucky. She's requested that we allow some, ah, *outside* help in this investigation."

"No private detectives."

"Hold your water, Boy. This woman has some serious juice. *Star Quest* is the top-rated show on the tube. Bringing it to Morgan was a major score for the brass at the Government Center. Bowles getting murdered here isn't going to make them happy."

"So, what's this Kennedy woman want? She has some specific hotshot private eye she wants to pull in?"

"Not exactly."

"What, then?"

"It seems she's one of…*his* clients."

"Not *Crapster*!"

I glanced at the television screen again, and there he was, waltzing through the crowd toward the crime scene. No more than five and a half feet tall, built like the Pillsbury Doughboy, resplendent in an Italian ice cream suit with a silk cravat and gleaming patent leather white shoes. His hair, cut in a sort of Caesar style with short, bleached bangs, was reflected in his silver Elvis sunglasses. He looked like a Good Humor Man in Key West.

"That's it," I said. "I'm handing in my badge."

"You'll do no such thing," Mulcahy said. "The City Council has implemented a hiring freeze, and I'm not honoring any resignations. I can't spare you, and I can't replace you, so you're stuck with the case."

"But...but it's *Crapster*! You promised me I'd never have to see him again."

"I don't understand your concern, Boy. He's always worked behind the scenes. He always gives the department credit for his work. I'd hate to think you resent him because you think he shows you up."

"He doesn't show me up. I'm just as sharp as he is on his best day. His methods are...well, I just can't control him."

"Are you watching the television?"

"Yeah."

"It looks like he's heading for the motor home. You'd better intercept him. And, for Pete's sake, be diplomatic. Every move you make from here on is probably going to be on television."

"Wonderful." I toggled the radio mike on my shoulder. "This is Boatright. Please detain that walking fashion disaster until I get there."

Bowie Crapster stood outside the yellow crime scene tape, accompanied by two uniform cops, when Baggs and I arrived. Most people probably would have been irritated at being detained. He seemed calm and composed.

He saw me round the corner and held out a delicately manicured hand.

"Detective Boatright!" he said, with an enthusiasm that sounded peevishly genuine. "How nice to see you again."

Aware that television cameras were watching, I shook hands with him.

"So," he said. "How was your recent vacation?"

"Enough hocus pocus," I said.

"Nothing magical or mysterious I'm afraid. Just good old psychic reading."

"Sure, sure. How do you know this Kennedy woman?"

"She's a client. Aida is a lovely woman, but her aura follows her around like a hovering cloud."

"Her aura."

"Yes. Quite brown, you know."

"Brown's bad."

"Just awful. She's carrying a truckload of past-life baggage that's simply trashing the karma in her present life. We're working through it."

"Along with her bank account."

"Karmic cleansing does not come cheap, Detective. Aida tells me that the dead man is Nigel Bowles."

"That's right."

"There's another fellow who'll have a lot to atone for in the next life. Do you watch the show?"

"No."

"You should at the tapes. I'd guess just about anyone could have killed Bowles. Almost everyone wanted to."

"And you know this…how?"

"By reading the papers, dear Boy."

"Don't call me that."

"*Dear*, or *Boy*?"

"The combination of the two. I don't want people to think we're dating."

"Don't be silly. You're not my type. Anyone can see that. May I see the crime scene?"

"Sure you can stomach it?"

"My eyes will be closed most of the time."

"Oh, yeah. Vibrations."

I held the crime scene tape up so that he could walk under it. I led him to the motor home and opened the door for him.

"All the black stuff on everything is fingerprint dust," I said. "It wouldn't do your suit any favors. There isn't much to see in the main room. The body was in the bathroom."

"Thank you, Detective."

He stepped into the motor home, and almost immediately seemed to reel.

"Such animosity," he said. "There's a lot of anger here."

"Vibrations, huh?"

"After a fashion. Look at the colors, the blacks and reds, and all the chrome. This is a cold place, filled with aggression."

"From what I hear, Bowles would have felt right at home."

"How true. It is disturbing, though. I'm afraid the native anger in this motor home might interfere with my ability to perceive the vibrations of what has passed."

"Gee, that's too bad, Crapster. Well, nothing to do for it. Sorry you came all this way for nothing. I'll see to it that the officers get you safely back to your car…"

"Wait. I didn't say I *couldn't* perceive them. It just won't be easy. How long had the late Mr. Bowles occupied this trailer?"

"According to the tour manager, just since they started the six-city road trip."

"Then four weeks or so?"

"That's pretty close."

"Not a lot of time to imprint a space with your own aura, but Mr. Bowles' aura was so overwhelming I'd suspect there's something of him left around."

"There's plenty. Wait until you see the bathroom."

"That's not what I meant, and you know it. Please be quiet, so I can concentrate."

He closed his eyes, spread out his arms, and went into this trance thing I'd seen him do a few times before. He slowly rotated, nodding slightly, apparently waiting for something to jump out of the ether.

"There were several arguments in here over the last two or three days. A great deal of emotion, most of it negative. Accusations. Recriminations. Threats. Very troubling."

"Any idea who was recriminating whom?"

"*Shush*."

He leaned toward the back of the motorhome.

"The vibrations are stronger in this direction."

"The bedroom," I said. "They usually are."

"*Please*, Detective."

He slowly walked through the trailer, and then stopped in front of the bathroom door.

"Here," he said. "This is where he was shot."

"No," I said. "He was shot in the bathtub."

"But the gun was fired from here, in the doorway. The killer didn't attempt to enter the bathroom."

"I suppose you're going to tell me how you know that?"

"I only sense one recent presence inside the bathroom, but two out here in the living area. The murderer was expected. He—or she, I can't tell for certain—entered the motor home through the door, and Mr. Bowles expected him."

"Or her."

"Yes."

"Can't tell man vibrations from woman vibrations, huh?"

He ignored me.

"Bowles wasn't necessarily shocked when he turned and saw the murderer in the doorway. Then he saw the gun, and he raised his hands. The killer fired, several times, and Mr. Bowles fell into the bathtub when he turned and attempted to avoid the bullets."

"Anything else?" I asked.

"Nothing for the moment. That's all there is."

"Great. Thank you for your input. On behalf of the Morgan Police Department, please allow me to extend our gratitude for your contribution to this case. Sorry you have to run along."

"Wait," he said. "I'm not going anywhere."

"Are you sure? You said that was all you had to contribute. I figured your job here was done."

"If I didn't know better, Detective, I'd imagine that you were trying to get rid of me."

"Guess you *are* psychic."

"Of course I am."

"You know," I said. "I've been around you long enough to know what you're doing. Let me offer you a few observations of my own. You spoke with Aida Kennedy before you came down here. She's invited you to assist in this case. She told you Nigel Bowles had been murdered, and she told you he had been shot several times. I'm pretty good at reading the signs myself. Bowles was found in the bathtub, fully clothed, so he wasn't taking a bath when he was shot. On the other hand, he didn't come out of the bathroom before being shot, so he must have thought that the person entering the motor home was relatively harmless. Ergo, he either knew his killer, or he was expecting the killer to visit.

"It's obvious that the murderer stood outside the bathroom and shot from here. You can see the powder marks on either side of the door, in the jamb and on the frame. The hand-raising thing is a nice touch, but it's reflexive. Nine out of ten people would do the same thing, which you count on, being such a shrewd observer of human behavior.

"Finally, it's easy to infer that there has been a great deal of rancor in this motor home, largely based on the fact that it was occupied by the deceased, who by all accounts was not a nice man. According to the other detective working this case, just about everybody would have enjoyed taking a pop at him. Now, how are *my* psychic observations?"

"Spot on, Detective. There's hope for you yet. What's our next move?"

"*My* next move is to interview people."

"In that case, might I tag along? You never know when I might get some interesting vibrations that might help your case."

Part of me wanted to toss him into the bathroom, draw my service pistol, and empty the magazine. But that would have really screwed up my crime scene. Also, the chief had ordered me to keep Crapster in the loop.

"Suit yourself," I said.

Aida Kennedy dabbed at her eyes with a tissue as we sat in her motor coach. Her mascara had run with the tears, making her look vaguely like a morose raccoon. She was a tiny woman. I could tell that—sans stage makeup—she had a piggish little face, all nose and buck teeth. The makeup artists on the show earned their paychecks with her. Crapster held her free hand, stroking it gently.

"Don't worry," he said, quietly "I don't think we're looking for someone with a grudge against the show. I felt very strongly when I read the crime scene that the attack was personal."

"About that," I said to her, "Are you aware of any significant arguments Mr. Bowles had over the last couple of days?"

"No," she said.

"Any threats?"

"Nigel and I—despite the way we were portrayed on television—weren't close. I didn't speak with him a lot."

"How are you portrayed on television?"

"The network likes to build up conflict among the judges," she said. "It's a subplot. The contest is legitimate, but to keep the show moving between singers the producers and writers like to invent arguments. It keeps viewers from switching channels."

"And some of these conflicts involved you and Mr. Bowles?"

"They'd have him leer at me, and I'd pretend to be offended."

"Were you offended?"

"Not at all. It's acting. Besides, Nigel leered at everyone. I'd be offended if he hadn't made a pass or two at me."

"Which he did."

"Once," she said. "He grabbed my ass during a commercial break in auditions. He never did it again."

"Why?" I asked.

"I slapped him, very hard, and told him…" She stopped.

"What?" I said. "What did you tell him?"

"Oh my God," she said, as she covered her mouth. "I said if he tried that again I'd kill him, but I didn't mean it. Really! It's just an expression."

"I see. Can you account for your whereabouts last night, between nine and midnight?"

The sentence wasn't out of my mouth before I saw the flush start at her ears and spread across her cheeks and chest. Even without Crapster's purported extra-sensory perception, I could tell I'd hit a sore spot.

"I could, if pressed, but I'd rather not."

"This is a murder investigation," I said.

Crapster held up his hand.

"I think I understand," he said. "Aida, you're saying that you have an alibi, but it would prove embarrassing for you to divulge it."

She nodded, a new well of tears forming on her lower eyelids.

"There is a person you were with at the time of the murder, and if that person's name is revealed, it could be a problem."

She nodded again, this time making a little squeak that might have been a stifled sob.

"And," Crapster said, "I believe this person's initials are…B.T."

She nodded violently and buried her face in a new handful of tissues.

"How in hell..." I said, but Crapster shook his head to stop me.

Then he mouthed the word *psychic*.

"If you're withholding evidence from me, I'll shove you in jail so fast you'll leave a grease stain on the back wall," I told Crapster as we left Aida Kennedy's trailer.

"I wouldn't dream of it. The person you want to speak with is Belinda Talbert."

"B.T. How'd you know?"

He handed me a sheet of paper torn from a small spiral notepad. Someone had written on it: *Please don't tell them about me. Thank you for last night. Belinda.* The *'i'* in Belinda was punctuated with a little heart.

"Where'd you get this?" I asked.

"Palmed it from the countertop. Apparently, Aida was so distraught she didn't think to destroy it."

"Who is she?"

"Belinda Talbert is one of the contestants. In fact, she's one of the frontrunners to win this year. Lovely young lady. Beautiful voice. I think she could become a major star."

"People from this show do that?"

"Oh, yes. They've won Grammy Awards and Oscars and Emmys. How can you be so out of touch?"

"Two of my three ex-wives asked me the same thing."

Belinda Talbert was tall and slim, with a caramel complexion and wide, dark eyes. She was rehearsing a song I didn't recognize as we walked into the theater. Her voice was light and clear, and I could see why people thought she was a winner. My first thought as she finished singing was of how I'd hate to put a talent like her in prison for murder.

Crapster followed me as I walked up to her and flashed my badge.

"Can we talk?" I asked.

At first, I thought she was going to faint. She swayed a bit, and her eyes glazed over, but she quickly recovered.

"I asked Aida not to tell you about me."

"She didn't. I brought my own swami. Knows all, sees all, can't shut him up. You could make my day by confessing you killed Nigel Bowles."

"I…" she started, but before she could finish, I felt a hand on my shoulder, pulling me around. This is generally a bad tactic for getting my attention. I grabbed the hand, pivoted on my right foot, pulled hard, and in a second had some kid in a hammerlock.

"You want a trip to the local lockup, grab me again," I growled.

The kid struggled a little, but I could tell it was mostly show for the girl. I slowly released him, grabbed a pair of cuffs from my pocket, and showed them to him. He was about my height but weighed maybe fifty pounds less. His head was arranged in dreadlocks. A stray matted tube of hair fell across his forehead.

"What's your name?" I asked.

"His name is Randy Locklear," Crapster said. "He's another contestant."

"What's the idea, Randy?" I asked.

"You were hassling Belinda. There's no need for that. I know why you're here. Everyone's heard about what happened to Nigel. You don't need to give her any grief. She didn't do it."

"How do you know?"

"Because she was with me all last night, in my hotel room."

"Oh, Randy," Belinda said, shaking her head. "You're going to screw everything up. He's lying. He's trying to protect me."

"Why?"

"Because…because we've been seeing each other. Please, don't tell anyone."

"Give me a reason," I said.

"It's against the contest rules. They don't like contestants hooking up."

"Beat it, Randy," I said. "I'll talk to you later."

Randy shuffled away, and I waited for him to leave the theater completely. There were a few chairs around the piano. I gestured to Belinda to take a seat. Crapster sat nearby. I pulled the note from Aida Kennedy's motor home out of my pocket and showed it to her.

"You wrote this?"

"Yes."

"What's it mean? Why didn't you want Aida to tell us you were in her trailer?"

"I just want to sing," she said. "All I ever wanted was to be a singer. It's hard. Breaking into this business can take years. There's a premium on youth. Nobody wants a breakout singer in her thirties. If you aren't discovered by the time you're twenty, you can probably kiss your chances of being a superstar goodbye."

"How old are you?" I asked.

"I'm twenty. The clock is ticking. If I'm going to be the next Mariah or Adele, I need to make a mark soon. This show is my chance."

Crapster stood and put his hand on her shoulder. He closed his eyes and bowed his head. I stifled my gag reflex. I'd seen this act before.

"I feel a conflict," he said, as if taking dictation from the spirit world. "You've discovered that there is more to this contest than talent or performance."

"You know?" she asked.

"I feel it. The vibrations are very strong, but they don't tell me specifics. Is someone putting pressure on you?"

"God, yes!" she said. "But I can't talk about that."

"You told Aida Kennedy about it," I said. "That's why you were in her motor home last night."

Belinda sat upright. "She didn't tell you that!"

"She didn't need to," I said. "Crapster here isn't the only person who can read between the lines. You were in Aida Kennedy's trailer, Nigel Bowles was murdered, and you left her a note asking her not to tell anyone about your visit. My guess is you were talking to her about something Bowles was doing to you."

"I overheard a conversation he had with Tyke Glenham."

"Who?"

"He hosts the show," Crapster said.

Belinda said, "Tyke and Nigel were talking behind the set the other day. They didn't know I was around the corner. I heard Nigel tell Tyke he was planning to fire Aida and Dawg."

"Dawg?" I asked.

"The third judge," Crapster explained. "Antone Gauchee. He's a rapper. His nickname is *Dawg*."

"Bowles was able to fire other judges?" I said.

Belinda said, "He's the executive producer of the show. He can fire anyone he wants. I heard Nigel tell Tyke he was planning to get rid of Aida and Dawg, and replace them with some judges who would appeal to younger viewers."

"Why?"

"Kids—teenyboppers—vote more than adults. Voting is done by calling telephone numbers for each of the contestants. If you want to vote for me, you call one number. If you want to vote for Randy, you call a different number."

"I think I get it," Crapster said. "These aren't toll-free numbers, are they?"

"No," Belinda said. "There's a charge for each call. The phone company gets a cut, and the show gets a cut."

"The more people vote, the more money the show makes," I said. "And, since Nigel Bowles essentially owned the show, more votes would mean more money for him. You think replacing the current judges would bring in that much more money?"

Belinda nodded and wiped at her eyes with a tissue. "Last year, the largest voting group was teenagers. They have cell phones and they don't pay the bills, so they never know how much their votes cost. By increasing that viewing demographic, the show—and Nigel—would make a killing."

"Intriguing choice of words," I said.

"There's more," she said. "I heard Nigel accuse Tyke of having an affair with Shirelle Forte."

"Last year's winner," I said. "The one from Morgan."

From the corner of my eye, I caught Crapster raising an eyebrow.

"One of my detectives told me," I said. "What about it? What difference does it make if Glenham is dating this girl?"

"No," Belinda said. "Not now. Back then. When she was a contestant."

It was my turn to raise an eyebrow.

"You said that the show has rules against contestants dating each other," I said. "I'd imagine they also frown on the host knocking boots with a contestant."

"It would be a huge scandal," Crapster said. "It would destroy the integrity of the show. Something like that might even cause the network to cancel it."

"Then this is something Glenham would want to keep a secret," I said.

"At the very least, they would fire Glenham to contain the damage."

"Glenham makes a lot of money for hosting this show?"

"High six figures, low seven."

I turned back to Belinda.

"You heard Bowles tell Glenham he knew about this affair?"

"Tyke told Nigel that he shouldn't fire them, and Nigel told him to stay out of it, or he'd get rid of Tyke too, and destroy Shirelle's career."

"When was this conversation?"

"Three days ago, just after we arrived in Morgan."

I looked over at Crapster. Neither of us needed supernatural powers to come to the same conclusion. The prospect of losing a seven-figure salary made Tyke Glenham a prime murder suspect.

"You said Nigel Bowles was pressuring you," Crapster said.

"He found out about me and Randy a couple of weeks ago. He thought it gave him some kind of power over me. He's invited me to his motor home several times, and he…" she stopped and covered her eyes with her hand, as if talking about it shamed her.

Crapster took over. "I can sense what happened. He thought, by threatening to expose your situation with Randy, he could coerce you into sleeping with him."

Without removing her hand, she nodded violently.

"That's why you went to Aida Kennedy's motor home last night?"

She sat silently for a few seconds, and then looked up. Her eyes were red and there were twin rivulets of tears on her cheeks.

"I thought she should know what Nigel was planning," she said. "It seemed like the right thing to do."

"And you told her about you and Randy, and about how Nigel was trying to blackmail you into sex with him," Crapster said.

"I thought she could tell me what to do."

"What did she suggest?" I said.

"She was shocked, and furious," she said, and then paused. "Do I really have to tell you all this?"

"This is a murder investigation," I said. "Everything is vital."

"I don't think she meant it, but she said she was so angry at Nigel she could kill him."

———

"I have a question," Crapster asked as we headed to the auditorium to find Tyke Glenham.

"What? Your psychic mind hasn't already answered it for you?"

"Of course not. Why isn't Belinda a suspect?"

"I didn't say she wasn't. She's a low-priority suspect. Same for Aida Kennedy."

"Because they can alibi each other?"

"That, and because Aida Kennedy believes you can see through walls and that you'd divine the killer immediately, so why would she ask your help if she was the murderer? It's possible she and Belinda killed Bowles together. They both clearly had motive. On the other hand, I'd rather try to find a killer that has both motive *and* opportunity."

"And access to a gun."

"Not just any gun. Bowles was killed with a .22. That narrows things a bit."

We found Tyke Glenham sitting in the first row of seats in the auditorium, sipping from a plastic coffee cup and staring intently at a clipboard on his lap. He was dressed in a crisp, tight-fitting Italian suit, which blended nicely with the tufts of tissue paper tucked into his shirt collar to keep makeup from staining his shirt. He was only of moderate height, coming perhaps to my chin, and his light brown hair was tinged with blonde highlights and tortuously combed and sprayed to stay in place under the hot television lights.

He saw us approach, placed the clipboard on the seat next to him, and stood to greet us.

"You're the police detective investigating Nigel's murder," he said, extending his hand in a fashion I had come to associate with car salesmen and undertakers.

"Amboy Boatright, Morgan Police Department," I said.

"Amboy."

"Most people call me *Boy* but feel free to call me *Detective.* This is an official inquiry."

"Of course, and you're Bowie Crapster. I saw you on the news report this morning. You made quite an entrance."

"He specializes in entrances," I said. "You two should get along nicely. He's in show business too."

"Aida told me about Mr. Crapster," Glenham said. "She told me I could talk openly with him, since he'll pretty much know what I'm thinking anyway."

"Let's get down to brass tacks," I said. "We know you were boffing this Forte woman last season and we know

Nigel Bowles threatened to reveal this and fire you if you didn't play ball with him. It would be in your best interests to be able to account for your whereabouts last night between—say—dinner and midnight."

His eyes, which had sparkled with debatable bonhomie as he had greeted us, suddenly went blank and dead.

"How…" he stammered.

"Excuse me, Detective," Crapster said. "Perhaps I can help. Nice to meet you, Mr. Glenham. I enjoy the show."

"Umm…thanks," he said.

"Aida Kennedy told you I'd know what you were thinking. She's wrong about that, of course, but I am pretty good at sensing feelings. As I watched the fifth season, I sensed a very strong connection between you and Shirelle Forte. I wasn't wrong, was I?"

"I really shouldn't talk about that," Glenham said. "There are rules."

"Of course there are, but the heart doesn't always abide by the rules." He placed a hand on Glenham's shoulder. "In fact, I'm getting very strong vibrations from you even as we speak. I sense that you wish to…*protect* someone. Nigel Bowles did find out about you and Shirelle, didn't he?"

I've been a cop for over twenty years. After a while you develop an instinctive understanding of when people are trying to be evasive. I couldn't figure out what Crapster was up to, though I've heard of stuff like neurolinguistic programming and the like. Somehow, he was connecting with Glenham. I let him go, because I couldn't see how that could be a bad thing.

"I…I didn't intend to start anything with Shirelle," Glenham said. "It just happened. Over the course of a season, the cast grows very close, but it's a fragile closeness. You never know from one week to the next who will be voted off the show. Shirelle was particularly vulnerable. She approached me for advice on handling the pressure. One thing led to another. I didn't intend it. Shirelle and I hid it as well as we could, but Nigel found out anyway. Shirelle's second album just released a month ago, and it's hot. Like blowtorch hot. If word got out that she and I were sleeping together during the show, everyone would begin to think that's why she won. It could kill her career."

"Nigel Bowles knew this," I said. "You told him not to fire Aida Kennedy and Dawg Gauchee, so he threatened Shirelle Forte's career to keep you in line."

"Sounds like motive, doesn't it?" Glenham said.

"I've seen people killed for less. Where were you between nine and midnight last night?"

"I was taping promos for the show from eight-thirty until about eleven, right here on the stage. I never left. The crew can vouch for me. From eleven o'clock until about midnight, I was at a late dinner with one of your local reporters, a woman named Lila Arcenaux. She drove me back to my hotel around twelve-thirty."

"Have you told Shirelle Forte about Mr. Bowles' threats?" I asked.

"By telephone. She's in Los Angeles, working on a new album. We haven't seen each other for a few weeks because of the tour."

"Motive, but no opportunity," Crapster chimed in.

"Yeah," I said. "You got that right."

———

I took a break for lunch at the Morgan Oyster Bar, two blocks from the Convention Center. I was about halfway through my club sandwich when Crapster walked up and plopped down in the seat across from me.

"I thought you'd be here," he said.

"How in hell did you find me?"

He gave me this *I'm psychic, you dope* gawp.

For a moment, I contemplated launching across the table, grabbing him by the lapels of his Givenchy linen jacket, and stuffing him into a napkin dispenser. Tempting as the image was, I rejected it.

Too many witnesses.

"Okay, I get it. You called Mulcahey, and he told you I was code seventy out here."

"I feel that I've done something to anger you."

"You get a *vibration* on that one? Maybe you are psychic after all."

"Of course I am."

"Balls." I gestured to the waitress for a tea refill. The waitress walked over and scooped up my glass.

"Anything for you, sweetie?" she asked Crapster.

"Cosmopolitan," he said. He pulled a silver dollar from his pocket. "I think you have the wrong idea about me. I was hoping to talk with you civilly, to explain what it is that I do."

"Oh, I got an eyeful of what you do this morning. Quite a show."

"Yes. A show." He rolled the dollar around his knuckles, the way Van Heflin did in that old movie *The Strange Loves of Martha Ivers*. "A large part of it *is* show. I have a product to sell, and the show is just the packaging. It's a great deal like what sleight of hand magicians do. You think you see what they're up to, and then they distract you."

He snapped his fingers on his free hand, as he closed the hand with the quarter in his palm. Then he opened it, and the silver dollar was gone.

"Cheap trick."

"The real trick is understanding people and observing everything."

"Observing," I said, as the waitress arrived with our drinks.

"Let's try an experiment," he said.

He pulled a small notepad from his jacket pocket, along with a thin gold Cross pen. He scribbled on the pad, tore the sheet out, and folded it carefully. Then he placed it in the center of the table.

"Think of a number between one and ten," he said.

"Oh, come on…" I protested.

"No, really. Think of a number."

I thought.

"Okay," I said.

"Open the piece of paper."

I reached over and opened the sheet. On it, he had written *seven*.

"That was the number you thought of," he said.

Part of me wanted to lie, just to toss it in his face. The cop part of me tried to figure out how he'd done it.

"So what?"

"So, it's a trick, of course."

"You had a one in ten chance of getting it right."

"Actually, I had about a seventy percent chance of getting it right. A person choosing a number between one and ten will most often choose seven. Why? I haven't a clue. I suppose it's hardwired into us. Maybe it's cultural. It is, however, dependable."

"Proving?"

"You can depend on human nature. These predictable patterns of behavior can be understood and, if you are *sensitive* to them, you can detect when the patterns are violated."

"What's all this to do with being psychic?"

"Everything. Psychics have gotten a bad rap over the years. Everyone expects that *'Read my mind, Uncle Martin'* stuff. I can't read minds. Rest assured, Detective, your thoughts are private. On the other hand, there are moments when I can be pretty certain what people are thinking, because – at least statistically – they *should* be thinking it."

"And you exploit that."

"*Exploit* is a harsh word. I allow that statistical probability to guide my own intuition. Extrasensory perception has nothing to do with hocus pocus. It's just a sensitivity and awareness of something being out of place that occurs outside the boundaries of the five senses. It's a synergistic response, and if you train yourself to recognize it for what it is you are, for all intents and purposes, training yourself to sense the *vibrations* around you."

"I still say *balls*."

"Which is why we make such a good team."

"I'm forced to put up with you by the whims of my Chief. I don't sense a lot of *teamwork* in that."

"We don't always get to choose our teammates," he said.

My cell phone beeped. It was Scotty Baggs.

"Boy, thought you'd want to hear about this soonest. We found out that Nigel Bowles owned a pistol. California registration."

"Twenty-two?" I asked.

"Yeah. We combed the motor home this morning. No sign of it. We also contacted the LAPD and asked them to do a search of his house there. Zilch."

"So he may have been killed with his own gun."

"Also, we got the results of the fingerprints in the motor home. There were matches for a lot of people on the show. I emailed you a list. He only lived in the motor home for a few weeks, but people apparently were streaming in and out of it like it was Grand Central. It's almost like Bowles was holding court in his RV."

"It's what royalty does," I said. "Okay. Put together a squad of uniformed officers. Warrant up and go through the hotel rooms of every person associated with the show."

"Not just the ones on the list I sent?"

"Everyone. Killer might have worn gloves, and it could have been his first visit. I still think someone on the show killed Bowles. The killer may have the gun stashed."

"I'll get right on it."

I checked the list Scotty had emailed me, and I turned to Crapster.

"You know where I can find this guy Dawg Gauchee?"

"I believe his motor home is the third one down from Nigel's. You're interviewing him next?"

"Yeah."

"Mind if I join you?"

"Can I stop you?"

"Unlikely."

"Come on, then."

Crapster followed me to Gauchee's RV. We found him next to it, going through tai chi exercises on a rug under the side awning. He was just under six feet tall and built like a gymnast. His skin was the color of café-au-lait, and his eyes were a surprising deep blue. His head was shaven. He wore a pair of sweatpants. He was in the Single Whip position when I flashed my badge.

"Antone Gauchee?" I asked.

He dropped his arms and squinted at me.

"Can't see a t'ing wit'out my glasses, mon. Who's there?" His voice had a Caribbean lilt.

"Detective Amboy Boatright. Morgan PD."

"Jus' a sec."

He stepped into the motor home, and emerged seconds later wearing a pair of black plastic-rimmed glasses. He had grabbed a short-sleeve Hawaiian shirt and slipped it on as he hopped to the ground. He left the shirt unbuttoned.

"Ah, that's better. Forgive me, please. Blind as a bat. Which one o' you gentlemen be the detective?"

I started to badge him again, but Crapster cut me off.

"This is Detective Boatright. My name is Bowie Crapster."

"Aida's psychic," Gauchee said.

"I work for a great many people."

"An' you wan' to know if I killed Nigel Bowles."

"We're interviewing all the people associated with the show," I said. "We didn't get to you this morning."

"Would you like to step inside?" He pointed toward the RV door.

We followed him up the steps. Gauchee's motor home was not nearly as ornate as Bowles', but it was nicely tricked out and the furniture was comfortable. Gauchee offered us bottled water. We declined, so he took a seat in a chair facing the sofa where we sat.

"Can you tell us where you were last night between nine and midnight?" I asked.

"I was right here," Gauchee said. "I did not leave here after dinner, until the police arrived this morning."

"Were you alone?" I asked.

"Sadly, yes."

"So, nobody to corroborate your whereabouts?"

"It would seem that way. Am I a suspect?"

"We know that Nigel Bowles intended to drop you from the show next season."

"This is news to me. Ah, I understan', mon. You think I might have killed him to keep my job."

"The thought occurred to us."

"Rest assured, gentlemen. I do not need this gig. In fact, I have considered quitting the show after this season. I need to get back into the studio, cut some tracks. I might have killed Nigel for any number of other reasons, but not to stay on the show. I probably would have sent him a case of Cristal instead."

"What would those other reasons be?" I asked.

"Mostly for bein' Nigel. T'at was one sorry waste of skin and bone. A truly despicable human being."

"Do you own a firearm?" I asked.

"I do. It's back in California. Feel free to inspect my temporary home. I have not'ing to hide."

"Nothing?" Crapster asked.

"You readin' my mind?" Gauchee said.

"Everyone has something to hide. There's a skeleton in every man's closet."

"You been talkin' to Aida."

"Of course," Crapster said.

"T'at woman, she talk a lot. Okay, so Nigel and me, we had a fight."

"What about?" I asked.

"Aida didn't say?"

"Let's say she was vague on the subject."

He settled back in his chair and rubbed his face a couple of times. When he spoke again, I noticed that his accent was gone.

"My name isn't Gauchee. I was born Michael Jones, in Wiesbaden, Germany. Army brat. Mom was from Granada. I learned the accent from her. There's a real Antone Gauchee, down in Jamaica. Met him a few years back, but he wouldn't recall me. We weren't friends. I stole his name and used the novelty of being a Caribbean rapper to stand out from the crowd. It worked. Somehow, Nigel found out about me. I wanted to leave the show two years ago, but he told me he'd divulge my real identity if I did. It served his purposes to keep me on. Like I said, though, even if he did plan to fire me, I wouldn't have killed him. I didn't want to be here anyway."

"Just one problem," I said.

"What's that?"

"You already told us you had no idea Bowles planned to dump you and Aida Kennedy. That means you still had motive to kill him."

"What motive?"

"With Bowles dead, there'd be nobody to keep you from jumping ship. You also had opportunity, since you claimed you were alone here in your motor home on the night Bowles died. That leaves means. I think I will search this place after all, and I think I'll have you tested for GSR."

"GSR?" Gauchee—or Jones—asked.

"Gunshot residue. It's only been seventeen hours, so there should still be some traces if you shot Bowles."

He leaned back in his chair and clasped his hands behind his head.

"Search all you want and test all you want," he said. "I didn't do it."

———

Maybe Gauchee/Jones killed Nigel Bowles, and maybe he didn't, but nothing in the motor home implicated him. We didn't find a gun, and the lab tech found no traces of powder residue on his hands. I advised him not to take any sudden trips, though, since he was the best suspect we'd found yet, but I was dubious of his guilt.

"An embarrassment of riches," Crapster said as we walked toward the Convention Center.

"Yeah. Lots of suspects, tons of motive, even a little opportunity here and there. How to narrow the field?"

"Perhaps I can help with that."

"How so?"

"A few parlor tricks, some sleight of hand, a little song, a little dance, a little seltzer down your pants. That sort of thing."

"You want to trick someone into confessing."

"*Trick* is a loaded word. I think I can influence the killer into revealing himself."

"Or herself."

"Of course."

"How would you manage that?" I asked.

"Adroitly. Can you round up everyone on the show for me? Perhaps on the stage in the Convention Center?"

"I'd like to know ahead of time what you plan to do."

"Me too," Crapster said. "But I'm making this up as I go."

Two hours later, I had the cast of *Star Quest* assembled on the stage. They sat in a circle of metal folding chairs. They glanced back and forth at each other nervously as Crapster and I walked up the steps from the auditorium.

"I'm reasonably certain that somebody on this stage is responsible for the death of Nigel Bowles," I announced. "With the assistance of Mr. Crapster, I intend to know who that person is before we leave the theater."

Crapster stepped into the center of the circle of chairs. I gave a prearranged hand signal to the crew in the booth at the back of the theater, and the house lights were doused. Seconds later, the stage lights dimmed. I'd like to claim credit for the dramatics, but they were Crapster's idea.

He held his arms out wide, closed his eyes, and slowly began to rotate.

"Yes," he whispered hoarsely. "The vibrations are very distinct. There is a killer among us."

I stifled my gag reflex.

Crapster pulled a religious medal on a thin gold chain from his pocket and held it out to show the people in the circle. Only he and I knew that he'd purchased it an hour earlier from a local five and dime.

"This belonged to Nigel Bowles," he explained. "It was given to him at his confirmation when he was only a child.

He wore it for over thirty years. Personal possessions take on the animal magnetism of the people who wear them. A gifted psychic can read those vibrations and learn a great deal about those possessions' owners. After many years, everything about the person is imprinted on a piece of jewelry as intimately connected to its owner as this one."

Having set the stage, he closed his eyes again, and his head fell backward. He allowed the medal to swing from one hand as he slowly rotated, once to his left, and then to his right. He suddenly stopped, the hand carrying the medal pointed directly at Aida Kennedy.

"Aida," he said. "As a dowsing rod bends to the power of water, the magnetism in this medal is drawn toward you. Opposites attract on a magnet, as they attract in the spiritual plane. You and Nigel Bowles were polar spiritual opposites."

"We couldn't have been more unlike one another," Aida said.

"Obviously so. That's how spiritual magnetism works. This medal is drawn toward those people with whom Nigel Bowles had the greatest conflicts. Imagine how it would respond to the person who took Bowles' life. Imagine!"

On cue, the lights changed color, to a deep, angry red. Most of the people sitting in the circle gasped. Crapster rolled his head on his shoulders as if going into a trance. He swayed first right and then left, did a nifty little pirouette, and then acted as if the medal was pulling him to his right. He stopped in front of Antone Gauchee.

"So much antipathy," he said, putting as much pain into his voice as possible, without overflowing into absurd melodrama. “There was great anger and conflict between you and the late Mr. Bowles.”

Before Gauchee could respond, Crapster seemed to be yanked away, toward the other side of the circle, where Belinda Talbert sat next to her dreadlocked secret boyfriend, Randy Locklear. Randy glared at him as he dangled the medal inches from their faces.

“Hmmm…” he murmured. He didn’t elaborate. His hand swung around again, and as if pulled by the medal he stepped five feet to his right and stopped right in front of Tyke Glenham.

“My, my,” he said. “No love lost between you and Nigel, was there?”

“You could say that,” Glenham said. “Doesn’t mean I killed him.”

“Doesn’t mean you didn’t either. Tell me, did Nigel Bowles know about your offer from the network?”

Glenham flinched for the smallest part of a second. It’s possible that most of the people in the circle didn’t catch it. I knew Crapster couldn’t have missed it.

“Nobody knows about…” Glenham started, and then stopped himself.

“Clearly, somebody does,” Crapster said. “You knew that Bowles planned to fire Aida and Dawg, but he wanted to keep you on. I seem to recall that you signed a new contract with *Star Quest* only last year. How long does it last?”

“Five years.”

“Ironclad, I’d imagine.”

“Nigel didn’t like to fool around,” Glenham said.

"That's bad for you. With four years out of a five-year contract still hanging over your head, I suppose it would be very difficult for you to take that network offer."

"I…" Glenham began, but before he could finish the sentence Crapster turned and feigned being pulled by the medal in another direction. He stopped before Aida Kennedy, the medal swinging back and forth before her eyes like a clock pendulum.

"I'm rethinking your situation," he said to her. "This medal likes you far too much for it to mean nothing. You had an alibi for the night Nigel was murdered. There's only one problem. Your alibi—Ms. Talbert—has *another* alibi. Randy Locklear claims she was with him that evening. She's a lovely young lady, immensely talented, but she can't be in two places at one time, can she?"

"You know she was with me!" Aida protested.

"Do I? Here's my problem. Either you are a liar, or Randy is."

He turned and stood in front of Randy Locklear. He dangled the medal in front of Randy's nose, as he placed a hand on the singer's shoulder.

"Right, Randy?" he said. "You can't both be telling the truth. And, if Belinda was with Aida in her motor home, that leaves your whereabouts up for grabs, doesn't it?"

"I don't have to answer that," Randy growled.

"But you already have," Crapster said. "Your dilated eyes and the increase in your heart rate gave you away. Of course, it didn't hurt that we found Nigel Bowles' pistol, right where you hid it!"

Randy jumped up, knocking his chair backward, and dashed toward the exit. Before he even got to the stage wings, two uniformed Morgan policemen stepped out and grabbed him. One held him securely while the other slapped on the cuffs.

"Randy!" Belinda Talbert wailed. "No!"

"Of course," Crapster said. "It makes sense."

"Maybe you can enlighten all of us, then," I said. "And what's this about a pistol?"

"Yesterday, when we interviewed Belinda, Randy became so upset he almost assaulted you. He claimed that he and Belinda had been together the entire evening when Bowles was murdered. When you asked why he lied, Belinda said he'd done it to protect her. The question is—from what was he protecting her? Why give her an alibi? She had no reason to kill Bowles, *unless*—"

"*Unless* he knew that Bowles had been pressuring Belinda to sleep with him," I finished. "Yeah, I get it. Belinda, did you tell Randy about Bowles' hitting on you?"

She wiped tears away from her eyes and nodded. "I told him about it on the way to Morgan, four days ago."

"So," Crapster said, "When Randy lied about being with Belinda on the night of the killing, he wasn't trying to give *her* an alibi."

"He was trying to protect *himself*," I said. "He hoped that Belinda would buy into the lie, which would get us off her back *and* give him an alibi. She couldn't, of course, because we already knew she had spent the evening in Aida's motor home."

Belinda crossed the stage to Randy, who stood between the two officers, his head down, ringlets of dreadlocks framing his face.

"You killed him for *me*?" she said.

"No," Randy said. "Well, yes, at first I went there to tell him to leave you alone. I told him I knew he'd been pressuring you to sleep with him, and that he should stop if he knew what was good for him. He just laughed. He said he had the power to rig the votes, and that he was going to see to it that I got voted off this week, to get me out of the way. Then he pulled his pistol from a drawer and told me to get out. I should have left, but I was furious. We wrestled, I got the gun from him, and I pushed him into the bathroom and shot him. It happened almost before I knew what I was doing."

He turned to me.

"How in hell did you get the gun? I hid it where I thought nobody would ever find it!"

"Ah," Crapster said. "Well, I might have lied myself. Just a little. With your help, though, we'll recover the pistol."

"Read him his rights," I told the cops. "We'll get an official statement from him down at the station."

I had just finished getting Randy's statement at the Morgan Police Department and was writing my report on the case when Crapster walked into my office.

"Good evening, Detective! I'm surprised to see you so hard at work, and so late in the day. Happy hour began an hour ago."

"So it did. I'm finishing up this report, so that Randy can be arraigned tomorrow morning. Perhaps you could fill in a few blanks."

"I'll be happy to help in any way I can."

"Let's start with this network contract business. Tyke Glenham never mentioned it to either of us."

"No, he didn't. I guessed. I have a large number of clients who work in show business. The more successful ones are always being offered contracts. *Star Quest* is one of the most popular shows on television, and Tyke gets very high ratings. I'd imagine he gets two or three offers a week. Some of them must be very attractive."

"And the gun? You guessed about that also?"

"Sort of. As I worked my way around the circle, I observed each person for autonomic signs of arousal—dilating eyes, flushing, increased heart rate."

"Like a lie detector."

"Yes. Of course, lie detectors have a very high error rate. On the other hand, if only one person registered significant arousal, that narrowed my field a bit."

"And Randy got aroused."

"As did Tyke. However, if you'll recall, Tyke had a perfect alibi for the night of the murder. He recorded promos, and then had dinner with your ex-girlfriend, Lila Arcenaux. I checked with Lila this afternoon, and she indicated that they were together far later than would have been necessary to clear Mr. Glenham."

"And that left Randy."

"Exactly. The more I pressed him, the edgier he became."

"But the bit about the gun. That was quite a chance you took."

"Not really. We were pretty sure Nigel was killed with his own pistol, which had disappeared. It stood to reason that the killer had hidden the gun somewhere. I decided to push Randy over the confessional cliff with a little creative mendacity."

"You lied to him."

"Didn't I just say that?"

"I suppose you did. Still seems like a risky move to me."

"Well, Detective, you know what they say."

"What's that?"

Crapster straightened his cuffs and tie, slipped on his sunglasses, and said, "If you want the marionette to dance, you have to know how to pull the strings."

BUSTING RED HEADS

by

Richard Helms

Author's Note: I've been a union supporter my entire adult life, and a proud member of SEIU. I always wanted to write a story about Pinkerton-style union busters in the 1920s. This story was originally intended to be part of a story collection about union organizer Joe Hill that never happened. I realized it was a corker as a standalone, and I submitted it to Ellery Queen Mystery Magazine. *First published in* EQMM's *March/April 2014 double issue, it went on to become a finalist in the SMFS Derringer Award, the ITW Thriller Award, and the PWA Shamus Award in 2015.*

R

Two years slogging through the trenches of France must not have been thrilling enough, so after tramping around the country for a year I went home and took a job as a Boston cop. It was easy. I was Irish, and the department was still recovering from the mess Commissioner Curtis had made of his dealings with the AFL sympathizers who went on strike in 1919. There were lots of openings for a mick with a hard head and a good billy arm.

That job lasted a couple of years, until I discovered that the striking cops had been right about one thing—cops were about three rungs down from stable boys on the salary ladder. I was lucky. I wasn't married like a lot of the lads, so the only mouth I had to feed was my own, but I still had needs. On my cop pay, I wasn't going to make a lot of headway in the world.

I was walking the beat one day in April, trying to figure out how to make some decent scratch without going on the take, like so many other guys had, when I ran across a window flyer that said the Horne Detective Agency was looking for operatives. I liked the idea of being a private detective, like Nick Carter maybe, so as soon as my watch ended, I dressed in my best suit and headed down for their office.

"Name?" the recruiter asked when I stepped up to his desk.

"Tommy Crane."

"Got any experience?"

"Fought in France. I've been a cop for the last twenty-seven months."

He looked up at me, and I think he actually saw me for the first time.

"You ain't one of them AFL strikers."

"I replaced one of 'em. I got no love for Bolshies."

He nodded and made a note on the paper in front of him.

"That's good. You'll see your share of them, you go to work for Horne. You got another suit?"

"I can find one."

"How long will it take you to separate from the force?"

"Just like that? You mean I'm hired?"

"We need guys like you. There's plenty of work to go around. I think you'll be happy with the pay, too. Much better than the pocket change you've been making on the force."

I'd walked in the door a cop, but I walked out a private dick.

When that recruiter said I'd see my share of reds, he wasn't kidding.

I thought I'd start out doing real investigating, collaring embezzlers and bootleggers and the like, but instead I got assigned to a strike-busting squad. In the wake of the Russian revolution, it seemed there were reds on every street corner. The Horne Agency was hired a lot by oil barons and wheat barons and rail barons—just about any fourteenth-floor type who thought his workforce was being infiltrated by Wobblies or Bolshies or some other kind of unionizing parasites, as we were taught to think about them.

One week, we'd bust up an IWW meeting in the Chicago stockyards. The next week, we'd take a train to Kentucky to drive off organizers encouraging coal miners to join the UMW. Wherever anti-capitalists showed their heads, we'd be there in a few days to bust them. The Horne Agency's goal was to crush the red menace before it took over the country, and it aimed my squad at them like a howitzer—with similar results.

Three of us—me, Everett Sloop, and Warren Johns, were sitting in the Kansas City office in August of 1923, trying to stay cool and counting the minutes until we could shove off and grab a cool beer down the street. Jess Coulter, our commander, walked in and scowled when he saw us.

"You guys packed?"

"We goin' somewhere?" Johns asked.

"Rawlings, Kentucky."

"Don't much care for Kentucky," Sloop said.

"There's the door," Coulter said. "Nobody's holding you here."

That shut Sloop up, but good.

"What's in Rawlings?" I asked.

"A rail yard. Makes passenger cars for trains. The Bolshies have been recruiting yard workers for a couple of years now, and they've formed an AFL affiliate. Call themselves the International Affiliated Railworkers, but there ain't no '*international*' about them. It's just a bunch of bluegrass shit-kickers got too big for their britches. They hit up the rail yard owner, guy named Stanley Marcus, for the usual—shorter hours, higher wages. Bunch of slackers and layabouts. Marcus told 'em to ram it, so they went on strike. Marcus has plenty of scabs ready to come in and work, but the IAR keeps blocking the entrance."

"So they want us to clear out the blockage?" I said.

"Yeah, Crane. The three of you get your stuff together. We got four more crews coming in from Chi, Cincy, Nashville, and Cleveland. I figure that should be enough to get the job done. You ship out in the morning."

The first day on the job in Rawlings, things got messy. A bunch of malcontents had formed a picket line at the front gate of the manufacturing plant, blocking the path for the honest workers who wanted to get in to make a day's pay.

The factory owner, Stanley Marcus, was also the local mayor in Rawlings, and he got a writ from a sympathetic judge ordering the strikers to disperse and allow the replacement workers in. The local sheriff, a guy named McWhorter, met us a block from the gate with the papers.

"Now, I'm gonna serve these here papers to the men at the gate," he said. "I want you boys to provide backup for me, just in case some o' them reds gets uppity. Think you can do that?"

"Same as back in Chicago," I said. "No problem."

It was a problem.

As soon as McWhorter walked up to the guys at the gate—with me, Sloop, and Johns in tow—the strikers formed a half circle. I had seen the tactic before, and I signaled the Horne guys to fall back a little.

As I expected, as soon as McWhorter stepped up to the gate, the half-circle collapsed into a ring, with McWhorter playing the finger. I saw someone toss a bottle toward his head. He must have sensed it, being a good cop, and ducked at the last second. So far, so good. Then he made his mistake. He unsnapped the holster flap and pulled his big Colt revolver.

I didn't have to say a word. Instantly Johns, Sloop, and I had our billys out, and we waded into the crowd, slapping knee tendons and elbows and the occasional head, laying out strikers right and left, until we reached McWhorter. The sheriff's face was beet-colored and his hair was hanging in strings as he tried to push and shove his way toward the gate. His campaign hat had disappeared at some point, trampled under the strikers' feet. He waved the gun around like he was swatting at hornets, and it was a sure bet that any second he was going to take off the top of some poor sap's head—probably mine. I'd seen what a .45 caliber slug could do to flesh and bone, and I wasn't eager to see it again. I reached out and grabbed the gun away from him.

"You crazy?" I said. "You got one gun, six bullets, and about eighty hungry men ready to rip the meat from your bones. Let's get. It ain't your day, Sheriff."

Warren and I dragged him away from the gate, while Sloop covered our tails. We kept dragging the poor guy about a half-block before we stopped.

"What kinda cowards are you?" he demanded, his face glowing so red I thought he was going to have a stroke.

"Realistic ones," Sloop said. "Don't worry, Sheriff. We ain't done yet. We just need to balance out the odds a little. Hold on to your legal papers. We'll be back."

I stayed with the sheriff until Warren and Everett could round up the crews from Cincy and Chi and Nashville, about twenty of us in all, and once we were all assembled, we walked the sheriff back down to the gate. This time we didn't bother hiding the billys. We wanted the strikers to see us coming from a distance, and to have a minute or two to consider what it would feel like to nurse a busted arm or nose.

We were all big Irish lugs, war veterans and battle-hardened. Could have played football if we'd been smart or rich enough to go to college, and we had all been hurt enough times to know it didn't last. The strikers, though, weren't used to the violent life. When they saw a score of us headed their way, they began to scatter. By the time we got to the gate, there were probably fifteen or so Wobs standing around trying to look menacing. They snarled a lot, but they'd lost their bite, and the sheriff was able to serve his papers and open the factory for the day.

That was the way it went for the first several days. The striking reds would get liquored up at night, building up their courage, and try to keep us from breaking the picket lines the next morning. They couldn't stand up to us, though, and it always ended the same way, with the workers getting into the factory and business as usual.

We were in the temporary office the Horne Agency had rented, about three blocks from the factory gates, maybe five days into the strike. It was morning, and we'd just tossed back some ham and eggs and biscuits. I was polishing off my second cup of coffee when Stanley Marcus walked into the office.

"Mr. Mayor," Sloop said. "Something we can do for you?"

"You boys have been doing a great job," Marcus said. "But it isn't enough."

"Don't reckon the Horne Agency can afford to send many more crews, unless you want to pay twice as much," I said.

"It's not that. You have the strikers handled. The problem is I can't get enough men to run the factory at capacity. We're running at about forty-five percent of the speed we need to keep up with orders. I don't just need the gates clear for the scab workers. I need more workers."

"Don't look at us," Warren Johns said. "I don't know what end of a monkey-wrench you blow in to."

"It's a thought," Marcus said. "Twenty able-bodied men, strong like you guys. No, though, I'm thinking about something else. The strikers were contented before that organizer and his red buddies came to town. Corcoran, his name is. He's running the whole strike, filling the workers' heads with all sorts of uppity notions. We take out Miles Corcoran, and the whole strike falls apart."

"What are you suggesting?" I asked.

"I'd like you guys to pay Corcoran and his partner Norris Hanks a visit. They have a rented office over on Bull Street, about half a mile from the factory. I've talked with McWhorter, and we've come to the conclusion that a raid like the one I'm describing could result in a great deal of damage—damage we'd find uninteresting in terms of prosecution, if you get my meaning."

"You're sayin' that if the IAR office gets torn to pieces, you'd overlook it," Sloop said.

"The IAR organizers are ruining this town," Marcus said. "Someone torches their offices and ties them to cow-catcher of the next train, I figure the town would have more important matters to attend to before seeking justice for 'em."

"We'll wait until dusk," Sloop said. "Make it harder for Corcoran and his pals to identify us."

It was the first of September, and the sun didn't go down until about eight at night. We cleared the gates that morning just like we had for the past week, and then I posted myself on a bench across the street from the International Affiliated Railways office on Bull Street.

There wasn't much to see. A couple of times during the day a guy left the office and headed down the street to the local hash house to get some takeout meals at lunch and dinner time. From the size of the boxes, he was feeding two or three people in the office. I made him for Norris, the number two man. That meant that Corcoran must be inside the office.

Along about eight-thirty, after it was good and dark, Everett Sloop walked up the boardwalk toward my bench. At the same time, I saw Warren Johns and one of the Cincy guys, a kid named Farris, approach the IAR office from the north, on the other side of the street.

"You know this kid, Farris?" I asked Sloop.

"Sure. He's all right. I asked him to help us out tonight. He'll get the job done."

Dispersing a gang of red strikers was easy and didn't call for much in the way of firepower. Invading an office after dark, when you didn't know who might be packing inside, carried enough uncertainty that we had come well equipped. I had my Colt 1911 automatic, the only one of us who carried one. Sloop had a Webley top-break .38 that he favored. Johns had a sawed-off twelve-gauge that could take the bark off an oak tree from thirty feet. The kid from Cincy—Farris—had a Smith and Wesson Police Special revolver hanging by his thigh, ready to swing it up at the first sign of danger.

They positioned themselves on either side of the IAR office. Johns glanced across the street at us, and I nodded that we were ready. Sloop and I started across the street. We were halfway there when Johns and Farris stormed the front door. We broke into a flat run, to form a second assault wave behind Johns, but we scattered at the boardwalk when we heard gunfire and shouting inside the office.

"I'm hit! I'm hit!" someone screamed, but I couldn't tell who. Then I heard the booming explosion from Johns' twelve-gauge, both barrels in rapid succession, before several more whipcracks of pistol fire. I heard several muffled voices, probably from the back of the office, and a door slamming.

"Back door!" I yelled to Sloop, but he was already dodging around the corner.

I sidled up next to the front door and peeked around the jamb. There was a single lamp in the back of the room, and in the shadows that fell jaggedly across the heart pine floor I saw Warren Johns and the kid from Cincy. A blind man could tell they were already gone. I choked back the acid that forced its way up my throat, a sensation I hadn't felt since the Battle of Marne in 1918.

The raid had gone very, very wrong.

Losing Warren Johns and the kid from Cincinnati was tough. Ev Sloop and I caught hell from the Horne home office, but only until Marcus rang them up and explained that we had been acting on his authority as mayor and—more importantly—Horne's client.

That didn't help me much. I felt awful that I hadn't been able to do more to prevent the killings. Ev Sloop and I were the senior members of our crew. By rights, we should have been the first to break the IAR offices' doors. What happened to Warren and Farris had been a bad draw of cards.

I was sitting in the temporary Horne offices several mornings after the raid, reading a copy of the *Police Gazette*, when the door opened and rail-thin man wearing a beaver bowler stepped inside.

"Help you?" I asked.

"Perhaps. My name is Jethro Schein."

"Tommy Crane. What can I do for you, Mr. Schein?"

"I am the attorney for Miles Corcoran and Norris Hanks. I would like to talk with you regarding their whereabouts."

"You know where they are?"

"Not…precisely. They have been in touch, but they haven't given me many details regarding their present location."

"That's a shame. I'd like to have a word with them, at least before they swing."

"Yes. I see. As it happens, that is precisely why I am here. There is a case to be made for their innocence, since they were not engaged in the violation of any laws when their offices were invaded."

"You want to explain that to Warren Johns' mother? I hear she'll be here end of the week to pick up his body. I'm sure she'd be very interested in how your clients' rights were violated, and how they lawfully blew her boy damn near through the nearest window. I'll introduce you, if you'd like."

"That won't be…uh, necessary. I just wanted to ask whether there is any circumstance in which you might consider that my clients might not have killed your friend."

"It was their office. I staked it out for most of the day. Saw your boy Hanks go in and out a couple of times."

"But you never saw Miles Corcoran."

"Asked around. Folks saw him go in that morning. Never saw him go out again."

"And where were my clients after your raid?"

"On the scoot. They ran out the back after shooting my boys."

"And you watched the back door the entire day, also?"

That stopped me. Johns and Sloop had been covering the factory entrance while I'd been sitting across the street from the IAR offices. I gave the matter a moment's thought.

"Weren't enough men to watch both doors," I said.

"And, yet, you believe that my clients were inside the offices when you and your hired guns broke in."

"I do," I said, but even I could hear the uncertainty in my voice.

"Here's my concern," Schein said. "Harboring a fugitive is a very bad crime, especially in a case of murder. I don't want my clients to wind up like Joe Hill did over in Utah a few years back. Nobody ever saw Hill rob that store, either, but he sure did take the heat for it. On the other hand, if I know where they are, and I don't do something about it, I could wind up being an accessory after the fact."

"You could."

"I surely could. I don't like the idea of that, especially if my clients are innocent. I just wanted you to know, Mr. Crane. If my boys stand trial, I intend to call you as a defense witness, and I expect you'll tell the jury exactly what you just told me, that there was nobody watching that rear door, and you never saw Miles Corcoran go in or out of the IAR offices."

"I don't think we have much else to talk about, Mr. Schein," I said.

He must not have thought so either, because he tipped his hat to me and left the office.

I thought about the conversation for a few minutes, and then grabbed my hat and locked the office doors behind me.

Coleman French, the town doctor, had his examining rooms about a half block from the Horne office. I found him stitching up a cut in the arm of a young boy who sat snuffling and trying to look brave. I waited patiently for French to finish.

After he'd sent the boy trotting off, French stared me down.

"You're one o' them detective fellows, aren't you?"

"Tommy Crane," I said, handing him my card. "Wanted to talk to you about the two boys we brought in the other night—the ones got shot."

"Come into my office."

I followed him through the hallway to a cramped room with a white oak rolltop desk and a few diplomas hanging on the wall. He took a seat at the desk, and I stood in the doorway.

"Want a place to sit?" he asked.

"I'm good. Those two boys. What killed them?"

"Why, they was shot."

"I know that part. I mean, what kind of bullets?"

"I'm a doctor, Mr. Crane. I don't know one bullet from another."

"Were they large bullets, or little ones?"

"Would you like to see them?"

"I would."

He swiveled his chair and rifled through a cabinet on the other side of his desk, until he found a one-pint mason jar. It rattled and clinked as he handed it to me.

"Thought it might be a good idea to hold on to them," he said. "You know. For evidence, if'n them boys ever come to trial."

I half-listened as I examined the jar. Inside were seven slugs. Bullets deform when they smack into flesh, and I've even seen them shatter, but these were intact enough for me to recognize them as thirty-eights and forty-fives.

"Now, this is interesting," French said. "The little ones there all came from the older fella. The big ones were all from the younger one."

"Two shooters," I said.

"Or, one man with two guns, maybe."

"These men were professionals," I said. "I examined the IAR offices after the raid. There wasn't a drop of blood anywhere in the room, except where our boys were lying. They broke down the door and got mowed down."

"Like someone expected them," French said.

"Yeah. Exactly like that."

I didn't like the implications, as I thought about the conversation on the way back to the Horne offices. When I got there, Stanley Marcus was waiting, sitting on the bench out front.

"Mr. Mayor," I said, while unlocking the door.

"Have an assignment for you," he said, after following me inside. He plopped down in the most comfortable seat in the room, without so much as an invitation.

"I take my orders from Jess Coulter."

"Then it's a good thing I already talked with him. We have a tip about Miles Corcoran and Norris Hanks. Word has it they're holed up in a hotel across the line in Cincinnati. I got the address and room number."

"Where'd you get it?"

"A reliable source. Very reliable."

"Well, that's good then. Guess the local police will round them up?"

"Not precisely. I want you to go get them."

"Why?"

"Because you have a stake in this. It was one of your boys who got killed."

"The Cincy crew lost a lad, too. Farris. Seems one of them would be a better choice. It's their turf."

"Coulter wants me to send you."

"Did he say why?"

"No. But he was clear about it. '*Send Crane!*' he told me. He was most emphatic about it."

"So, you want me to take a train to Cincy, grab your reds for you, and bring them back. No extradition papers, no red tape."

"I think you're beginning to understand. Ohio is a union state. That damned red Gompers started the AFL there forty years ago. The police there might not be sympathetic to extraditing a couple of card-carrying Bolshies."

"You want me to kidnap them."

"I want them retrieved and brought back here to face justice, Crane. The Horne Agency works for me. You work for the Horne Agency. You're working on my orders, bringing them boys back."

"I want papers I can flash, if there's any misunderstanding."

"You'll get them."

"And I want to be deputized for the duration."

"What?"

"I want papers and a badge. They open a lot of doors my Horne Agency card might not breach."

The next evening, I hopped off a train at the Baymiller Street Station and made my way to the address Marcus had given me. It was a cheap hotel, but not a slum by any stretch, about ten blocks from the station.

If the information Marcus had passed along was any good, I'd find Corcoran and Hanks in a corner room on the fourth floor. I knew what Hanks looked like, but I'd never laid eyes on Corcoran, so Marcus had scrounged up a picture from some union newspaper. It wasn't a very clear likeness, but it was enough for me to make a fair comparison if Corcoran was in the room.

I stood outside the door and listened cautiously for several minutes but didn't hear any conversation inside. It was still early, but maybe my two fugitives were asleep.

I knocked on the door twice. There was a rustling sound inside, and after a few seconds someone said, "Who is it?"

"Front desk," I said. "Telegram for Mr. Corcoran."

The door swung open, and a bleary-eyed man looked around it at me.

"I'm Corcoran."

I snapped my hand out, grabbed him by the front of his shirt, and jerked him from the room. With my elbow, I pinned him to the wall by his throat, and I held my Colt against his cheekbone.

"Hanks," I said. "He's inside?"

"Gone," Corcoran rasped. "Just this morning."

"You'd better not be lying to me."

"Gone, I told you."

I lifted him off the ground, pivoted, and put him on the floor nose-down. Before he could make much more fuss, I had him cuffed from behind. I pulled him to his feet by the waistband of his pants, and shoved him inside the room as a shield, as I scanned it for any other inhabitants.

The room was empty. There were two beds, one unmade, and a nightstand with a bowl and a water pitcher. In the middle of the room was a cherry table and a couple of chairs. A cracked mirror hung over the dresser. The closet door was open, and there was no bathroom in sight. The windows were both closed.

"See," Corcoran said. "I told you. I'm all alone."

"I'm taking you back to Rawlings," I said.

"You can't do that."

"Try me."

"They'll hang me for sure."

"That's tough for you, Corcoran. You should have thought about that before shooting my partners."

"You have no authority!"

I pulled back my jacket to show him the Rawlings Deputy Sheriff badge.

"Oh, God," he blubbered. "I am dead for certain now."

He seemed to calm down a bit by the time we got to the train station. We made a bit of a scene, as I pushed him through the depot with his hands cuffed behind him. Nobody tried to stop us, though.

I paid for a sleeper berth and hustled him on board the train. Once there, I took the cuffs off one hand, and secured him to a cast-iron bar that ran the length of the inside wall of the berth.

"It's a short trip," I told him. "You won't need to lie down or anything."

He didn't say a word, not then or even as the train began to leave the station. We were in Covington before he opened his mouth.

"It's funny," he said.

"Glad you think so."

"This train car. It was built at the rail yard in Rawlings. Like it's going home."

"What of it?"

"The men I represent built this car. Want to know what they were paid?"

"No."

"Fifty cents an hour. That's how much. If they're lucky, they make a thousand dollars a year. The U.S. government says it takes a minimum of twenty-two hundred dollars to feed and house a family of four. Steel costs thirty-four dollars a ton. At that price, the steel in this rail car is worth more than all the wages of the men who built it."

"They chose their work."

"And they have a right to fair compensation. And what happens if one of them gets sick or injured on the job? What happens to a man when he gets too old or worn down to work anymore, years before his time?"

"It's a hard world," I said. "But you aren't going to sway me with your Bolshevik talk. I've heard it all."

"What is your agency paying you? Bet it's a damned sight more than fifty cents an hour. Your clothes give that away. I figure you're making five, six thousand a year to beat on honest working men who just want to feed their families."

I couldn't stop myself. "Then they should be working, not walking a picket line."

"Walking the picket line is the only way to get a fair wage. A single man has no power. Four or five men can be fired and replaced in half a day. But an entire workforce walking off the job puts them into a position to negotiate, and if nothing is being built a railroad sheikh like Marcus has no choice but to sit down and talk. If he'd done that in the first place, he could have saved himself a lot of money, rather than paying a squad of thugs like you to clear the gates for the scab skeleton crews."

"What do you know about it?"

"I know his production is down over seventy percent since the start of the strike, even with the scabs working the lines. I know he sent you and your buddies to the IAR offices because he thought he could end the strike and get the men back to work by getting rid of the organizers. Tell me I'm wrong."

He wasn't, so I just clammed up.

"There's just one problem," he said. "I wasn't in that office when your boys broke in. Neither was Hanks. We'd cleared out already."

"Why?"

"Because we were warned. Someone called on the telephone about fifteen minutes before your raid. Told us we were about to get taken down. We ran out the back to a house half a block away, on the other side of the vacant field, and we watched. When we saw the guns flashing and heard the explosions, we knew who was going to take the blame for it if someone died, so we hopped a northbound train and rode it all the way to Cincinnati."

"I like my version of the story better."

"Funny thing about the telephone system in Rawlings," he said.

"What's that?"

"You gotta make a call through an operator. You look like a square guy, even if you're in the wrong profession."

"I like my work."

"You like the money, sure, but it's not an honest man's work, and I think you're an honest man"

"Don't bet too heavily on my honesty."

"You have the face. I can tell you want to do the right thing. You just don't know what that thing is, not yet. Marcus isn't going to lift a finger to help me. McWhorter is in Marcus's back pocket. Someone in town knows about the call warning us about the raid. Listen to me, Crane. What do you think is going to happen when you get me back to Rawlings?"

"They'll toss you in jail and hold a trial the next time the circuit judge rides through, and then they'll stretch your neck."

"Ain't going to be any trial. I've seen this before. This is a frame job. You may not see it, yet, but if they put me in that jail, I won't see the weekend. One way or the other, Marcus will see to it I'm shut up, but good. You claim to want justice. You get to the telephone operator, and I bet she'll tell you about that call. You do it as soon as you can, and maybe you can help keep me alive long enough to get a real trial."

We arrived back in Rawlings first thing the next morning. I walked Corcoran off the train and down the block to the jailhouse. I'd telegraphed Marcus from the station in Cincy that we were on our way, so I wasn't surprised to see the lawyer, Schein, waiting for us as we entered the jail. McWhorter was there, too, waiting with a set of leg irons and a replacement pair of cuffs.

"Sheriff, I'd like to post bail for Mr. Corcoran," Schein said, after McWhorter had escorted the organizer back to the cells.

"Nothing to post," McWhorter said. "Bond is set by the judge, who won't be here for another week. Can't even arraign this red bastard until then. Don't you worry, though. We'll take real good care of him."

Schein seemed put out at the sheriff, but there was nothing he could do about it, so he stomped out of the jail.

"You remember what I said!" Corcoran yelled to me from the cells at the back of the jail. "Don't you forget!"

I caught my midday meal at a diner near the rail yard. It was a blue-plate special, some kind of meat that was mostly gristle and some runny mash and boiled green beans. It was awful, but there was a lot of it, and for most guys I imagine that's the main thing with food.

As I sat at the diner window and gnawed on my lunch, I watched the scabs at the rail yard across the street take their fifteen-minute meal break. They were a pitiful lot, to be certain—mostly older men who'd retired from the yard years earlier, or young lads who hadn't been smart enough to stay in school, and even a few guys who looked as if they'd just walked off a failing farm somewhere. One of them chewed contentedly on a brick of dark brown bread and drank water he pumped himself with the hand crank, catching it in his hand because he didn't even have a tin cup from which to drink.

Something didn't feel right. That morning I had joined Ev Sloop and the rest of the gang in clearing the gates for the scabs. There was the usual jostling and flailing, and all of the lads got in their fair share of whacks with the billy clubs. I realized in the middle of it all, though, that I was pulling my punches. I had the chance to crack a couple of skulls good, but instead I had grabbed them by the collars of their cheap canvas jackets and I'd tossed them clear of the gate.

I wasn't sure why I'd gone easy on the reds. I didn't owe them a thing. So what if they were making only a sawbuck a day, and not even that while they were on strike? It's a hard world. They were hungry? Fine! Work was just a few feet away, through the gates. Nobody was holding them back.

And, yet, I had given some of them a break, mostly the older ones, the ones who looked half-addled to begin with, and the little guys. Didn't make sense. I'd been a detective and a strike-breaker for months. Why was I going soft now?

I kept hearing Miles Corcoran's voice in my ears, too. *'Don't you forget!'* he'd yelled. What did he mean by that? What had we shared that I'd want to remember? He was just a red, another Wob organizer, another Bolshie troublemaker. We were about as similar as Mutt and Jeff.

I couldn't get him out of my mind, though.

After lunch, I walked up the street to McWhorter's office. One of his deputies, a fellow named Revell, was minding the jail. He leaned back in a swivel chair, his feet perched on the white oak desk. I pointed toward the back with my chin.

"Prisoner doing okay?"

"Sure. He's dandy. We're feeding him like a king. Fattening him up for the judge. Something I can do for you?"

"You still have Warren Johns' twelve gauge about? It belongs to the Horne Agency."

"I reckon it's around here somewhere. Give me a minute."

He walked to the back of the jail and returned a moment later with the shotgun.

"Oh," I said. "I almost forgot. The kid from Cincinnati. Farris. He had a Police Special revolver. I'm going to need that one, too."

"Why didn't you say so before I walked all the way back up here?" he grumbled.

"My mistake. Sorry."

He brought me the revolver, and placed it on the desk.

"Nice weapon," he said, as he gazed at the almost-new bluing.

"Yes," I said. "Very nice."

I picked up the revolver and looked it over. It was a 1905 model in the five-inch barrel, but of recent manufacture. The crosshatched walnut grip was barely worn. I flipped open the cylinder and ejected the cartridges into my hand. Farris had kept an empty cylinder for the hammer to rest on, so there were five cartridges. One was unfired. Strange. I'd been in a battle or two in my time, and the tendency was to squeeze the trigger until the gun didn't go 'bang' anymore, and then reload.

The kid had shot four times and stopped. Why?

Maybe that was when he was shot. Maybe the first bullet that hit him cut all his wires, and he dropped on the spot.

Four shots fired. The remaining cartridge was a standard .38 black powder round.

Warren Johns had been killed by four standard .38 rounds.

Had the kid from Cincy accidentally shot my buddy in the confusion? Four times? It seemed unlikely. And, if it wasn't an accident…

That was too much for me to get my thick Irish skull around. I stowed the pistol in my jacket pocket and cradled Warren's twelve-gauge under my arm, thanked the deputy, and headed back to my office.

The word came the next morning. During the night Miles Corcoran had hanged himself in his jail cell.

According to scuttlebutt, the sheriff hadn't relieved him of his belt, and he'd looped it through the bars, high enough to keep his feet off the ground so he couldn't back out if the thought occurred to him, and he'd stepped off the bed to dangle for a few tough minutes before dying.

It didn't sound right. As a cop I'd seen guys kill themselves in jail, but most of them had been losers, the type who always took the easy way out. Corcoran didn't seem right for it. I also recalled what he had told me on the train from Cincy.

'If they put me in that jail I won't see the weekend. One way or the other, Marcus will see to it I'm shut up, but good.'

Why would the mayor want to shut Corcoran up? What did Corcoran know, but wasn't telling? One thing was certain—now I'd never know. Whatever it was had been choked back forever when he danced at the end of his own belt.

The belt Sheriff McWhorter hadn't taken from him.

That implied that—if Corcoran had been right, and Marcus wanted to keep him quiet—Marcus and McWhorter had conspired to kill Corcoran. I didn't buy that suicide story for a second. Corcoran had seemed desperate for a chance to tell his side, but in a court of law where he could at least hope for an impartial judge.

Corcoran had been right about one thing. I *was* an honest cop on the beat, and I liked to think that I had been an honest detective with the Horne Agency. Something about Corcoran's death smelled awful. It was none of my business, really. As soon as the strike ended, Ev Sloop and I would head on down the road to a new assignment somewhere, and probably never see Rawlings, Kentucky again.

On the other hand, I had this gnawing suspicion that justice had been sidestepped, and as an honest cop that feeling settled in my stomach like a paving stone. There was only one way to relieve it. I had to know the truth.

The telephone operator for the entire town was housed in the Main Line Hotel lobby. The operator was a jolly, overly-plump, middle-aged woman named Hortense Trimble. It was the right job for her, since I discovered soon enough after meeting her that she loved to talk and—perhaps more importantly—loved to know things that others didn't.

I bought her dinner in the hotel dining room. She was suspicious at first, but I'd already figured that food was the best way to loosen her tongue. By her second pork chop, she was ready to tell me anything I wanted to know.

"Curious thing," I said. "On the night my partner was killed, I heard that someone called those awful union organizers on the telephone just before dusk."

"Really?" she said, between bites. She was acting coy, but I could see the twinkle in her eye. She knew exactly what I was talking about.

"Yes," I said. "Another roll?"

She took it gleefully and slathered two pats of butter on it. I admired her appetite.

"Do you recall putting calls through to the IAR offices?"

"Oh, yes. All the time. It was mostly long-distance, though. A lot of calls from Ohio and New York."

"How about local calls?" I said, as I passed her the bowl of mashed potatoes.

"A few. They weren't terribly popular in Rawlings, you know."

"I don't know a thing about the telephone business," I said. "Let's say I wanted to call Mayor Marcus. You know I work for him, right?"

"Sure I do."

"So, if I were to call Mayor Marcus from my office phone, it would have to go through your switchboard, right?"

"Surely. Every telephone in town is wired into my switchboard. All fifty or so of them."

"So, you'd know that I was the person calling."

"I would now," she said, batting her eyes at me. I fended her advances off by handing her the bowl of creamed corn.

"For certain, you'd know it was someone from my office."

"Yes."

"And, if you recognized *my* voice, you'd probably say something to me before putting my call through, right?"

"Passing the time of day," she said.

"Exactly. Tell me something, Hortense."

"Oh, anything, Mr. Crane…Tommy."

"That evening, when we raided the IAR offices. Did someone local call them, sometime around sundown?"

She stopped chewing. For a moment I thought I'd tried for too much too fast. Then, she glanced around the room to see if anyone was listening, and leaned forward.

"You know, they make a mean strawberry shortcake here," she said.

"Would you like some?"

"I'd *love* some."

"Tell me who called the IAR offices, and I'll get you two helpings."

I thought she was going to swoon right there at the table.

And then she told me.

There weren't enough scabs to run three full shifts, so we only had to clear away the strikers in the morning and afternoon. After that, the evening was ours.

I deposited Hortense back behind her switchboard, stuffed and sated, and took a walk down the street toward the courthouse. There were four or five benches situated around the courthouse square, so I settled onto one and waited as the sun went down and the lights began to come on in the offices.

Shortly after eight o'clock, Jethro Schein locked up his office and started to walk away from the square. I shadowed him for a block or so, and then made a point of catching up.

"Mr. Schein!" I said, as I walked up behind him. "A pleasant evening to you."

He stopped and turned to me, his face at first etched with fear. Then he recognized me.

"Crane, right? The detective fellow?"

"That's me. Tommy Crane. Mind if I walk with you for a block or so? I'm headed over to the Horne Agency office."

"No. That is, I don't mind."

"Tough deal about your client."

"Which one?"

"The dead one. Corcoran."

"Yes," Schein said. "Very sad. I never took him for a suicide."

"Me either. Rode all the way from Cincy with him on the train. He never mentioned the idea of killing himself. Not even once. Hell of a shock."

"Yes. I suppose he couldn't deal with the idea of a public execution."

"So you expected he'd be convicted, then."

"I'd have done my best to prevent it, but I'm afraid it would have been a lost cause. The circuit judge hereabouts doesn't take kindly to union rabble-rousers."

"How about you? How do you feel about them?"

Schein stopped short.

"Why do you ask?"

"Well, you seemed in an awful hurry to defend Corcoran. Even wanted to bail him out as soon as I brought him back. I got the impression you had a soft spot for him."

"How do you mean?"

"As a client."

"I still don't understand."

"Forget it. Just making small talk. Guess things will be getting back to normal around here now that the organizers are gone. Strike can't go on much longer."

"I suppose you're right."

"Funny thing. Corcoran and I were talking on the train. He said that he and Hanks weren't even in the IAR offices when we raided them. Can you beat that?"

"Really?"

"Sure. We talked about it, remember? I told you I watched that office all day long, and never saw Corcoran leave. Watched Hanks run up the street for some grub once or twice, but otherwise nobody entered or left the building. Something you said got me thinking, though."

"What's that?"

"The back door. They could have left through the back door."

"That was going to be a key component of my defense."

"So you said. And, you know, you might be right."

"You think?"

"Yes," I said. "Corcoran told me, on the train, that *someone* called the IAR office about fifteen minutes before the raid and warned him and Hanks. Told them to run. Of course, he might have been lying about that, trying to save his hide."

"Or not."

"As you say. Sure beats the hell out of me, though. For someone to warn Corcoran, they'd have to know about the raid itself. Seems to me the only people who had that information were me, my boys, Mayor Marcus, and the sheriff."

"Do tell?"

"That's about it, as far as I can recall. But there's more. Let's say someone did warn those lads, and they did scoot out the back door. That still doesn't explain the fact that there was *someone* in the office when we crashed it. *Somebody* killed my partner and that kid from Ohio."

"I see," Schein said.

"It's a puzzle, right?"

"It sure is."

"Well, here's my office. Nice to pass the evening with you, Mr. Schein. Get a good night's sleep."

I watched Schein through the drawn curtains of the Horne Agency office as he shuffled down the boardwalk. He stopped once or twice and glanced back toward me, but of course he couldn't see me watching him. When he had put enough distance between us, I stepped back out onto the street and put a tail on him.

Following a person isn't so hard unless you don't want to be caught doing it. A decent tail needs two or three guys to pull off right, and I only had myself.

I dodged to the backside of the main street and navigated my way through alleys, running from intersection to intersection to get ahead of Schein. Then I hid in the shadows until he walked by on the main drag, and I did it all again.

Finally, I hit an intersection where he didn't show. I made my way to the main street and found myself in a section of row houses. Schein had to be inside one of them. I crossed the street, slipped into the dark recess of a storefront, and waited. If I were right, Schein wouldn't stay put for long.

About a half hour later, he locked his front door behind him, and started back down the street in the direction from which we had come. He had no reason to suspect I was behind him, so I kept a decent distance and stayed close to the buildings, ducking into doorways as necessary. He walked three blocks and stopped at a squat, one-story office. I held back as he opened the door and stepped inside. After a few seconds, a light came on in the office, and I settled back to see what happened.

It took about fifteen minutes. I heard a car turn the corner three blocks up, and watched as it parked in front of the office. Seconds later, Stanley Marcus and Sheriff McWhorter stepped out and walked into the building.

I crossed to their side of the street and crept into the alley next to the office. It was September, but it was still warm at night. There were several windows open to the alley for ventilation. I pulled up a milk crate and stood on it so I could peer through one of the open windows.

Schein was pacing nervously. The mayor had taken a seat at a desk, and McWhorter seemed to be standing guard near the door.

"He knows, I tell you!" Schein said. "He practically accused me of warning Corcoran about the raid!"

"What does that prove?" Marcus said. "You were the reds' lawyer. Of course you'd want to protect them."

"But how would I know about the raid in the first place? Crane said that only he, the other Horne operatives, you and McWhorter knew about it. The only way I could find out would be if I had thrown in with you."

"He's a strike-breaker," McWhorter said. "Not much more than a hired thug. You're crediting him with too many brains."

"There was no other way," Marcus said to Schein. "We had to get Corcoran and Hanks out. That man Johns knew too much. He already knew we'd been paying you to rat out your red buddies. We needed the cover of the raid to get rid of him."

I felt a hand on my back, and I whirled around, my Colt automatic already in my hand. Ev Sloop put a finger to his lips, and I relaxed. I slipped the automatic back into my holster.

"What in hell are you doing?" he whispered.

"I found out what happened at the raid," I rasped back. "That lawyer fellow, Schein, was working with Marcus and the sheriff. They killed Warren because he'd learned too much."

Just then, through the window, I heard Schein say, "What are we going to do about Sloop?"

"What about him?" Marcus asked.

"What if he gets a bad case of the guilts? What if he decides to go to the cops?"

"This is a hanging state," Marcus said. "He goes to the cops, it's his own neck's gettin' stretched."

Before I could react, I felt something hard press against my ribs. It was Ev Sloop's Webley revolver. His free hand snaked around my waist and he removed the Colt from my holster.

"I sure wish you hadn't heard that," he said. "Now I gotta do something about it."

"Now it makes sense," I said. "I sent you around the back of the IAR office, but you said you didn't see anyone. You saw someone, all right. You saw plenty."

"I think we need to continue this conversation inside," Sloop said. He prodded me with the revolver. "Let's go."

He followed me around the corner to the door and held the gun on me as he pushed me inside.

"What in hell!" Schein yelped when he saw us. "What's he doing here?"

"He heard the whole thing," Sloop said. "He knows all about the raid."

"This is a problem," Marcus said.

"It's all making sense to me now," I said.

"Okay," Marcus said. "You're so smart. What do you think you know?"

"Corcoran and Hanks believed that Schein was working for them. In reality, he was paid off by you and Sheriff McWhorter to spy on the union and provide information. Somehow, Warren found out about it, and he had to be killed. After we planned the raid, Sloop here recruited Farris to go in with Warren and kill him in the heat of the battle. How much did you pay him, Ev?"

"It doesn't matter," Sloop said. "He never saw a penny of it."

"No, because lawyer Schein had called Corcoran and Hanks and warned them about the raid. They'd already gone on the run long before we breached the front door. My guess is that right after they fled, the sheriff here used the back door of the IAR office to get inside and lie in wait."

"How do you figure that?" McWhorter asked.

"Farris was killed by .45 ACP rounds. I recognized them when I saw them at the doctor's office. Remember the scuffle at the front gate of the factory the other day, Sheriff? You pulled your gun? It was a Colt New Service revolver, a .45 caliber. None of the Horne boys carry one. After Farris killed Warren, you figured you'd keep him quiet, permanently. That was the third set of shots I heard from outside. As he was dying, not knowing where the bullets that killed him had come from, Warren let loose with both barrels of his twelve-gauge. Soon as you knew he was spent, you came out of hiding and fired on Farris, killing him. Then you ran out the back door. Ev here saw you, but he was in on the game, so you were safe. What I don't understand is why?"

"Warren Johns was dumb," Sloop said. "He thought he could play both sides of the street. He was busting them red heads, but then he tried to shake down the guy who's payin' our salaries. Stupid. Me, there ain't a shred of pink in me. If these Bolshie organizers go to the gibbet, then I done my job."

"Clean," I said. "Corcoran and Hanks get blamed for the killings. I get sent to Cincy to bring them back, and the local hanging judge shuts them up for good."

"It would break the back of the union," Marcus said. "We found a way to kill two birds with one stone."

"So why kill Corcoran in his jail cell?"

"He got mouthy," McWhorter said from the corner. "He started talking about getting warned off the raid. He had to be shut up. When we find Hanks, the same will happen to him."

"They were innocent!" I argued.

"They're *reds*!" Sloop yelled back. "You better figure out what side you're on, Tommy boy. I got paid good by Marcus for what I done. There's more where that come from. I sure don't want to park one in your back, but if you got any thoughts of turnin' on your old buddy…"

He stopped, suddenly. In all the shouting, we hadn't noticed the growing sound of voices in the street, and the advancing sound of boots on the boardwalk.

"What's that?" Marcus said.

"People," McWhorter said, as he glanced through the door. "Lots of them. Some kind of mob. They're coming this way."

"What in hell?" Marcus said, and he joined McWhorter at the door. "It's the men from the rail yard! The picketers! They've left the front gate and they're headed here!"

Sloop couldn't help but take a look for himself. He had my automatic, but he hadn't bothered to check my jacket pocket for Farris's .38. As soon as his head turned, I had it out and pressed into his ear.

"Give me the guns," I said, hoping McWhorter couldn't hear me.

"This is a bad idea," Ev said.

"Not giving me the guns is a worse one. Hand them over."

I stashed Ev's Webley in my jacket and had my automatic in one hand and Farris's revolver in the other.

"Hands up, Sheriff!" I yelled.

He spun, ready to shoot me, but stopped when he saw two weapons pointed at him, and he dropped the .45 to the floor.

The mob was close now, the shouting in the street nearly impossible to hear over. I herded McWhorter, Schein, Marcus, and Sloop through the front door to the porch, just as the union workers reached the building.

They were led by Norris Hanks.

"Thought you might need help," he told me. "Guess I was wrong."

"You've been following me?"

"Ever since Cincinnati. I was hiding when you came to get Corcoran. I realized that Schein must be on the take, since he was the only person we'd contacted. Then I remembered that he had called to warn us about the raid, and I couldn't figure that one out, since there was no way he could know about the raid unless he was in cahoots with Marcus. I was on the train with you, and I followed you from a distance as you went around town trying to put the pieces together. I watched you get shoved into the office here a little while ago and figured you could use some support."

"Thanks."

"I suppose you can explain everything that happened?"

I could, and I did. I told the entire crowd how Schein had sold the union down the river, how a brave man named Warren Johns had tried to stop him and had paid for it with his life, and why Corcoran had been killed. For a few minutes, I was afraid the union would become a lynch mob, but Hanks calmed them down. He joined me on the porch and gave an eloquent and moving speech about equality and the rights of man, and he concluded with this:

"We aren't going to become the kind of men Marcus and the sheriff are. We are going to live by the law. As of this moment, these men are under arrest. We are going to escort them to the jail, and they'll be cared for better than they'd take care of any of us, until the circuit judge comes to town and can lawfully try their cases."

Then, Hanks turned to me.

"I'm not certain how we can maintain peace in this town until after the trial. Mr. Crane, do you reckon you would consider being the Acting Sheriff until the judge can sort all this out?"

Well, what could I say, after all? I'm an honest cop.

The only decent thing I could do was take the job.

SEE HUMBLE AND DIE

by

Richard Helms

Author's Note: This story first appeared in ***The Eyes of Texas, edited by Michael Bracken****, an anthology of stories about Lone Star State private investigators. It was written specifically for that collection, but it also gave me the opportunity—as an aging writer—to explore the life of a retired law enforcement officer trying desperately to stave off boredom and the call to action. This story was a finalist for the 2021 SMFS Derringer Award, and was selected by Otto Penzler and C.J. Box to appear in* ***Best American Mystery Stories 2020****, published by Houghton-Mifflin-Harcourt.*

R

A summons. A dumb subpoena. All I had to do was slap it into the guy's hand, tell him he'd been served, and pocket the forty-seven-fifty for the job. Should have been simple as a wet dream, especially for a former Texas Ranger looking for something to stave off boredom after punching out with thirty-two years' service.

Sick and tired of sitting around, watching TV, and waiting for something critical to break and put me on the dark side of the grass, I registered a DBA with the Houston Clerk of Court, and hung out a private investigator shingle. It was something to do. I put a listing in the Yellow Pages, my granddaughter made a web page, and business trickled in from time to time. Maybe every two or three weeks, some drab, nervous housewife would sidle through the door, her makeup smeared with tears, and demand that I catch her husband banging his secretary. I usually gave them a one-week turnaround. Sometimes, if the philandering husband was a real horndog, I wrapped the case before the end of the evening news.

I met an insurance guy in a bar in Sugar Land, just west of Houston, about a year back. We struck up a conversation. When he found out I had been a Ranger, he started asking me a lot of questions. Then he found out I was a private cop. He almost peed himself.

"No shit?" he said. "You're like a real private eye? Don't get me wrong. I don't mean nothing by it, but aren't you a little...well...*old* to be a private eye?"

"Want to arm wrestle?" I said. "My usual opponent is still in a cast. I stay in shape. And I know things."

"Like what?"

"Wear a badge for three decades, and you learn tricks. It's not all about knuckles. There's a lot of know-how to the game. Besides, it ain't like you see on the TV. My days of tracking felons and punks are in the past. Most of what I do these days is sit around and wait for someone to do something stupid."

"I think I can get you some work," he said.

"Yeah? What kind?"

"Insurance fraud," he said. "Let's order another round and talk about it."

So, every month or so, I get a call from Dallas to check on a claim. I once accidentally rear-ended a guy in San Angelo. It was nothing. A couple of crinkled bumpers at a stoplight. I couldn't have been going more than three miles per hour. I hopped out of the car and checked on the other driver, who said he was perfectly fine. No problem. By the time the uniform cop arrived to take a report for the insurance companies, the other driver was holding his neck and declaring that he had shooting pains going all down his arm. I shrugged and handed my information over to the cop.

Two days later, I caught the guy on my dashcam, doing backflips on a trampoline in his backyard. Needless to say, his personal injury claim died on the spot.

That was the kind of work I got from Dallas. Lots of folks trying to put one over on the insurance company. Some of them were legit. Most were bullshit. I saved the insurance company in Dallas a lot of money.

Then there was the process serving. An old friend at the courthouse called me one day. Said he'd heard I'd opened an office. Wondered whether I'd like to pick up a hundred or so a week to serve warrants and subpoenas. Probably wouldn't take more than a couple of hours.

I bit. The pay is pocket change, but like I said I'm not in this for the money. Not entirely.

I drop by his office each Monday morning, and he has three or four orders to be served waiting for me. It's usually local stuff. I served a guy just down the street from me a couple of months ago. Walked over after dinner, found him in his front yard mowing his dirt. Slapped him with a subpoena and was back in my house, all in ten minutes. They're not all that easy. In most cases, though, it's a piece of cake.

People don't walk around expecting legal papers to drop out of the sky. It's a cinch to get close to them. The easiest are the ones you catch at home. Ring the bell, ask for Mr. About-To-Be-Served, tell him you're a courier, and hand him the envelope. Bingo bango, dinner for two at Golden Corral in your back pocket, with a few bucks left over for ice cream.

I'm partial to ice cream.

Sometimes, you catch a guy who's been given a heads-up. This is especially true in divorce cases, where the wife has already screamed something like, "I will steal your fucking dreams, you cheating son of a bitch!" Those guys are on the lookout. Getting to them sometimes takes a little finesse.

I know a woman in town who's in the process-serving game. Her name's Amy. She's middle aged, but time has been kind to her, and she still gets lots of looks from guys half her age. She snags a lot of divorce paper services. Her game is to catch the subject in a bar, start up a conversation. Somewhere along the line, she gives him a fake name, and he—naturally—gives his real one. She repeats the name, as if she's heard it before. The guy says, "Yep, that's me!" and she lays it on him. He goes home with a subpoena in one hand and his dick in the other. Works every time. Nobody expects a hot southern lady to come bearing a summons. She has perfect camouflage.

Won't work in my case, unless I'm serving divorce papers to little old ladies in rest homes. I work the codger angle. There's always a guy out there willing to talk about the good old days. Sometimes they buy me a beer before I serve them. It's not really ethical, but I hate to be antisocial.

The boss at the courthouse knows what kind of guys are likely to respond to Amy, and which will respond to me. He's kind of psychic that way. He gives Amy the young guys, and I get the old-timers.

I received the call on a Wednesday morning.

"Got a job for you, Huck," my guy said.

I'm Huck. Huck Spence. It's short for Huckleberry, my middle name.

"What's the job?" I asked.

"Guy named Ralph Oakley. Should be a milk run, no big deal. He skipped out on jury duty. Chose exactly the week the district judge's diverticulitis was flaring up. Judge was in the mood to knock broomsticks up some asses. He issued orders to bring in every scofflaw who failed to show for the jury pool, so they could account for their lack of civic engagement, but mostly so he could rake them over the coals and vent his spleen. There's a fine for dumping out on the call, also."

"I'm familiar with it," I told him. "Word in the halls is the money goes into a fund that's split evenly among the judges at the end of the year."

"Beats me," he said. "I have no idea whether it's true, but I've heard the same rumor."

Ralph Oakley lived in Humble, about fifteen miles north of the center of Houston. Humble is the ghost of an oil boom town, which lent its name to an oil brand at some time in the murky past. A hundred years ago, it was the richest-producing field in the entire state. The oil dried up, and the petro circus pulled up stakes and moved on, leaving Humble very humble indeed. At its height, Humble burst at the seams with roughnecks and wildcatters and mud loggers and doodlebuggers making small fortunes by pulling dead stuff out of the ground. These days, population tops out around twelve thousand, mostly truck farmers and day laborers and field workers and timbermen, the kind of people who sweat out their paychecks and try to raise families on the precipice of poverty. It's your typical small suburban Texas town, a simple satellite of the metropolis to the south. It's a hundred square miles of desperation and hope and churches and resignation, with a few bars thrown in to keep the sidewalks flat on Saturday night. The best thing Humble has going for it is a high school football stadium that would make most college fields weep with envy. They take high school football extra serious in Humble.

It also has twice the average crime rate for towns its size. It's that kind of place.

I had an address for Ralph Oakley. It was close to the city limits with an unincorporated community called Borderville, close enough to the freeway to hear the cars zooming by. To get there, I had to drive through the center of

Old Humble, a section that might have inspired Anarene in *The Last Picture Show.*

I pulled up in front of the house where Oakley lived. A woman wearing a flowered house robe answered the door. She looked like someone had wrapped a refrigerator. Her voice sounded like someone grooming a cat with a belt sander.

"Yeah?"

"I'm looking for Ralph Oakley," I said.

"Ralph? Ralph ain't lived here for a year and a half. Can't say I'm sad about it, either. Guy was a fuckin' cheapskate, pardon my French. Practically had to beat the rent out of him every month. Why you want him? What's he done?"

"Just wanted to catch up. Do you know where he moved?"

"You're a friend of his, you should know."

"I haven't seen him in years. I'm just passing through. This was the last address I had for him."

"Well, you might catch him at work, if he ain't been fired yet. Check out Borum's Butcher Shop. Five blocks thataway. Cain't miss it. Got a big plywood bull hanging out over the sidewalk. Last I saw him, he was working in the back."

She was right. There was no missing Borum's Butcher Shop. I walked through the front door. Texans pride themselves on their beef, and Borum was no exception. The floor was spotless. The cases were polished to a sheen, the glass crystal clear. Cuts of ribeye, thick as man's wrist, were stacked inside. I walked down the case, building an appetite.

Porterhouses, New York strips, filets. I started thinking about grilling that night.

"Help you?" a man said as he walked in from the back room. He was shorter than me, but massively built, in the way you get cutting up two-hundred-pound steer carcasses for a couple of decades. His face was open and smiling, that fake sort of grin people slap on their faces when they want to sell something.

"Ralph Oakley?" I said.

"Bob Borum. You a cop?"

"Nope. Are you?"

He grinned for real this time. "Was, once. Long time ago. Thought I smelled it on you."

"Leftover from my days in the Rangers, but that was a long time ago, too. Ralph wouldn't be around, would he?"

"Off today. Mind if I ask your business with him?"

"Some legal stuff. Nothing big."

"None of my business anyway, right? It's cool. Way Ralph's been moping around and skipping out on work lately, he probably won't be working here much longer. What happens to him is on him, right?"

"Couldn't agree more. I dropped by the address I had for him, but they said he moved away."

"He's in a motel, three streets over. Been living there for quite a while now. Not a bad deal, I suppose. Fresh towels every day, fresh sheets every week, and you don't have to lift a finger. Not a lot of square footage, but how much room does a man need, anyway?"

"I reckon we all wind up with more or less the same space," I said.

"Ain't it the truth?"

"Let me take care of this business with Ralph, and I'll drop back by. That ribeye there looks like it's got designs on my stomach. Think you can wrap it and have it ready for me? I don't want to leave it in the car."

"You got it."

The place was what we used to call a "drive-up motel." It wasn't a chain place. It had likely been around for half a century. The entire motel was on a single level, all the room doors opening directly onto the parking lot. The outside walls were painted cinderblock. An ice machine with a wheezing, rattling compressor stood against the outer wall alongside a Pepsi machine. All the "sold out" lights on the machine were lit.

Bob Borum had given me Oakley's room number, so I didn't have to shine on the desk clerk. I backed my car into a space across the lot, facing his door.

A couple of years back, a process jockey in Houston was beaten to death with a baseball bat when he tried to serve divorce papers on a guy who'd stoked back too many PBRs. Since then, I carry a GoPro camera on my dashboard. It's motion-activated and connected to a drive that can record up to a week of images at a time. If I ever catch the off-world shuttle on the job, I figure someone might find evidence on the camera to catch the guy who did it. It also protects me from claims that I dump paper in the trash and still claim the pay for serving it. It's happened.

The whole deal took less than a minute. I slipped an oil change receipt from my glove compartment onto a clipboard, added the subpoena, turned on the dashcam, and crossed the lot to his door. A Latina cleaning woman stepped out of the room two doors up just as I rapped on Oakley's door and said, "Maintenance!" The cleaning woman looked at me strangely. Guess she never saw a maintenance guy in a corduroy jacket and a Stetson before. I held a finger to my mouth and pointed at the door. She nodded and retreated into the room she had been cleaning. That door closed, and I heard the lock trip. Guess it was that sort of neighborhood.

Oakley opened the door. He was about an inch shorter than me, maybe six feet in his socks. He was blond, his hair shaggy and maybe a little stringy, and otherwise an attractive sort, as best as men can determine that about other men. He looked sweaty and nervous. His eyes were red, and I caught a whiff of weed from the room. None of my business.

"Got a call about your AC," I said.

"I didn't call nobody," he said.

I checked the oil change receipt on my clipboard, which looked official enough if you didn't examine it too closely.

"Ralph Oakley?" I asked.

"Yeah, that's me."

I took the envelope with the subpoena and held it out. "This is for you."

He took it, reflexively. My job was done.

"The original notice of jury duty was sent to your old address. They didn't know where to forward it. Tell the judge that story, and you might talk your way out of a fine."

"What?" he asked, but by then I'd turned and walked away. His rose-colored eyes told me he wouldn't remember the advice anyway.

He closed the door. I sat in the front seat of my car and filled out the service log detailing when I'd completed the job. As I did, a Honda Accord pulled into the parking slot in front of Ralphie's room. A woman stepped out. From behind, she had a decent figure. Nice legs. She wore a scarf over her hair, which I thought strange, but then she knocked on Ralph's door. He opened it and she looked over the parking lot furtively, but she was in shadow, and I couldn't make out her face. I thought she stared at me for a long time, then stepped inside, and it all made sense. I'd spent time sitting outside motels spying on philanderers for longer than was healthy. I recognized a clandestine rendezvous when I saw one.

I drove back to Borum's, where Bob had my steak wrapped and rung up.

"How'd it go?" he asked, as he made change.

"Smooth. No biggie. A misunderstanding. He seems a nervous sort."

"Ralph? Never noticed."

"Maybe it's because his girlfriend was on the way over."

"Didn't know he had one. Hey, you enjoy that steak, y'hear?"

———

Sunday morning, I was lounging on the screened porch at the back of my house, reading the newspaper. I'd dispensed with the sports and the funnies and was perusing the local section. I keep an eye on the obituaries these days, mostly because it's become sort of a game for me to outlive people. I had just taken a sip of coffee, and I nearly sprayed it all over the newsprint when I saw the notice.

Ralph Mark Oakley. Age forty-three. Butcher. Died on Friday, May sixteenth. A smattering of survivors. Services to be held, so forth and so on. Two paragraphs. Forty-three years of breathing, and his entire life had been digested into two paragraphs. Short paragraphs at that. No cause of death listed. The picture looked like the guy I'd served at the motel, except the hair was shorter.

I had Saturday's newspaper still in the rack in the den. I'd been working Saturday and had only glanced at it. I yanked out the local section and searched it. Found the story on page three. A cleaning woman—probably the one I'd scared—found Ralph's body in his hotel room late on Friday afternoon, after seeing the door slightly open. The reporter tried to pretty things up, but it was easy to read between the lines. It had been gory. Ralph had been bludgeoned and stabbed multiple times. He had to be identified by his prints. Police were investigating, but there were no suspects.

I sat on the porch, scratching my aging cat Boudreaux's lumpy head as she basked in the sunlight, and I thought. Bob Borum had told me he didn't know Oakley had a girlfriend. I wondered if anyone else knew? I had seen the woman visit him surreptitiously in his motel room. People who sneak around have things to hide. What if the woman thought she had been discovered? She had looked right at me. Maybe she thought I was spying on her, and she decided to eliminate her cheating problem. It didn't gel completely in my head, but it was something to work on.

And, I had a way to find her.

I retrieved the dash camera from my car. It took a couple of minutes to hook it up to my laptop computer.

I was in luck. Since I'd parked directly across the lot from Oakley's door, I had a full-on view of his visitor's car when she parked in front of me. I jotted down the license number and saved the file on my computer.

Here's the thing about being a retired Texas Ranger. It's like being in the mob. You might cash out, but you never really leave. Looking back, I probably should have gone directly to the Humble Police Department. I'm a cop, though—or at least I used to be—and the tendency to do it yourself is kind of strong in cops. I called my old office. It was Sunday, but there was always someone on duty. I was lucky. I got Wade Stanfield. We used to call him Wade the Blade because, in his day, he was definitely the sharpest knife in the drawer. That was a long time ago. We've all dropped a half-step toward second since then, which was probably why they had him working the slowest day of the week.

"Blade, need you to run a license for me."

"What's up?" he asked.

"Don't know. Could be something. Might be nothing."

"Like always. Gimme the number."

What we were doing was technically illegal. Like I said, though, once a Ranger, always a Ranger. You never completely punch out. It would have been a lot worse if Wade had checked a license for some guy on the street who had never worn a badge or body armor. I read the number off the paper and heard him muttering a little.

"No can do, podjo," he said. "System's down for maintenance. Ain't that the way? They always do these things on Sundays. Should be up tomorrow morning. Maybe later tonight. Tell you what. I'll run it as soon as I can, and I'll call you. Gonna cost you two beers and a burger."

"Cheap at half the price," I said. "You're on."

Sunday turned into Monday, and no word from Wade the Blade. I wasn't surprised. Like most government agencies, the Rangers were stuck with a computer system that should have been junked years ago. Sometimes, shutting it down made it lazy about booting up again.

I had nothing to do, and the Rangers didn't have the only computer system in the state, so I drove over to Humble and introduced myself to the detective who'd caught Oakley's murder.

His name was Ken Sheeran. My bona fides as an ex-Ranger got me into this office pronto. He was in his middle-forties, a lifer. He was thick around the middle. His shirt gapped between the buttons when he sat down, probably because he saw extra-large shirts as an assault on his vanity.

He had thick pewter hair and a gaze that could cut glass. The first time I saw him, I had a feeling he was a good cop. You get a sense for these things.

"How can I help you?" he asked.

"Maybe I can help you. I served papers on Ralph Oakley last week, a couple of days before he died."

"Did you, now?" Sheeran asked. "So, you're the one. Yeah. I see it now. You match the description."

"Description."

"Tall, lean guy like you, in his late sixties, with silver hair and a thick salt-and-pepper mustache. Voice like a cement mixer. Wearing a cream Stetson just like the one in your lap there. Sure. Several folks came forward and said you were poking around town last week asking about Ralph Oakley. Serving papers, you say?"

I showed him my PI license, and a copy of my process service log. "He ditched out on jury duty. Judge wanted to have a word with him."

"Guess that ship has sailed. I do recall some legal papers we retrieved from the trash can in his room. You scared the piss out of that cleaning woman at the motel. I mean, like, literally. She peed her pants when you came knocking on Oakley's door. She thought you were there to kill him. Don't suppose you were. That would make my day."

"Here's the thing," I said. "I was sitting in my car at the motel where he was shacked, and a woman came to visit him. It looked like she didn't want to be seen entering his room. Has anyone said anything about him having a girlfriend?"

"Not as I recall. Can you describe this woman?"

"Five-five, nice figure. Good legs. I only saw her clearly from behind. I got her license number, though. Caught it on my dash cam."

I handed him the slip of paper with the number and a thumb drive with the video segment from the cam.

"We'll run this right away. I'd like to thank you for coming in," he extended his hand. "This could be a big help."

I started to shake hands, but my telephone beeped. It was Wade Stanfield. I held up a finger to Sheeran and answered.

"Sorry it took so long to run that number, buddy," he said. "Computers just came back up this morning, and I had a backlog."

"Did you get a hit?"

"Sure did."

He told me the car owner's name. I glanced at Sheeran.

"You need to do a safety check," I said.

He tried to make me wait at the station, but we both knew that was unlikely. I followed him across town in my car. We parked in front of a wood frame house with a deep covered gallery. I followed him up the steps to the front door.

A woman answered when he knocked. I had never seen her face before, but the figure was familiar.

"Mrs. Borum?" Sheeran asked, flashing his shield. "Mrs. Margery Borum?"

"Oh, my God!" she said, her hand rising to her mouth. "What's happened?"

"I think you know," I said. Sheeran shot me a warning look.

"You," she said to me. "I recognize you. You were the man sitting outside..." she stopped, cutting off the very end of the last word.

"Mrs. Borum," Sheeran said. "We need to talk."

She led us inside. She was flustered and sweaty, and she nearly forgot her manners. Finally, she asked us to sit and even offered iced tea. We declined.

"Tell us about Ralph Oakley," Sheeran said.

"He worked for my husband," she said.

"He wasn't working last Wednesday," I said. "I know, because I served him a subpoena at his motel room. I saw you there minutes later. Were you in the habit of visiting him when your husband was at work?"

She started to cry. I sat back and let her. I did hand her a box of tissues from the table next to the couch. Her entire world was crumbling. I'd seen it a thousand times. It never got easy, but sometimes you just had to wait it out.

After a few minutes, she calmed a little.

"We...Ralph and I...started seeing each other a few months back. It got out of hand, but I couldn't stop. He couldn't stop. We were talking about running off together. It seems silly, now that he's dead. It never would have worked."

"Why?" Sheeran asked.

"No money. Cash just burns holes in Ralph's pockets. He can't hold onto it. I don't know what I was thinking."

"Where were you on Friday?" I asked.

"In Houston, visiting a friend. We went shopping and had some drinks at a restaurant there. I know what you're thinking. I was nowhere near Ralph on Friday. By the time I returned, around eight on Friday evening, the news was spreading around town. I've been a nervous wreck ever since."

"Where's your husband?" I asked.

"He's at work, of course. He'll be there until six."

Sheeran told her not to call her husband. I followed him several streets over to the Borum Butcher Shop. When we walked through the door, the sales floor was empty. I pointed toward the door to the back.

"I'm calling for backup," Sheeran said as he pulled a walkie from his pocket. I moved toward the door to check the parking lot. Sheeran started to follow me. I heard the blow that dropped him. It sounded like beating a watermelon with a whiffle bat. I turned. Sheeran was sprawled out on the floor, a pool of blood spreading from the back of his head, his eyes oddly unfocused. He twitched and jerked on the linoleum. Bob Borum stood over him, holding a honing steel, which dripped blood. In his other hand was a cleaver.

"You!" he shouted when he saw my face. "This is all your fault!"

"What did you do?" I knelt next to Sheeran and checked his wounds.

"Why in hell did you have to say anything about Ralph's girlfriend?" Borum pleaded. There were tears in his eyes. "Twenty-three years. We been married twenty-three great years. Then you come in and tell me Ralph's knocking off a little, so I decide I'll swing by and see who he's shagging. Thought it'd give me something to rib him about. I get to the motel, and there's my own car sitting out front of his room. I followed her the next night, when she told me she was going out to a Grange meeting with her friend Sally. Sure enough, she went straight to that bastard Ralph."

I backed toward the door. The confines of the butcher shop were too close for comfort. I pined for the open air, where I could dodge any swipes he might want to make with the cleaver. I had palmed Sheeran's walkie. As I backed up, I quickly raised it and made an officer down call, adding the butcher shop address. I suddenly wished I'd also palmed his gun. I don't carry one.

I hit the door, but it didn't budge. I recalled that it opened inward from the street.

"You ruined my life, you son of a bitch!" Borum cried as he strode toward me, real tears streaming from his eyes. "Ain't nothin' left for me here. I either go on the road or on the gurney. Cain't kill me twice, can they? I done took out Ralph, and now I done a cop. Ain't nothin' to keep me from doing you too."

"When did you kill him?" I asked, trying to buy time.

"The next morning, on the way to work. I called his phone. Told him I'd drop by, give him a lift. I gave him a lift, all right. Lifted his cheatin' ass all the way to fucking Heaven!"

He dropped the bloody honing steel and raised his hand to wipe at the tears running down his face. I took the opportunity and charged him, the way a tackle sacks a quarterback. My shoulder rammed into his midsection, just below the ribs, crushing against his solar plexus. The air rushed out of him in an explosive gasp. In the back of my mind, I heard the sirens in the distance. I felt a sharp, searing pain along my left shoulder blade. He had swung at me with the cleaver and had connected. The cleaver hit the floor and skittered across it into the corner under a baseboard heater. My stomach lurched, and I tasted metal in the back of my throat. My heart raced as I grappled with the burly butcher, him trying to suck air into his lungs, and me trying to hold him down. We rolled and scrabbled about in Sheeran's blood. I got in two good punches just as the cruisers pulled into the parking lot, and I saw his eyes roll up in their sockets as he went slack beneath me.

It was touch-and-go for Ken Sheeran. They had to remove part of his skull because his brain was swelling. He was unconscious for almost a week, but slowly came around. He took a disability retirement. I had a call from him a few weeks back. He was thinking about the PI game. Wanted to know how to get a foothold. My long silence spoke volumes.

Bob Borum's lawyer managed to make a deal for aggravated manslaughter mitigated by passion, but he'll still spend the better part of the rest of his life in prison.

His wife divorced him while he was in jail waiting for trial. She moved away; I think to San Antonio. She showed up to testify, but otherwise nobody in Humble saw her again.

It took seventeen stitches to close the gash in my shoulder. Borum also fractured my scapula, so I was in a sling for a couple of months. You heal slower as you get old. It put a crimp in my PI activities, but that was okay. I needed a while to process things.

Bob Borum wasn't a bad guy. Neither was Ralph Oakley. They weren't criminals. They weren't evil. They were two men in love with the same woman, and I walked into their lives, a stranger come to town who innocently catalyzed their self-destruction. There were no bad guys in this, just people set on the path of disparate fates.

Borum blamed me for his life turning to shit. In a way, he was right. If I'd kept my mouth shut about seeing the woman go into Ralph Oakley's motel room, probably none of this would have happened. At least, it wouldn't have happened because of me. Humble's a small town. Sooner or later, one way or the other, the word would have gotten back to him. Killing Oakley was on him. I triggered it, though. That's a lot of responsibility to carry around.

I would have to learn to live with that.

THE CRIPPLEGATE APPREHENSION

by

Richard Helms

Author's Note: The idea for this story came to me in a sushi bar in Matthews, North Carolina, where I was enjoying a snack and reading Josephine Tey's ***The Daughter of Time****. As a college professor, I had lectured my Forensic Psychology students just that afternoon about the strange case of Daniel M'Naghten, who murdered the private secretary of British Prime Minister Robert Peel in 1843. I thought I might enjoy writing a mystery built around M'Naghten's famous trial, and an hour later Vicar Brekonridge was born. Brekonridge is a thief-taker in Victorian London, and the protagonist of my next novel, eponymously titled* ***Vicar Brekonridge****. This story first appeared in* Ellery Queen Mystery Magazine *and was a finalist for the SMFS Derringer Award in 2020.*

R

Vicar Brekonridge pulled his thick wool greatcoat closer around him as he strode in two inches of snow past St. Alphege's Church near the Cripplegate in Islington. He was headed toward the Whitecross Street Market on a gloomy

Sunday morning. The Market was only held on Sundays, when vendors erected booths and tents to sell wares ranging from food, to beer and ale, to miscellaneous sundries including baskets, scarves, refurbished boots, woolen stockings, root vegetables in the winter and fresh produce in the summer, poultry, mutton, discarded furniture, and linens from the beds of recently deceased noblemen.

Despite his name—a smirking conceit by his parents—Vicar Brekonridge was no clergyman. Brekonridge was looking for something other than grace as he turned onto Whitecross Street from Beech and plunged immediately into a sea of barkers and fishmongers. He bought two parcels of hot roasted chestnuts from a vendor for a penny, and immediately stuffed them into each of his greatcoat pockets to keep his hands warm. A block further down Whitecross, he purchased a dozen oysters wrapped in oiled parchment paper and perched himself on a wall in front of a decrepit church to eat them.

Brekonridge would have been a striking figure even if he hadn't been taller than the average man. At slightly over six feet, he stood almost a head above the men who surrounded him wherever he went. In public, he favored a conventional—if shopworn—beaver felt John Bull hat that added another half foot to his stature.

His hair, still remarkably jet black as he neared fifty, was pulled into a queue, but thick strands of it evaded the ribbon he used to tie it back and fell sloppily over his ears. His watery blue eyes seemed to miss nothing around him. Even as he pried open and slurped the briny oysters, his gaze darted back and forth, scanning the crowd.

His most notable feature was one he dearly wished he could hide. His left profile, dominated by a long, pointed nose and strong chin, was attractive enough. At times in his life he had even been regarded as ruggedly handsome. When he turned, the right side of his face revealed a congealed mass of bubbled scars extending from over what remained of his ear down across his jaw line, up into the hair, and down the back of his head into his neck. The stray locks of hair hid some of the deformity, but not enough for him to look at himself in the mirror with comfort.

He had earned his scars nobly, rescuing three small children in an apartment fire in which he had also lost all his earthly possessions. During the winter, he tried to conceal them by wrapping his neck and lower face in a long, moth-eaten wool scarf. In the summer, there was no way to adequately hide the disfigurement, so he simply endured the looks on people's faces when he walked abroad.

He finished the oysters, dumped the shells into a growing pile behind the vendor's tent, and went in search of ale. He pulled out his white porcelain football pipe filled with hemp and lighted it with one of Ashford's new phosphorous friction matches. The acrid smoke wafted around his head. Within seconds he relaxed and became completely focused on the crowd around him.

On any Sunday, Whitecross Market might contain as many as fifteen hundred vendors, and three times as many shoppers who loaded up on staples and non-perishable foods for the coming week, or simply strolled from booth to tent inspecting the newest wares. Children played in the snowdrifts piled up along the road and slid precariously on patches of blackened ice they found on the rare hard surface.

Brekonridge stopped at an ale booth and ordered a pewter flagon, which he drank standing there. He placed the container back on the wooden plank that served as a bar, wiped his mouth with his scarf, and resumed his search for the man who had brought him out on such a wretchedly cold day.

As he strode the length of Whitecross Street, cries from salespeople and artisans rang in his ears.

"Old for some but new for you! As little as tuppence for fine linens!"

"Roast chestnuts hot and sweet, a penny a score!"

"Fresh guinea fowl! Mutton! Joints of beef! Buy, buy--bu-u-uy!"

"Lovely bonnets, only fourpence! Two for six!"

"Bootlaces! Three pair for a ha'penny! Bootlaces!"

"Fresh and succulent whelks! None finer in all of London! Penny a lot!"

Men, hunched at the back after years of laborious hauling, struggled past shoving barrows piled high with shellfish, trying to urge the wooden wheels through the snow. A man walked by with two muslin sacks over each shoulder, one in front and one in back, loaded with loaves of bread baked fresh that morning. A shivering woman sat on a sun-bleached milk box in front of four baskets filled with dried flowers. The din of commerce went on block after block as vendors desperately endeavored to make enough money to survive until the next Sunday market.

Brekonridge's pipe had gone cold. He tamped the cinders into a snowbank and stuffed it into his inner jacket pocket. He knew the face of the man he sought, and he continued to scan the street, every darkened booth, every alleyway, and every doorway for the man's features. He was able to screen out the ruckus of the crowd and focus only on locating his quarry.

Vicar Brekonridge was a thief-taker.

Broadly speaking, thief-takers were part bounty hunter and part private detective, though neither term existed in the first half of the nineteenth century. Their duties ranged from assisting police officers in the apprehension of criminals, to acting as private agents for victims of crime, to—in some cases—shaking down wanted criminals as a form of extortion.

In the middle eighteenth century, Henry Fielding penned a series of diatribes decrying the unregulated nature of thief-taking and called for a better-organized group of citizen law enforcers to take the place of private vigilantes. Those screeds resulted in the formation of the Bow Street Runners, unofficial and marginally better-organized law enforcers.

Vicar Brekonridge had joined the Runners in 1827. He had served with the Royal Navy in his early teens, including a stint in the United States during the War of 1812, before working for another decade as a ship's carpenter. Upon leaving the sea, he discovered he had a talent for apprehending criminals. He remained with the Runners for over a decade, at which point the entire unit was absorbed into the new Metropolitan London Police Force founded by Sir Robert Peel.

Brekonridge never discussed why he left Scotland Yard. Some said his tactics were overly violent, typified by his attack on the son of Lord Barbury, who was admittedly in the process of choking the life out of a prostitute at the time. His fellow officers maintained Brekonridge had saved the life of a defenseless—if not innocent—woman. Their superiors were outraged that a member of the noble class might be subjected to corporal injury at the hands of a uniformed constable. Other reports suggested his ouster was the result of a failure to follow direct orders when those orders violated his personal standards. An alternate history suggested he was cashiered because of his habitual use of ganja to ward off pain from a life filled with battle injuries and his more recent burns. While perfectly legal, hemp was still regarded as an intoxicant, and habitual use was frowned upon among Prime Minister Peel's bobbies.

Regardless of the actual reason for leaving the force, Brekonridge relinquished his badge, cuffs, and clacker in 1839 after only four years in uniform. Left with a lifetime of experience in sailing, soldiering, and policing, and having no desire to return to sea or take up arms, he had resorted to hiring out his policing skills to the highest bidder, or for rewards offered by the Bow Street Magistrate's Court for the apprehension of wanted criminals.

It could be a surprisingly lucrative line of work, with bounties as high as a hundred pounds for some miscreants, in an age when the average working man was fortunate to see three hundred pounds in an entire year.

He would make nowhere near that sum with the man he was pursuing in Cripplegate on this particular Sunday in February, but Brekonridge had amassed an enviably tidy bank account ten or twelve pounds at a time.

The newspapers were dominated by the assassination of Prime Minister Robert Peel's private secretary Edward Drummond, by some radical journeyman woodturner from Glasgow named M'Naghten. Assuming the heightened police activity around Buckingham, Downing Street, and the Admiralty would result in a privation of constables elsewhere in the city, and therefore an increased number of warrants for arrest, Brekonridge had ventured to the Bow Street Assizes where such warrants were posted. He found the usual collection of sneak-thieves, cutpurses, highwaymen, cheats, and swindlers, along with a smattering of anarchists, Anti-Corn Law League agitators, and everyday ne'er-do-wells.

One warrant in particular caught his eye, not so much because of the bounty, but because he knew the man.

> *January 29th, 1843. A warrant for arrest has been issued for MATTHEW MARK LUKE JOHN MAYHEW, late of 46 Bishopsgate-street. Five feet, two or three inches in height. Pockmarked complexion, thinning hair, sometimes wears a beard. Absconded, charged on a warrant with stealing monies.*

Well-known to the London Police as a pickpocket and embezzler. Five pounds paid directly to the man who delivers him to the Bow Street Magistrate's Court, and a bonus of ten pounds in gratitude from the theft victim.

Mayhew had been hired by a tavern owner to keep the floors and tables clean and the spittoons emptied, in return for three shillings a week, a cot in the backroom of the tavern, and free access to sandwiches and pottage put out for the customers. Mayhew had repaid the barkeep's generosity by raiding a moneybox after the tavern closed and vanishing into the night.

Fifteen pounds was far from the largest reward Brekonridge had chased in his highly successful career as a private policeman, but it would keep coal in his firebox and food in his belly for weeks.

He had apprehended Mayhew on two other occasions and had spoken about him in passing with another acquaintance only a day or so before. That acquaintance, Jericho Pratt, most likely knew of Mayhew's whereabouts. Jericho Pratt was a pure-finder. He sought his fortune in the world by roaming the streets of London with a bucket, one hand clad in a heavy leather glove, collecting dog waste to sell to tanners who used the chemicals in the feces to produce leather.

If Jericho Pratt had an idea where to find Mayhew, Brekonridge figured he could complete the job in a few hours and have Mayhew in irons before dinner. He claimed the warrant and set out from Bow Street to begin his hunt.

Brekonridge marveled at how much of his business was conducted in the East End, with its industrial population, dense greasy fogs, and horrid odors. His first stop was a tanner's shop on Morocco Street in Bermonsey. Pratt was a freelance pure-finder, so it was likely every tanner in the district knew him. The shop proprietor was a man named Bouton. He greeted Brekonridge as the thief-taker ducked through the short doorway of the tannery office.

"I'm looking for Jericho Pratt," Brekonridge announced.

"Haven't seen him in days," Bouton said. "Word has it he's in Newgate Prison. Can't tell you why."

The last time Brekonridge had been on the Newgate Prison grounds was on a brutally hot July day in 1840, when he had joined an estimated forty thousand other Londoners to witness the widely publicized hanging of Francois Courvoisier for the murder of Lord William Russell.

Newgate was an imposing place, and in fact had been designed for the purpose of frightening would-be criminals away from their intended acts. For centuries, dating back almost to the reign of King Henry II, the building had been regarded as a place of horror and torture, from the dungeons in which men had been shackled to walls for years to the outdoor public space for executions, the *architecture terrible* design was intended to drive thoughts of malfeasance from the minds of potential lawbreakers.

Not everyone heeded the warnings. The prison was typically full to overflowing, its inmates divided into two populations. The first—the Commoners—were street thieves and blackmailers and common ruffians who could not afford better accommodations, and likely never would. They tended to be housed in groups, chained to walls and standpipes to prevent them from attacking one another, living in communal filth and degradation, eating from a common trough filled with tavern slop each evening.

The other population was housed in the State wing. These were offenders who had the means to afford slightly more comfortable quarters—the term "comfortable" in this case was more relative to the Commons area than to everyday life. Even so, State inmates enjoyed the dubious luxury of being jailed one to a cell.

Brekonridge stepped up to the massive front door and lifted a large black iron knocker, which he allowed to drop to a striker plate. He had been there enough to know one knock was sufficient to draw the attention of the gatekeeper, who arrived quickly and swung the door open. Brekonridge presented the Bow Street warrant.

"My name is Vicar Brekonridge. I am attempting to apprehend a thief, and I believe one of your inmates, a man named Jericho Pratt, can point me in his direction."

The outer door closed with a dramatic crash. Brekonridge, no stranger to violence, and generally resistant to fear, could not stifle a shudder. He comforted himself with the knowledge that—unlike the unfortunate Mr. Pratt—he could leave any time he wished.

The gatekeeper fished through his ring of keys and opened another door at the opposite end of the Keeper's House, which led into an atrium.

As the turnkey escorted Brekonridge beyond heavy iron doors into the ward where the prisoners were held, the thief-taker's nose wrinkled at a sudden sour smell. It was a combination of damp earth, mold, sweat, human waste, and a brief whisper of decomposition, an odor Brekonridge knew only too well from his wartime days.

To Brekonridge's surprise, Jericho Pratt's cell was in the relatively comfortable State wing, near the end of a long, second-level catwalk, accessed by stairs from a central hallway. The door to the cell was constructed of heavy cast-iron plates and straps, brazed together and fastened with massive iron bolts. The turnkey opened the door. Brekonridge peered inside.

The room was twice as long as it was wide, the walls and arched ceiling built of kiln-fired bricks and heavy mortar. An iron bed covered with a thin blanket was bolted to the brick and concrete floor. A small table with a single chair had been provided, where Pratt could eat his meals and write any letters he might wish to send. At the end of the cell, some eight feet above the ground, was a glass window with a mildly arched top, bars and steel mesh attached to the inside to prevent prisoners from getting to the glass. At midday, sunlight streamed into the cell. There were no candles or gaslights. Brekonridge could only imagine how dark the place must become after sundown. A bucket in the corner served as Pratt's sanitary facilities.

Pratt looked up as Brekonridge filled the doorway. An expression of alarm crossed his face. He was a slight man, rail-thin and pale. The top of his head was entirely bald, ringed by a long fringe of colorless, wispy hair. The turnkey reappeared with a second chair.

"I wish to be alone with the prisoner," Brekonridge said. "You may close the door and leave us here."

"I don't know, sir," the turnkey said. "This one is a murderer, you know."

"Look at me. Look at him. Can you doubt I will be perfectly safe? In any case my interview with the man will be fruitless if he believes he is being spied upon. When I am ready to leave, I will knock on the door and call for you."

"It's your neck, sir," the man said. "I do feel obligated to report this to the Superintendent."

"Yes. Please do so. I would not wish you to be remiss in your duties."

The turnkey retreated, closing and locking the door behind him.

"Jericho," Brekonridge said, shaking his head. "Who did you kill?"

"I didn't kill anyone, Mr. Brekonridge. This is all a horrible mistake. Nobody has told me anything. All I know is some police officers barged into my rooms two nights ago and dragged me off. I haven't seen another person since they slammed that door. When you walked in, I thought maybe you had some news."

"I'm sorry. I don't know anything. How did you arrange to be housed in the State wing?"

"It's a long story, and in truth I can't tell you the answer. I have means. I was born into a good family. I'm an educated man, despite my lowbrow employment. Times are difficult. One takes the work presented. Someone must have told the authorities that I had resources the prison could attach to pay for my accommodations." He swept his hand in the air to indicate his quarters. "Are you here investigating my case?"

"I'm on a different matter. A few days ago, we spoke of Matt Mayhew. I'm looking for him."

"I can't help you. As I mentioned the other day, I haven't seen him in weeks. There is a man, though. He is closer to Mayhew than I. I'm told he's come to visit me several times since I was incarcerated, but they won't allow him back."

"His name?"

"Not so fast. I'm innocent, I tell you. I have no idea whom the authorities think I've murdered, but I swear to you I haven't harmed anyone. If I tell you the man's name, you have to agree to help me. I have some money. Not a lot, but you will not go uncompensated for your endeavors on my behalf."

"Agreed," Brekonridge said, happy for the opportunity to add to his bounty for apprehending Mayhew.

"His name is Albert Camp. He's another pure-finder, but he grew up with Mayhew. If anyone can point you toward Mayhew, it's Camp. Don't forget me, though. You promised to help me."

"And my promise will be kept. As soon as I catch Mayhew, I'll return."

"Bless you, Mr. Brekonridge. You may have the face of a devil, but your heart is angelically pure."

"Don't count so much on my heart. I have to eat like everyone else."

Brekonridge stopped on the steps of Newgate prison to wrap his face—and his egregious scars—with his woolen scarf. He began to walk toward Newington, and then stopped when a motion in his peripheral vision caught his attention. It could have been a shadow, but he was certain he had seen a man duck into an alleyway ahead of him, on the other side of the street.

He sat on a bench and pulled the football pipe from his jacket. He had already packed it with a pinch of the new East Indian hemp he had acquired from his chemist, so he lighted it and began to puff idly, staring seemingly off into space.

He saw the movement again, at the corner of his eye. He tilted his head back, as if trying to catch as many of the sun's rays as possible, but in doing so he also turned his head so that he could get a better view of the alley.

A small, gnarled man emerged from the space and walked briskly down Newgate, affecting a slight limp. As Brekonridge watched, the man stopped at the Cross and Key Public House and stepped inside.

Brekonridge tamped out the pipe and walked back to the prison. A few seconds after he rapped at the door again, the gatekeeper opened and peered out at him.

"I am sorry to disturb you again. A moment of your time? According to Jericho Pratt, a man has visited him several times since Pratt was jailed. Do you recall the man's physical features?"

"I should say so."

"Was he, then, a short man with a balding head, and a thick upturned nose, face lined with wrinkles, and a club foot?"

"That's the man, precisely! How can you know all that?"

"The description fits the features of a person I've run across quite recently. Thank you, sir."

The transition as Brekonridge entered the Cross and Key Public House was jarring. It was like walking into a dreary cave. A small bar stood in one corner of the main room. The owner had installed two gas lights, one on either side of the bar. Behind the bar was a doorway to a back room where, no doubt, food and barrels of stout and wine were stored. The walls were ancient brick painted many times over, the floor thick oak planks with spaces between them wide enough to sweep the crumbs at the end of the day. A number of tables were scattered around a fireplace in which a few logs crackled and spit. A black iron cauldron of Welsh cawl hung on a hook at the inglenook, its savory contents simmering heartily and filling the otherwise dingy room with a delightful aroma.

Brekonridge quickly surveyed the five or six men sitting lazily around the pub. The short man he had observed ducking inside was sitting alone on an L-shaped bench built into a far corner. He was still bundled in his thick winter coat.

Brekonridge walked to the bar and ordered a tankard of cider and asked for a bowl and a spoon. He crossed to the hearth and ladled from the cauldron until the bowl was three-quarters full. Cawl was the Welsh equivalent to the ancient pottage that had maintained British and French families through most of the Middle Ages. It was a never-ending stew made from various meats, root vegetables, cabbage, herbs and spices. The cauldron had likely not been completely empty in years. Something—a bunch of chopped carrots, a handful of parsley, the remnants of a roast guinea hen, a head of cabbage, or any other variety of foodstuffs—was added every day, along with enough water to keep the stew from boiling down to sludge. It was particularly popular in public houses because it was cheap to make, cheap to maintain, and eating it kept the customers ordering beer and ale. He cut a thick slice from a huge loaf of soda bread and dropped it into the bowl.

Brekonridge took his meal to the corner where the little man sat nursing an ale, and he sat at the next table, taking care to ensure that his mass prevented convenient egress. The little man stared at Brekonridge, though it was impossible to tell whether it was due to suspicion or the fact that Brekonridge, by design, had sat with his scars facing the man. Brekonridge began to attack the cawl, shoveling large spoonsful into this mouth, and making sounds of contentment.

"Like my mother used to make," he said to the little man. "Would you believe I grew up in a tavern?"

The man looked at him but didn't respond.

"You should get some of this to go with your ale," Brekonridge said. "This is a meal to warm the soul, it is."

And, in fact, it was. Brekonridge had sampled pottage, stews and cawl all over the British Isles. The example he enjoyed now was superlative. It was nice not to have to feign delight while forcing back swill. He smacked his lips as he stuffed in another spoonful, then wiped his right hand on his jacket and extended it.

"Brekonridge," he said.

The little man recoiled slightly, then caught himself, and leaned forward. More out of curiosity than cordiality, he put out his own hand.

"Camp."

"Nice to meet you, Mr. Camp. Yes, I've spent many a happy hour in public houses like this one, recalling the warmth and comfort of my childhood. One thing about growing up in a tavern, it ain't like being the cobbler's children. There's never a shortage of food. What can beat the sense of contentment a child enjoys when his belly is full? Am I right?"

"I suppose," Camp said. He had lost interest in the conversation, and in Brekonridge, who made a show of slurping down the cawl, alternating it with sips from the cider. When Brekonridge was convinced the man had begun to ignore him, he took out the Bow Street Magistrate's Court warrant for apprehension on Mayhew and slid it across the table. Camp glanced down at it, at first disinterested, and then he read the text.

"You must be burning up," Brekonridge said, the bonhomie suddenly missing from his tone. "Take off your coat. Stay a while."

Camp's expression grew panicked. He stood to run, but the only route he had from his corner seat meant getting by Brekonridge, who kicked out his leg and slammed his boot into the wall, effectively blocking the man's exit.

"No. Really. I mean it," Brekonridge said. "Take off your coat and have a seat, Mr. Camp. Do not be alarmed. I have no interest in harming you, but I believe you can tell me things I would like to know."

Camp tried to protest, but Brekonridge noted that he did not do so enthusiastically. He saw Camp glance toward the barkeep, and then back at Brekonridge, who shook his head and gave Camp his most intimidating scowl. The little man sat back down. He unbuttoned his coat but did not remove it.

"Your first name, Mr. Camp?" he began.

"Albert," the man muttered, defeated.

"You've attempted to visit Jericho Pratt in Newgate Prison?"

"Is that a crime?"

"None that I know of. I'm curious. Why?"

"What matter is it of yours?"

"Mr. Pratt is an acquaintance, who has just enlisted my assistance in proving his innocence. If you have information that will assist me, I would recommend you share it."

"He's a friend! Isn't that enough?"

"He's been charged with a murder."

"I know."

"Who did he kill?"

"Jericho didn't kill nobody," Camp whined. "They say he stabbed a man named Fenwick, but he didn't."

"Who did?"

"I don't know."

"Who do you suspect?"

"Not a clue. I swear to you, sir. This man Fenwick is a tanner in Bermonsey. He and Pratt got into a fight because Fenwick was underpaying for Pratt's dog dirt. The next night, Fenwick turns up dead on the floor of his tannery, a knife in his chest. Someone saw him fighting with Pratt and told the bobbies. Now you know as much as I do."

"Not entirely. I understand you are close to Matt Mayhew. I need to find him. Where might he be?"

"I don't know for sure. Last I heard, he was down in Cripplegate. He's a cutpurse, Mr. Brekonridge. You want to find him? Market Day is the place. He's sure to be there, plyin' his trade."

———

"They say you killed a man named Fenwick," Brekonridge told Pratt after returning to Newgate.

"Fenwick! He's dead?"

"A knife in his chest."

"I see." Pratt settled on his bed. "Fenwick and I argued. Loudly. He was cheating me. It's bad enough that a man of manners must resort to pure-finding to avoid destitution, but when a customer shortchanges you, the pain is almost unendurable."

"Did you make threats toward the man?"

"Probably. Who can recall exactly what they say during a pique of anger?"

"Did you strike him?"

"Of course not! After venting my spleen, I told him I would never do business with him again. There is a surfeit of tanners in Bermonsey."

"And you can account for your time in the day or so before you were apprehended?"

"Not all of it. I'm afraid, after I got into it with Mr. Fenwick, I went on something of a tear. There are parts of those two days I don't recall accurately, and some I cannot retrieve at all."

"But you are certain that—in your inebriation—you did not return to Mr. Fenwick's tannery and do him in?"

"I cannot swear to it, but I cannot imagine a state of mind, impaired or not, in which I would undertake such violence. It is not in my nature."

"All right, then," Brekonridge said. "I have a man to apprehend, and once I've deposited him at Bow Street I shall turn all of my attention to your situation."

Matthew Mark Luke John Mayhew's name was longer than he was tall. The adopted son of an Anglican priest whose teachings were wasted on the boy, Matt Mayhew had grown up to be an accomplished sneak-thief, shoplifter, pickpocket, and—when the need arose—arsonist. When he couldn't make ends meet through criminal pursuits, he hired himself out to any business that would take him and was in the rare position of being unaware of his larcenous nature.

The midday bells had barely stopped chiming in the belfry of St. Giles Cripplegate when Mayhew emerged from a stable, with the apparent goal of picking pockets. Brekonridge watched as Mayhew stalked any well-dressed man he could spy in the crowd, looking for an opportunity to make off with a few shillings or even a pound or two.

Mayhew was no more than five feet tall, skinny as a fence stake. His rat-like appearance included a protruding brow, overly long and upturned nose, recessed chin, and buck teeth you could use to dig a trench. Brekonridge caught sight of him within seconds after he stepped out into the street.

Within two minutes he watched the wretched little man lift one wallet, surreptitiously grab several coins from a wool-merchant's money box when the man was briefly turned away, cut the strings to a coin purse on an oyster-barrowman, and cadge two apples from a fruit stand. After making some quick mental calculations, it occurred to Brekonridge that he might have chosen the wrong career.

A gentleman accompanying a lovely and much younger woman stepped out of a cab near the corner of Whitecross and Roscoe and helped his companion to the street. The man was dressed in the latest fashion from Paris, the woman clad in a bell-shaped dress in silk and satin, cinched furiously at the waist. She grasped the man by the hand and directed his attention toward a booth selling bolts of brocade and lace. He tossed the hack driver tuppence to wait.

Brekonridge imagined Mayhew was unconsciously drawn to the gentleman the way southern climes compel geese to migrate in the winter. Even from a distance, he could see the outline of the man's wallet in the inside breast pocket of his greatcoat.

Brekonridge increased his pace and rapidly closed the distance between himself and the brocade merchant's booth. He stood behind Mayhew, careful not to draw the thief's attention, and waited for his move.

It didn't take long. While the man's attention was directed by the woman toward a silhouette artist snipping away at black paper with scissors at potentially dismembering speed, Mayhew grabbed a bucket and silently slid it behind the man's heels. Momentarily, as he turned to move along, the man stumbled over the bucket and tumbled into a pile of snow at the edge of the street.

Mayhew was upon him in an instant.

"I say, Guvnor, are you all right? That's a right nasty fall you took. No, please, don't try to get up too quickly. Me cousin tripped over a bucket once't and he was bedridden for days. Here, allow me to brush some of this snow off your lovely coat."

He made a show of straightening the man's jacket and helping him back to his feet. The man offered his thanks, and the woman took his arm in a nurturing fashion, and also thanked Mayhew for his kindness.

"Think nothin' of it, my lady," Mayhew said. "It's the Sabbath ain't it? No better day to do a fellow traveler a favor. Please enjoy your afternoon."

He waved and turned to walk away. Instead, he ran straight into Vicar Brekonridge, his rodent nose crushing against the thief-taker's chest.

"If you break my pipe, you'll buy me a new one," Brekonridge said, his voice gravel-like, with a hint of a Scottish accent.

"Oh, damn," was all Mayhew could manage. "Brekonridge. Beggin' your leave, sir. I had no intent of violating your person."

Mayhew tipped his cloth cap and tried to sidestep Brekonridge, who grabbed the man by his collar.

"Matthew Mark Luke John Mayhew, there's a warrant for your apprehension at Bow Street. I'm to deliver you to the jail to await arraignment. I would appreciate it if we could handle this with as little resistance as possible."

"What resistance could I possibly offer? You're a bloody giant, and a right ugly one."

"Give me the wallet you took off the gentleman."

"My hearing ain't so good, Mr. Thief-Taker. I didn't catch what you said."

"You lifted the man's wallet while you were brushing off his jacket. I should be charitable and offer it was a right masterly job of it you did. You are an artist, if I may be permitted to say so."

"I am gratified at your appreciation of my craft. Is there any way we can come to an agreement that don't include you delivering me to the assizes? I have no desire to return to Newgate. It is a poor place for a soul to pass a winter."

"Give me the wallet," Brekonridge repeated.

"I see," Mayhew replied. "I see perfectly. I can't say I am enamored of the idea of parting with this delightful prize, but if it is the cost of my freedom, it's cheap indeed. You can have it."

He reached into a slit cut in the lining of his scuffed greatcoat, withdrew the gentleman's wallet, and handed it over to Brekonridge. As he extended his hand, Brekonridge grabbed it, slipped an iron handcuff over the thief's hand, and screwed down the lock.

"What's this then? You're going to rob me and still turn me over to the magistrate?"

"Not at all," Brekonridge said, as he attached the other end of the cuff to his own wrist. As soon as they were securely yoked to one another, Brekonridge dragged the little man up Whitecross Street toward the intersection with Roscoe, where the gentleman's cab sat waiting.

They waited, together, until the gentleman walked into view, looking distraught as he rushed the young woman back toward the silhouette booth. Brekonridge pulled on the cuff, bringing Mayhew to his feet, and forced him to walk toward the same booth. Halfway there, the gentleman saw them and pointed a finger as he stumbled through the snow in their direction. Brekonridge held up the man's wallet.

"Good afternoon, sir," he said. The woman caught up to them and then recoiled when she saw the right side of Brekonridge's head. "My name is Vicar Brekonridge. The gentleman chained to my wrist is Mr. Matthew Mark Luke John Mayhew, a wanted thief. I am hired to detain him and deliver him to the Bow Street Magistrate's Court. However, as I approached him to apply the irons, I saw him take this from your coat. Please allow me to return it."

The gentleman grabbed for the wallet and inspected it as if it might contain the secrets to existence itself. Satisfied, he slipped it back into his pocket.

"I thank you, Mr. Brekonridge. A less scrupulous man might have kept it as the spoils of war."

"The spoils you speak of are most often bitter compensation for the loss of your soul. I could have kept your wallet, but nothing comes for free. I'd have had to give up something more precious in compensation for it. I'll take my leave of you, sir. Please do have a pleasant afternoon."

He started to turn, but the gentleman hailed him. Brekonridge looked over his shoulder. The man held out a gold sovereign.

"For your trouble, Mr. Brekonridge. And for your honesty."

"I'm not proud, sir, I will accept your gratitude." Brekonridge pocketed the coin. "And good day to you, sir." He led Mayhew away toward Banner Street and tried not to think about the way the woman had shivered as she turned from him.

"Are you demented?" Mayhew demanded as he tried desperately to keep up with Brekonridge's long stride. "There was twenty quid easy in the man's wallet. You gave it up for a sovereign. What kind of fool are you, anyway?"

"One who sleeps at night. Turning you in will net me a reward of fifteen pounds. Added to the gentleman's largesse, I'd only be out four quid, and my conscience will not torment me over it. Be quiet or I'll walk more rapidly."

"Wait, wait," Mayhew said. He pulled gently against the handcuffs. Brekonridge stopped and glared at him. "An idea has occurred to me. Do you realize, in the last ten minutes, you've made a pound?"

"You noticed."

"And you didn't have to cut a purse or put the cosh to anyone. A pound! This idea only now formed in me mind. We could team up, you and me. I pick the pockets, you catch me and tell the victim you're taking me to justice, we return the goods, and split the rewards. It's brilliant, I tell you. Brilliant. And legal!"

"Except for the thievery," Brekonridge said.

"We give it back! Why, at the worst it would be borrowing, and there's no ordinance against borrowing is there? Why, we could do the act ten, maybe twenty times a day. Think of it, Mr. Thief-Taker. We could be living like lords in a few weeks' time."

"Forget it."

"It's the opportunity of a lifetime. The opportunity of a lifetime, I say!"

"Not my lifetime," Brekonridge said, and continued the long trudge toward Bow Street, Mayhew's short legs churning in the snow to keep pace. "Besides, I have enough on my plate. As soon as I drop you off at Bow Street, I must return to Newgate Prison, where a man awaits my services."

Stop!" Mayhew said, and dug his heels into a snowbank. "Would you be talking about Jericho Pratt?"

Brekonridge glared down at him. "You know Pratt?"

"We are of long acquaintance, the pure-finder and me. We've bent elbows in many a tavern over the years. Only yesterday, I heard Pratt had been transported to Newgate for the murder of the unfortunate tanner Fenwick."

Brekonridge continued walking. "What do you know about it?"

"More than you, I'd guess. People talk, Mr. Brekonridge. Secrets are passed across the tables of taverns and public houses. A man who keeps his eyes low and his ears open can hear things."

"Such as?"

Mayhew stopped and shook his head. "Not so fast and not nearly so easy. Everything has a price."

"I suppose you wish me to forget about the warrant for your arrest, and allow you to go free."

"I am not so foolish. Your reputation precedes you. We have a history, you an me, and I know you are incorruptible. However…"

"Yes?"

"If I am to pass the cold months chained to a standpipe in Newgate prison, I see no reason to share my information with you. To think, a single sovereign could buy me a bed—however humble and mean—in the State wing. I believe that would make my inevitable incarceration tolerable."

Brekonridge pulled the sovereign he had received as reward from the gentleman and held it above Mayhew's head. It sparkled in the sunlight. Mayhew made a grab for it, but Brekonridge lifted it above the little man's reach.

"If the information is good," he said.

"Yes," Mayhew said. "Since my unfortunate departure from my last employment, I have been sleeping in the loft of the stables on Whitecross. There is no warmth in a stable loft, so I found it necessary to fortify my blood with a few glasses of Irish whisky. I was in the St. Ives tavern several nights ago, biding my time. I overheard a conversation between Fenwick and another tanner named Bouton."

"I've met Mr. Bouton," Brekonridge said.

"Then you know him to be a sizable and powerful man."

"He seemed pleasant enough."

"He was sober. Bouton has a reputation for being a nasty drunk. On the night I saw him and Fenwick, they were arguing."

"About what?"

"Jericho Pratt. It seems Mr. Pratt has been a longtime provider of dog dirt for both Mr. Bouton and Mr. Fenwick. However, Fenwick tried to cheat him, claiming the product Pratt sold him was of poor quality. Come on, Mr. Brekonridge. It's shite. How good could it be? Am I right?"

"Go on."

"I heard Fenwick attempt to conspire with Mr. Bouton to cheat Pratt. It seems Pratt refused to sell his product to Mr. Fenwick, and said he'd take all his business in the future to Mr. Bouton. Fenwick suggested that he and Bouton fix the price, so Pratt would have to continue selling to both. Bouton went into a rage at the suggestion. I asked the tavernkeeper about them, purely out of curiosity, and was told Bouton and Fenwick have a troubled past. Seems they have been at loggerheads for years over some woman. So, I'm talking to the barkeep, minding my own business, when Bouton slams his mug into the table, stands, and roars, "I'll see you dead before I throw in with the likes of you!" to Fenwick.

"You know the name of the tavernkeeper?" Brekonridge asked.

"Smythe. Tolerance Smythe. A big, round man. You can't miss him."

They arrived at Bow Street, where Brekonridge presented Mayhew to the magistrate for arraignment and transport to Newgate. As he turned to leave, five pounds reward money newly lining his pocket, Brekonridge was stopped by Mayhew.

"What about my money?" Mayhew asked.

"I will speak with Smythe," Brekonridge said. "If he corroborates your story, I will return to Newgate and pay for a room for you on the State wing. If you're lying…"

"I'm a cutpurse and a pickpocket," Mayhew protested. "Don't make me a lying man. Everything I told you was the truth."

"In that case, you can look forward to a winter that is only mildly tolerable, compared to the miserable, unbearable season you faced otherwise. Good fortune to you, Mr. Mayhew. I have no doubt, one way or another, we shall meet again."

"Until that time, Mr. Brekonridge. Until that time."

The St. Ives Tavern on Roscoe Street was dim and quiet when Brekonridge entered. It was middle afternoon on a Sunday, not the peak time for public alehouses. He stepped to the bar and rapped on the wooden top twice. Seconds later, a rotund man almost as tall as Brekonridge emerged from the back rooms. Brekonridge ordered an ale. As the man drew it, Brekonridge said, "You'd be Tolerance Smythe?"

"I would. And I believe you to be Vicar Brekonridge."

"Have we met?"

"No, I am happy to say. If we had, it might mean I had run afoul of the magistrates. I'm an honest man, sir. However, your reputation among some of my customers is well-established. I recognized you by…" he pointed to the right side of his head.

"Only this afternoon, I apprehended a sneak thief named Matt Mayhew. Do you know the man?"

"Indeed I do. So they finally caught Mayhew? Can't say I'm happy. I've pocketed a great deal of his money over the years. Always pays cash."

"Someone else's cash," Brekonridge corrected.

"All money has been or will be someone else's money," Smythe said, smiling. "Shite's no good unless you pass it 'round."

"Do you also know Jericho Pratt?"

Smythe shook his head. "Only by name. Word has it he killed the poor tanner, Fenwick."

"Whose word?"

"Nobody in particular. Word on the street. Heard he was picked up by bobbies and transported to Newgate for the crime."

"Mayhew tells me Fenwick was a customer here."

"Indeed he was."

"And the tanner, Bouton?"

"I know the man."

"According to Mayhew, Bouton and Fenwick argued in this tavern two nights before Fenwick was murdered."

"Now that you mention it, I believe they did. Refresh your tankard?"

"Thank you." Brekonridge handed it to Smythe. "From what I heard, during that argument, Bouton threatened to kill Fenwick."

"Yes." Smythe slid the pewter tankard back across the bar. "I recall threats being made. Didn't think much of it at the time, or since. As long as it doesn't come to blows or cause damage to the tavern, I let it go. Men in their cups say things they later regret. Especially those two."

"So, otherwise, Bouton and Fenwick were friends?"

"Far from it. They've been bickering for years. As is often the case in stories like theirs, there is a woman involved."

"A romantic triangle."

"Not anymore. Years ago. Both Fenwick and Bouton were interested in the same girl, Ivy Cornwell. Bouton won her, but realized quickly she was no prize. The girl was a shrew, only Bouton didn't discover that until after they were married. Fenwick later told him he had learned her true nature early and had voluntarily relinquished her to Bouton' arms. Bouton always believed he'd been cheated into an unhappy marriage. He thought Fenwick should have warned him about his intended spouse. He blamed Fenwick for all his various woes."

"And Mrs. Bouton? I would like to know her location."

"In a churchyard somewhere, I should think. She died several years back. Can't remember how many."

Brekonridge thanked the man, paid for his ale, and set out for Bermonsey and Bouton's tannery. As he strolled, he lit his pipe again and allowed the smoke to focus his mind, as he tried to see how all the pieces of the story of Fenwick's demise meshed. He discovered there were several critical pieces missing. Foremost among them was Jericho Pratt's story of losing two days on a drinking bender. He had known Pratt, however tangentially, for several years, and had never known him to give in to dissipation.

On a hunch, Brekonridge stopped in at the Bermonsey constable station of the London Metropolitan Police. He was fortunate. An officer manning the main desk recognized him from his days wearing a badge.

"As I live and breathe, it's Mr. Brekonridge!" the constable, Caleb Toll, said when Brekonridge walked through the door. "I haven't seen you in five years." He shook Brekonridge's hand vigorously.

After they hurriedly caught up with each other's lives, Brekonridge became serious. "I'm in the midst of an apprehension, perhaps," he said.

"Perhaps?"

"As it happens, a man is already in Newgate awaiting trial for the crime, but I believe he may have been accused falsely. Are you familiar with the murder of the tanner, Fenwick?"

"Am I? I was among the officers who took Jericho Pratt into custody."

"How did you find him?"

"Nearly unconscious with drink. We could have nabbed him with a single officer."

"And how did you determine Jericho Pratt was your prime suspect in the murder?"

"We had a tip. A man reported he had seen Pratt in a horrible row with Mr. Fenwick, during which Pratt said he would kill the man. Made a promise, he did, and two days later Fenwick was dead. Seems an open and shut case to me, if you ask."

"If it would not violate a confidence," Brekonridge asked, "Could you divulge the name of the man who informed on Mr. Pratt?"

"Wouldn't violate confidence at all. After all, I reckon the man will be called to the dock during Pratt's trial."

He told Brekonridge the name. Brekonridge was not surprised.

Brekonridge arrived at the tannery, and his eyes watered at the stench. The process of turning living flesh into leather was better left to the imagination. The clouds of ammonia-laden air surrounding the tannery were oppressive and nauseating. Outside the tannery, piles upon piles of bound tree bark awaited rendering for tannic acid. Inside the tannery, large wells of stinking chemicals roiled and churned, skins undulating in the foul liquid as they were preserved and softened. Workers, dressed in loose linen shirts and trousers rolled to the knee, waded in the tanks with long poles, continuously pushing the skins deep into the tanning solution. Other workers tied the treated skins to drying racks, sweat pouring off their faces and arms as they hefted the hides.

Brekonridge found Bouton in the same office he'd visited earlier in the day. The tanner was a large man, thick through the waist, with shoulders and biceps swollen from years of wielding a tanning pole and lifting sodden skins from vats. He sported a full beard, which he had allowed to grow lusciously over his lower face to the point that his mouth was barely visible through hair. He looked up as Brekonridge walked through the door.

"Mr. Brekonridge! I suppose you located Jericho Pratt."

"I did. As you suggested, he was at Newgate Prison. I was distressed to learn you had lied to me."

"Lied? In what way?"

"When we met earlier today, you told me Pratt was in Newgate, but you also said you had no idea why."

"So?"

"In fact, you knew quite well why Pratt was incarcerated. You were the person who told the police that Pratt was in a horrible fight with Mr. Fenwick, and you told them where Pratt could be located for arrest. I also checked in at the Dove and Turtle public house down the street. You are familiar with the establishment?"

"I've visited a few times over the years."

"According to the tavernkeeper, you and Pratt drank heavily there the night before Fenwick was murdered. More precisely, he told me Pratt drank heavily, and you paid for the ale. He said you had to carry Pratt out of the pub, because the man could barely walk. The next day, after Fenwick's body was discovered, you turned Pratt over to the constables. Perhaps you could explain how a man who couldn't stand upright managed to plunge a knife into Fenwick's chest."

"I have no need to explain anything," Bouton said. "I merely told the police what I had seen."

"Did you witness Pratt threaten to kill Mr. Fenwick before or after you made similar threats yourself?"

Bouton cocked his head and glared at Brekonridge.

"Say that again."

"It may well be the case that Jericho Pratt argued with Fenwick. He might even have threatened the man. However, the only witness the police have to such a confrontation is you. I have two witnesses who saw you threaten Fenwick in the St. Ives Tavern in Cripplegate, two nights before Fenwick died. In the course of my investigation, I learned you and Fenwick have been enemies for years, after he tricked you into wedding Ivy Cornwell. Trapped in a horrid marriage, you blamed him for all your troubles. I think you heard about the threats made toward Fenwick by Jericho Pratt. I think you got Pratt dead drunk, so he could not account for his time, deposited him in his lodgings, and then set out for a final showdown with Fenwick. I think you drove the knife into his heart, and then blamed the murder on an insignificant, innocent pure-finder."

"You have no proof," Bouton stammered.

"Don't need it. I'm not a magistrate or a judge. It appears to me, however, that the preponderance of evidence against you far outweighs that against poor Mr. Pratt. I recommend charging both of you. Let Bow Street sort it out."

Brekonridge was prepared when Bouton launched himself from his office chair, fists clenched, and arms raised to strike. The two grappled in the office. Bouton tried to grasp Brekonridge's head and struggled to gouge the thief-taker's eyes with his thumbs. Brekonridge broke his grasp and slapped at one of Bouton' ears with his open hand, rupturing the man's eardrum. Bouton fell to the floor, howling in pain, but had the presence of mind to lash out at Brekonridge's knee with his heavily booted foot.

Brekonridge tried to sidestep the kick, but still caught the boot on the outside of his knee. He collapsed to the floor, rolling to get away from his attacker, as Bouton gained his feet and ran toward the door exiting the tannery.

He ran directly into the waiting arms of Constable Caleb Toll and two other London bobbies. They wrestled him to the ground and were applying the irons as Brekonridge limped outside to join them.

"As I suspected," Brekonridge huffed. "When confronted with the evidence against him, he attacked me and attempted to flee. It's as strong an indicator of guilt as I've seen."

"I didn't murder nobody!" Bouton protested. "It was self-defense, it was. I fought with Fenwick, sure, but he was the one who drew the knife. I took it from him, and he came at me with a length of chain. I had no choice but to stab him. It was him or me."

"If so, you may be spared Tyburn Tree," Brekonridge told him. "But I wouldn't count on it."

The next day, Jericho Pratt, a free man, walked out of Newgate Prison with Vicar Brekonridge.

"I cannot thank you enough," Pratt declared, shaking Brekonridge's hand ferociously.

"Fortunately," Brekonridge said, "your information led me to Mayhew, whose apprehension in Cripplegate will cover my expenses for some weeks to come. The ten pounds you promised to free you is extra, and thanks enough. Oh. I almost forgot."

Brekonridge returned to the imposing front door of the prison, struck the knocker, and waited for the gatekeeper to appear. When he did, Brekonridge pressed a gold sovereign into the man's hand. "This is to pay for a cell on the State wing for Matthew Mark Luke John Mayhew. He earned it. Please see to it that he is moved to Mr. Pratt's old cell as soon as possible. I will return in several days' time to ensure my wishes have been carried out."

Back on the street, Brekonridge lit his pipe and started his long walk to his rooms. He had walked about three blocks when a carriage pulled alongside. The driver stopped the horses.

"Mr. Brekonridge," a man said from inside.

Brekonridge stopped and peered through the window.

"It's Mr. Cockburn, is it not?" he asked.

"Indeed. May I offer you a ride?"

Small and slight, but with a head seemingly too large for his body, Alexander Cockburn was known as a ladies' man, as well as being one of the foremost litigators in Britain. Queen Victoria herself had named him Queen's Counsel. Brekonridge stooped and pulled himself up into the seat facing the barrister. His John Bull hat nearly touched the velvet-covered headliner.

"I saw you at Bow Street," Cockburn said. "Delivering a prisoner. I had hoped to speak with you there, but I was waylaid by another attorney who needed information. By the time we were finished, you had gone."

"You need a man caught?" Brekonridge asked.

"He's already been caught. Are you familiar with the case of Daniel M'Naghten?"

"A man kills another, under the delusion he's shooting the Prime Minister? Word gets around. May I presume you are representing Mr. M'Naghten?"

"I am among a team of barristers working on his case. His trial is on March third."

"Five weeks away."

"The only defense option sparing the man from execution is insanity. The prosecution is going to bring witnesses, including medical doctors, who will attest M'Naghten is as sane as you or me."

"Speak for yourself, sir."

"I think not. Your reputation precedes you, Mr. Brekonridge. You are a perceptive man, a man of remarkable resources, and you are pragmatic. We have a short time to build our defense, and you could provide the key pieces for it."

"How so?"

"Familiar with Glasgow, are you?"

"I've passed out in a public house or two there."

"We would like you to act as an investigator for our team. You would interview M'Naghten's acquaintances. Gather as much information on the man as you can. We need witnesses who can testify to a general and steady decline in Mr. M'Naghten's faculties over time, leading to a loss of reason, ultimately leading him to fire upon poor Mr. Drummond in a fit of delusion."

"And you want me to go to Glasgow."

"Yes."

Brekonridge fell silent and stared out the window at passersby. Presently, he shook his head.

"I must be mad," he said. "I could walk into Bow Street today and take my pick from any number of warrants. I do not need to go to Glasgow to make my way and fill my belly. I do not care for travel beyond the streets of London. I grow weary of the expressions of strangers when they first see my disfigurement. I prefer solitude. However, I will take this case on one condition."

"That being?"

"You will represent Mr. Bouton at the Bow Street assizes next week. He has been charged with murder, but his story leaves some room for an argument that he acted in self-defense. If he is to slip the Tyburn noose, he will require an able barrister."

"Done," Cockburn said. "And you will leave for Glasgow on the morrow?"

They shook on it.

"May I drop you at your lodgings?"

"If you please, I prefer to walk. I have things to think about."

Brekonridge stepped down from the carriage and watched as it disappeared around the corner. He pulled his football pipe from his greatcoat pocket and set a match to it, inhaling the acrid hemp smoke deep into his lungs.

All in all, it had been a productive week.

SWEEPS WEEK

by

Richard Helms

Author's Note: Sometimes, an author types The End *on a story, and just knows they have created something special. This was the case with* "Sweeps Week", *which first appeared in* Ellery Queen Mystery Magazine *in 2021. I knew the instant I sent it in that it was destined for great things, and I wasn't wrong. There's a lot of personal baggage woven into this story, and a lot of stories I picked up from homeless people over the years. This story won the PWA Shamus Award and the MRI Macavity Award in 2022, but—more importantly, it highlights the plight of the homeless in this country, especially in big cities. I am happy and proud to close out this collection of award-winning and award-nominated stories with this fine tale.*

R

I'm the Invisible Man.

You've probably seen me many times, but I'm still invisible. I'm the wretch standing in the median with a cardboard sign. I'm the pair of legs sticking from behind a dumpster as you pass an alley. I'm the guy sleeping in the subway station while people hustle by on the way to their trains. I sit on the bench at Hudson Park with two huge black garbage bags. You sneered at me when you walked by and I was taking a dump behind a cardboard box screen. I'm the woman down on Christopher Street, standing in the middle of the road and directing imaginary traffic. I'm the guy who washed your windshield the other day, and you stiffed me.

Remember me now?

Of course not. Too busy. Too frightened. Too embarrassed. Too heartless. Too self-absorbed. Too close to one paycheck from being homeless yourself, and you deny those of us who have already fallen through the cracks, as if homelessness were contagious.

Sure. I get it. Please. Don't apologize. I know you don't mean it anyway. You're just not used to invisible men suddenly becoming visible. You want me to vanish as quickly as possible. That's how it is with people like me. You can stroll past, see me without acknowledging my existence, walk on to wherever you're headed, and forget me half a minute later.

Surprise. I'm still here. I haven't gone anywhere just because you made me vanish in your head. A day after you've forgotten me, you'll probably walk by me again, without recognizing our prior relationship. That can hurt. One does like to believe that one leaves an impression on the Earth.

Who am I kidding? The great majority of us are destined to strut for a few short years before being consigned in every possible way to oblivion. Only one in a million leaves an impression on this planet that lasts beyond the lives of his grandchildren. Don't believe me? Tell me everything you know about your great-grandfather. I'll give you fifteen seconds. You want to toss a quarter in my direction once in a while, we'll be jake. I'm way too busy surviving to give a damn whether you recognize me. A minute after you've forgotten my face, I'm still wondering how I'm going to eat today.

Not *what.*

How.

Presuming I've settled the issue of eating versus going hungry, there's the matter of where I'll lay my head for the night. It isn't a foregone conclusion. There are only so many bridge overpasses, even in big city, and there are buttloads of invisible men and women. One must be creative, especially during the extreme seasons.

We all have stories, you know. For most of us, we are the protagonists in our stories. The invisible are no different. We've fallen on tough times, or we drew the smelly end of the sanity stick, or there's simply nobody left who knows us or cares whether we live or die. There are as many stories teaching us how to fail as there are failures. Nobody ever looks down at a cooing baby, only weeks out of the womb, and says, "Gonna make a fine bum someday!" Nobody aspires to homelessness. There's no future in it. If we've hit bottom, we all believe it's only temporary. Things have to get better. Right?

Every social stratum has its own structure, its own hierarchy. Within every socioeconomic status, there are those who have, and those who want. I remember one of my old college professors—

What? You're surprised I went to college? Stick around. You might learn a thing or two.

So, this professor used to say, "This is the way all social interaction works. You have all the money in the world. I have a fifty-caliber machine gun. Sooner or later, that money is gonna change hands."

Suppose you not only don't have all the money in the world, but barely have two nickels to rub together? What if all you have to your name is a devoted little dog? Or a pair of shoes without holes in the sole? Or a warm blanket without any rips? There are all kinds of currency in this world.

It was late summer. I'd spent the day on a temp job clearing a lot where a house had burned. I'm a big guy, and I try to keep myself up, so when gypsy labor recruiters show up at the local home improvement store looking for help, I'm usually among the first picks. They fed us a decent lunch, which was a nice change. I made thirty bucks. I didn't have to worry about eating for two or three days if I kept it cheap.

My wardrobe was filthy and shopworn, so I dropped by a thrift shop and bought a new bag of underwear, a lightweight cotton sport shirt, some socks, and a pair of khaki cargo shorts with the tag still attached. Hard to imagine some people donate stuff they never even wore. Total outlay: $3.85. I paid another quarter for a pack of disposable razors that would last me a month.

There's a hostel nearby. It's a nice flop for budget-minded travelers, international tourists, and Ken Kesey addicts taking their act on the road. I did some favors for the owner back when I was on the job, so he lets me use their showers. Sometimes, if business is slow, he lets me flop on one of the bunks. I always offer to pay. He always refuses. Both of us know I couldn't afford it anyway.

A few hours later, showered, shaved, and dressed in my new duds, I lounged on a bench in a park near the hostel, reading the latest issue of a weekly newspaper peddled free in boxes all over town. The lead story, sandwiched between theater reviews and ads for outcall escorts, was about the political convention coming to town. It worried me. Political conventions mean television cameras and lots of them, and are bad news for people like me.

As I read, a man sat next to me.

Chuey Espinoza was a wizened little guy in his sixties. Or, perhaps, he was only in his early forties. The streets have a way of aging a person. He had served in the military, in some capacity about which he refused to speak. At night loud noises roused him screaming from his sleep. Otherwise, I never heard his voice rise above a whisper.

Chuey had two things going for him. First, he was a veteran, which entitled him to free medical care, of a sort. In the street life, that's a luxury.

Second, he had a buddy.

On the street, safety lies in numbers. If you aren't tough and battle-seasoned, like me, you're a victim. Kids get drunk and decide to roll a bum. A panhandler hassles the wrong guy, who settles the issue with a baseball bat. Shit happens, and it seems to happen a lot more frequently to the invisible men. If you have a buddy, people keep their distance, because people in general are cowards who wilt in the face of superior numbers.

Not that Chuey's buddy was going to be much help in a back-alley brawl. We called him Sonny. Nobody really knew his first or last name. Sonny had an interesting childhood.

His father was a chemist in the 1960s, but not the kind who worked for Dow or Monsanto. It was the hippie generation. Everyone was chasing the alphabet soup trips. LSD, DMT, MDA—it was the heyday of better living through chemistry. Nobody knows Sonny's father's real name, either, but his underground alias was Commander X. He had a partner, fellow known as Necromancer. They liked to putter around in the lab producing hallucinogens for a new generation of pleasure seekers. Some of the concoctions were hits. Some were busts. All of them were tested on Commander X's eight-year-old son, because Commander X was already a psychopath long before he burned out his synapses snorting Drano crystals, and he didn't have the emotional capacity to distinguish his boy from a lab rat. From the time he was twenty, Sonny wandered the streets of the city, carrying all his earthly possessions in a cigar box and a permanent angelic smile on his face. People said he could see fairies and demons, but people like to talk.

Sonny was in his late fifties, and still as oblivious to reality as an empty Coke bottle. He was tall and thin and scraggly, with a long wispy beard and watery blue eyes that always seemed focused on a plane of reality denied the rest of us. Sometime in the past decade, he and Chuey hooked up. Nobody knows when or how, but they had become inseparable. Sonny wasn't going to be much help if the black flag went up, since his brain operates in a distant time zone, but other people didn't know that, and he looked just crazy enough to be dangerous. Chuey took care of Sonny, and Sonny unwittingly protected Chuey.

Chuey looked worried, sitting next to me on the bench.

"You seen Sonny?" he asked.

"Nope. Figured he's always with you," I said.

"Don't like it." Chuey fidgeted on the bench. "We got separated yesterday. I was asleep, and he wandered off. Haven't seen him since."

"Sonny's been wandering for forty years," I said. "He'll show up."

"I dunno," Chuey said. "With this convention in town…"

I knew what he meant. Among the League of Invisible Men, the days before a huge city-wide event like a political convention are known as Sweeps Week. The city does everything it can to paint its face for the cameras, and that means getting rid of as many homeless people as possible. Sometimes, the removal is relatively benign, with the city opening temporary shelters to house us for the duration. Sometimes, we get Greyhound therapy—a bus ticket, a fistful of ones, and an invitation to infest another city. On other occasions, the purge is brutal and unannounced. Cops descend on tent villages and highway underpasses and public parks like Cossacks in a pogrom, wrecking or confiscating precious possessions it took months to acquire. The message in all the cases was clear. *Our welcome mat does not apply to you.*

"Maybe he got swept," I said. "Might be in a nice temp shelter, snoozing on a cot."

It was unlikely, but stranger things happened all the time.

"It's summer. Shelters are closed. You heard about any new ones springing up?" Chuey said.

"No. But the convention doesn't start for another week."

"I think something happened to him. It ain't like Sonny to stay gone for so long. I was wondering. Think you might help me find him?"

"Me?"

"You was a cop. You know how to do stuff like that."

"I was a dirty cop," I said. It was true. At least I wasn't in denial about it. That should count for something. "I spent more time on the take than I did tracking down missing persons."

"But you know the ropes, how to find people. You still got connections."

"None who want to admit it."

Chuey gave me this look, his rheumy eyes brimming with tears. He was in a whole new zip code of desperation.

"I'll…I'll pay you," he said.

"You want to hire me to find Sonny? You don't have enough cash for a hot dog."

"I…I got a place where I get food. Good food. I'll share it with you."

"What kind of place?" I asked.

"New restaurant, three or four blocks over. The chef used to be one of us. Slept on the streets for a year before someone hired him. We helped each other out, back when he had nothin'. He and I, we got a deal going. He leaves me and Sonny a box dinner behind the dumpster each night. You find Sonny, and you can have a third."

Like I said. On the streets, there are all kinds of currency.

Times being what they were, I took the job.

There was still a chance Sonny was in a shelter somewhere, dozing on a cot. I didn't know of any that were open. But, with sweeps due to start any day, maybe I was wrong.

Not everyone in the NYPD hated me. I still had a friend or two. One was Sean Bayless, a beat cop in Hell's Kitchen. He thinks I saved his life in a raid a few years back, but that's another story. The down and dirty was he still felt like he owed me. I tried not to abuse our relationship. Unlike me, Sean is a straight arrow. It might not be good for his career to be seen too often in my company.

I found him the next morning as he walked out of a bodega carrying a cup of coffee, and I fell into step beside him.

"How's it hangin' Sean?" I asked.

He glanced at me and did a double-take. He isn't used to seeing me in fresh clothes.

"You back on your feet?" he asked.

"Same ol', same ol'," I said. "You caught me on a good day. Won't bother you long."

"Ain't no bother," he said. "Good to know you're still alive."

"Not many people feel that way. Just need some information. I'm doing a job for a friend. His buddy's missing."

"You a private detective now?"

"You didn't see my half-page ad in the *Times?*"

"You can file a report at the precinct, you know."

"This missing person, the cops wouldn't be interested in finding."

"A homeless guy?"

"You remember Sonny? Chuey's buddy? The burnout?"

"Sure. How's the little fella? Oh. Wait. You mean..."

"Chuey hasn't seen him in a couple of days. With the convention coming to town, I thought maybe the city's opened a new shelter to round us up and keep us away from the cameras, and Sonny might be there."

Sean shook his head. "Sorry, man. No shelters. Word at the department is bus tickets are a lot cheaper."

"You know where they're going?"

"Boston. Philly. Anyplace Yankee fans hate. Some are going down south, but sweeps haven't started yet. If Sonny's missing, it isn't because he got picked up. Have you checked the hospitals? Maybe he got hit by a car or something. Off in his own world all the time, he never looks both ways."

"There are over sixty ERs in this city. Only one of you. Figured I'd start with the easy stuff. Thanks, Sean. I'll check the indigent clinics first."

"Hey. You okay? Really? You need any money?" Sean asked.

"Hell, I'd just blow it on food and clothes. What fun would that be?"

Sean held out his hand. I took it and wasn't surprised to find folded bills in it. I let go and stuffed the bills in my pocket.

"I'm not proud," I said. "Thank you. I gotta hustle. Keep it on the straight and narrow, Sean. Let me be an object lesson."

I started to peel off, but he placed a hand on my shoulder.

"You know, you don't have to live like this," he said. "You get picked up in the sweeps and they put you on a bus, why don't you stay where it drops you? You could start over someplace where you don't have so many guys in blue with a hard-on for you. I mean, you can't be a cop anymore, but there are lots of other ways to put food on the table."

"What?" I said, as I waved goodbye. "And leave New York?"

Sonny was a wanderer, for sure, but he never wandered far. His attention span was too short to make long-range plans. On the off chance he wound up in a hospital somewhere, I made a spiral search, starting with the one closest to the place Sonny and Chuey usually squat for the night.

Hospital ER waiting rooms are like resort spas for homeless guys. You get AC, free TV—even if they always seem to be tuned to The Disney Channel—and a place to sit unmolested as long as you don't draw attention to yourself.

Even so, I thought I might get further with the front desk staff if I spiffed up a little. I dropped a couple of Sean's dollars at the thrift store on a like-new pair of khakis, so I wouldn't look like a vagrant, and I showered and shaved at the hostel before I started hiking.

Spent the afternoon talking to check-in desk clerks. Described Sonny to each of them. I think they figured I was his social worker or something. Nobody asked for any *bona fides*.

I did this for two days running. Thought I had a hit at one place. I was glad it wasn't him, because the guy the clerk thought was Sonny had died waiting to be seen by a doctor. Turned out he was homeless, all right, but he was in his eighties. Beats me how they could tell. Maybe they counted his rings during the autopsy.

"He isn't in a shelter, and he isn't in any hospital for thirty blocks in any direction," I told Chuey the next afternoon. "Sonny hardly ever wanders farther than that, so unless he got lost, he's probably still breathing."

"Now you got me real worried," Chuey said. "Don't know what I'll do if we can't find him. You hungry?"

It was like asking if I was still breathing. I'd been pounding concrete for three days looking for Sonny. A guy my size runs through a tank in no time, and the time I'd spent looking for Chuey's buddy was time I hadn't spent clearing the building lot and putting a little coin in my pocket. I was running low on cash.

"Come with me," Chuey said. I shadowed him several blocks over. He directed me down a service alley. "This is the place I told you about. The restaurant. Lemme see…"

Chuey ducked behind a dumpster and came back out with a biodegradable recycled cardboard take-out carton wrapped in cling plastic to keep out the rats and roaches.

"That's the food the chef leaves for you and Sonny?" I asked.

"Sure thing. He's a nice guy. Sonny's not here. Figured you could take half."

He opened the container, and sure enough there was plenty inside for two people. The guy even included two little wax paper baggies with napkins and bamboo utensils. Environmentally conscious. Chuey used one of the forks to separate the food into two piles. It smelled good, much better than the stuff I can usually afford. I told him to eat his fill, and I'd take the rest, and I stood watch while he wolfed his bit down. I was staring out the alley into the street when I heard a voice behind us.

"Who's this?"

I turned around to face a man about my height, dressed in a chef's jacket and a pair of jeans. His head was shaven bald, and he wore big glasses with black plastic frames, the kind you get at the VA.

"Friend of mine," Chuey said, through a mouth full of half-chewed food.

I held out my hand and introduced myself.

"Carroll Sampley," he said, as he took it. "You Chuey's social worker?"

"Just a friend, like he said," I replied.

"That's good. It's important to have friends on the street. Hold tight. Be right back."

He disappeared through the back door of the restaurant and returned a minute later to hand us two take-out paper cups of iced tea, with paper straws. Carroll Sampley took great pains to protect the world, I figured.

"I told him you was homeless like us once," Chuey said between bites.

"That's a fact," Sampley said. "Fell on hard times after I got back from three tours in the Sandbox."

"Three?" I asked.

"National Guard. One weekend a month my ass. I was stop-lossed. Twice."

"Raw deal," I said.

"At least I got three hots and a cot for my trouble, even if the food was MREs and it was hard to sleep in hundred-degree heat at midnight. Biggest worry was getting splattered by an IED or fragged by a random sniper round. Once I bounced back stateside, nobody gave me much of a damn."

"*'Thank you for your service,'*" I said, sarcastically.

"Thanks was about all I got. Before I was called up, I had some culinary training. Took me months, but I finally found a restaurant that would put me to work without a formal address. Worked my way up to this place. Chuey here was nice to me when I was on the streets, so I try to take care of him and Sonny. What's your story?"

I told him. He didn't appear disturbed. When I got to the part about being driven from the NYPD for taking bribes, he just nodded.

"It happens," he said. "Hold tight. Got something for Chuey here."

He ducked back inside the restaurant, and reappeared seconds later with Sonny's cigar box.

"Found this a few dozen feet away couple of nights ago, when I was signing for a delivery. It's Sonny's, right?"

Chuey stared at the box like it might hold his buddy's ashes. He nodded, his mouth hanging open.

"Figured you could give it to him," Sampley said. "Where is he, anyway?"

"We've been looking for him," I said. "He's been gone several days."

"Thought you weren't a cop anymore."

Chuey handed me the food container, and took Sonny's cigar box as I dug in. He cradled it like a newborn baby.

"I hired him," Chuey said. "Told him I'd give him Sonny's share of the food until he gets found, and then we'd split it three ways."

Sampley shook his head.

"That's the most pathetic thing I've heard this week. Tell you what. You find Sonny, and I'll see to it there's food enough for three of you. Just don't let it get around."

"You won't get in trouble for handing out free dinners?" I asked.

"I got a dishwasher inside. Good kid, but maybe a little down on his luck. I know he doesn't get a lot to eat away from the place. He and I got an arrangement. If he needs a bite, he just calls into the kitchen and says, *'Burn one.'* I leave a hotdog or a burger on the flattop for half a minute too long and shuttle it back to him. I figure helping a buddy is no worse than that, and if you find Sonny, you'll be a buddy. Besides, I own part of the place. Won't be any trouble, but I don't want to become famous for this. Know what I mean?"

"Sure," I said. "And I don't mind telling you, you're a hell of a cook. When did you see Sonny last?"

"Probably last Monday, with Chuey. Yeah. It was Monday. I remember because I was off on Tuesday."

Chuey looked at me. "Sonny wandered off on Tuesday. He had his cigar box with him. He always had his box."

"Why were you off on Tuesday, Carroll?" I said.

He shrugged.

"I'm always off on Tuesday. I work six days a week. Our heaviest business is on the weekend, so my partner takes off Monday, and I take off Tuesday."

"Yeah," Chuey said. "Sonny and me, we know not to come around Tuesdays."

"Maybe Sonny forgot," I said.

Chuey nodded. Sonny forgot a lot of things.

"What night did you find the box?" I asked Sampley.

"Wednesday," he said.

"And you just remembered it tonight?"

"What are you saying?" Sampley asked.

"It ain't that," Chuey broke in. "I ain't been here since Monday myself. Been too busy looking for Sonny."

"I was wondering why the meals hadn't been picked up," Sampley added, "Most nights I don't see either Chuey or Sonny. Too busy inside. I stowed the box in my office until I ran across either of them in the alley. Would have missed the two of you tonight if I hadn't stepped out to grab a smoke."

"I see," I said. "So Sonny left his cigar box here between Tuesday afternoon and Wednesday night."

"Is that important?" Sampley asked.

"Beats me," I said. "It does narrow our time frame."

"You talk like a cop," Sampley said.

"Old habits die hard. Thanks for the food, and the offer of more for finding Sonny. I hope I can take you up on it."

I was in luck. My hostel buddy had a vacant bunk that night. I should have been content, but I tossed and turned as I ran through the little information I'd learned so far.

I gathered my stuff together just before sunup the next morning, made myself a large plastic cup of instant java, left a thank-you note for the manager, and grabbed a quick cheap bite at the market on the next corner. A banana and a two-pack of PopTarts. Strawberry. Breakfast of champions.

A half hour later, I found myself back in the alley behind Carroll Sampley's restaurant. I wasn't sure why, but I was drawn to the last spot I knew Sonny had visited. The dead-end alley was quiet and deserted. I strolled down one side, staring at the ground, looking for anything that resembled a clue.

The dumpster people must have been there before me. When I raised the lid, all I found was bare, stained sheet steel and a rotting stink of old food and rancid milk, like every dumpster I'd ever opened. I released the lid and let it slam with a metallic clang. There was a second dumpster about fifty feet farther down the alley. Empty as well, but when I walked around it, I saw a stain on the pavement that was sickeningly familiar.

Once you've seen a pool of blood, you never forget it. It's like nothing else in nature. This was old, at least several days, but there was a lot of it. It had dried on the pavement into a dark ochre splotch about the size of a manhole cover.

I opened the dumpster again and examined it more closely. It was hard to tell, with the collage of ancient food stains on the floor, but I thought I could make out several fresh splotches the size of canning jar lids, the same color as the pool on the asphalt.

"Hold it right there," someone said. I turned and found two beat cops standing twenty feet away. The older guy was husky but not fat, the way athletes get when they give up training. His name was Feeney. We had a history.

"Keep your hands where we can see 'em," the young one said, with the cocky swagger you sometimes see in rookies who had recently discovered the real power bestowed on a man who carries a gun and a badge. He had his hand on his service piece, mostly to intimidate me.

I don't intimidate easily.

Feeney placed a hand on the young cop's shoulder. "Hold up, Ted. I know this one."

He didn't have to tell Ted to back him up. It was understood. Feeney sauntered toward me, never taking his eyes off my face. Ted stayed in place, in a ready stance, waiting for me to do anything untoward. Feeney stopped a yard or so away.

"You remember me telling you about the guy who sent my partner to prison?" Feeney said, over his shoulder.

"Yeah," Ted said.

"Well, this is him."

I forgot to mention that, in addition to being a dirty cop, I was also a rat. I'd been a cop long enough to know the first guy to squeal gets a break, and when the IAD boys slapped the cuffs on me, I immediately called my attorney and cut a deal. In return for time served in holding, I'd pled guilty to police corruption and put the finger on my partners. Feeney wasn't dirty, but his partner—a guy named Adcock—was up to his elbows in it. Adcock went away, along with three or four other guys I hoped never to meet again. I got to hang around, which I'd been doing, more or less, for five years.

"Assume the position," Feeney commanded. I complied. He patted me down, but all he found was a few meager folded bills and a small pocketknife I used to pare my nails. He confiscated the knife but was smart enough not to pocket my cash in front of his partner. Might have muddied the waters. He stuffed the money back in my pocket and stepped back but didn't tell me I could take my hands off the filthy bricks. I stayed leaned up against the building.

"It's one thing to be a bad cop," Feeney told his partner. "It's another to roll over on your brothers." He surveyed my new clothes. "Heard you were homeless."

"Yeah."

"Don't look homeless." He leaned forward and sniffed. "Don't smell homeless."

"I'm doing it better than most guys," I said.

"Check the street," Feeney told Ted. When Ted turned around, Feeney gave it to me hard, right in the kidneys. Even the most stand-up tough guy can't handle a stout kidney punch. I went down, my face scraping against the rough bricks. I felt my new khakis rip as my knee banged into the asphalt. By the time Ted turned back around, I was curled on the pavement, and Feeney had stepped back, as if he'd never walloped me.

"Stand up," Feeney said. As soon as I was confident I wouldn't lose my breakfast, I pulled myself up against the wall and stared him down, panting. "We got a call from the restaurant over there about some vagrant rummaging through dumpsters."

"From Carroll Sampley?" I wheezed.

"Who in hell is Carroll Sampley?" Feeney asked.

"My co-owner," said a new voice from the back door of the restaurant. The man standing in the doorway was built like a pro wrestler, biceps straining the fabric of his short-sleeved shirt. He wore a stained kitchen apron and one of those old-timey paper diner caps. "I'm John Delacorte. How do you know Carroll?"

"Met him last night," I said. "I'm looking for a guy he knows."

"What do you mean, *'looking for'*?" Feeney asked. "You a private cop now?"

"You think they'd give me a license, with my record? I'm doing a favor for a friend."

"This Sampley fella?" Feeney said.

"No. Another homeless guy. His buddy is missing. Sampley knows about it."

"What's this missing bum's name?" Feeney asked.

"I don't know his real name. We call him Sonny. He wandered off a few days back. Hasn't been seen since." I was still trying to catch my breath, and the words came out between gasps.

"So why were you looking around this alley for him?" Delacorte demanded.

"I'll ask the questions," Feeney said. "But, yeah. Why here?"

"Like I said, Carroll Sampley's been helping Sonny and his buddy Chuey. They're friends from back when Sampley was living on the streets. I talked to him about it last night. Sonny's got a lot of frayed aluminum wiring in his head. He doesn't see the world the way you and I do. He carries all his possessions in a cigar box. Sonny disappeared on Tuesday. On Wednesday night, Sampley found his cigar box here in the alley."

"So?" Feeney said. "Bums dump stuff all the time."

"There's more," I said. "Look here."

I showed him the apparent blood pool on the pavement, and I lifted the dumpster lid to show him the stains on the floor inside.

"Sure looks like blood to me. Maybe it's Sonny's, maybe it's not. Maybe Sonny wandered into this alley and got attacked, then dumped into the trash." I turned to Delacorte. "You haven't seen him, have you? Skinny guy, about five-eight. Has long greasy gray hair, a straggly beard, and a clouded eye. Might have been carrying a cigar box."

"No," Delacorte said, hesitantly. "That could be any of a thousand bums in this city. I find these derelicts dumpster diving back here all the time. When I do, I run 'em off."

"Sure that's all you do?" I asked. "Feeney, this looks like blood to me. A lot of blood. Someone got hurt bad here, I bet. Maybe killed. What are you gonna do about it?"

"You may be right," Feeney said. "Tell you what. I'll call it in, see if the Homicide Squad guys can send out a CSI team to comb the alley and look for evidence. They just been sitting around the precinct twiddling their thumbs for days now, looking for something to do. I'm sure they'll jump all over the case of some freakin' bum who got himself rolled and dumped in a trash can." You could have painted a room with the sarcasm in his voice, with one coat.

"You aren't going to do shit," I said.

"You're smart for a rat," Feeney said. "Maybe I'll run you in for vagrancy. A night or two in holding might teach you to mind your own business and not bother upstanding entrepreneurs like Mr. Delacorte here. On second thought, you aren't worth the paperwork. You're pissing up a rope.

Nobody gives a damn about some missing bum. Best thing you can do is move along. River's that way. Why don't you jump in?"

The way John Delacorte got nervous when I described Sonny and his cigar box bothered me. Maybe it was just my rusty cop instincts, but I suspected he knew more than he was saying. He'd admitted strong-arming homeless guys in the alley before. While my kidneys weren't fond of the idea of crossing Feeney and his eager-beaver rookie partner again, I liked the idea of Chuey grabbing his dinner alone even less. From what I could tell, Delacorte worked days and Sampley took the evenings, so I walked Chuey over when I figured it was safe.

There were two boxes behind the dumpster. We had just started chowing down when Sampley stepped outside.

"Any news?" he asked.

"Met your partner today," I said.

"John?"

"Looks like he bench presses Volkswagens."

"That's him."

"He's a walking poster child for 'roid rage. Sounded like he gets his jollies rousting homeless guys," I said.

Sampley nodded but didn't say anything.

"There's more. Come take a look." I closed the lid on my dinner box and led him down to the alley to the second dumpster. "I was checking out the alley this morning and found this…"

I stopped. The bloody splotch was gone. The area looked as if it had been washed down with a fire hose. I lifted the lid of the dumpster. There was a shallow layer of trash in the bottom, but not enough to cover the entire floor. The puddles of blood were missing as well. There were still areas of standing water.

"Damn!" I muttered.

"What?" Sampley asked.

"There were stains here that looked like dried blood this morning. I showed them to the beat cop. He kidney-punched me. Delacorte saw them too. Now they're gone. Someone went to a lot of trouble to hose them down."

"Are you sure?"

"Of course. Look around. The rest of the alley should be quarantined, but the area near this dumpster is sparkling clean."

Sampley walked me back to the back steps of his diner. "I believe you," he said. "At least the part about the blood. John, though? I don't know, man."

"I get it," I said. "He's your partner. But listen. When I described Sonny, he changed. He knew who I was talking about."

"What are you suggesting?"

"You've met Sonny. He doesn't know what century it is, let alone what day. Chuey knows not to show up on Tuesday nights, because you're off. Sonny only knew that this was the place to come for food. Maybe, while Chuey was napping last Tuesday, Sonny got hungry. Decided to come here to eat. Maybe he got upset when there was no box behind the dumpster, and he banged on the back door here. Delacorte answered, and Sonny asked for his meal. You take it from there."

Sampley sat on the back steps and rubbed his chin.

"Yeah," he said quietly. "I could see it. John's a good man, in most ways, but he has some screwy ideas about how to make it in the world. A guy like Sonny? John might see him as disposable. And you're right. I've seen him in rages. They're brief, but scary."

"It only takes a minute."

"I don't know what to think," Sampley said. "It took me several years to pull myself out, build a new life. John gave me a shot at the dream. Without him, I wouldn't own half this diner. If you're right, I could lose all that."

"If I'm right, Sonny already lost everything," I said.

"You'd have to prove it. Show me evidence, and I'll back you all the way. Sonny would deserve it."

He pulled a hard pack of Marlboros from his pocket and lit up. He held the pack out to me. I waved it off.

"I have an idea," I said. "Use your phone?"

The next Tuesday night, Sampley's night off, I left my good clothes in a locker at the hostel and put on my ratty work stuff. I hadn't shaved since my meeting with Sampley. I looked scruffy as hell.

Twenty minutes later, I was back at the alley. I made a show of rummaging through the dumpsters, banging the lids down after sorting through the garbage, and swearing a lot. I wanted to be noticed.

As I expected, John Delacorte stepped into the alley from the back restaurant door. He carried a length of cast iron pipe.

"Hey! You!" he called out. "Beat it!"

I faced him. "You talking to me?"

"Yeah, you deadbeat. Take off."

"Free country, man. I'm just looking for something to eat," I said. I tried to make myself look small and weak, like an easy target.

"How about I give you a mouthful of this?" he said, slapping the pipe against his meaty paw.

I stared him down. "Like you did the guy last week?"

"What? Who are you?" Slowly, he recognized me. "Wait. I know you. You were the guy in the alley the other day. The one I called the cops on."

"Must be mistaking me for someone else. I'm just a hungry guy. I'm invisible, you know. We all are. Nobody sees us unless they're looking. I saw you, though. I saw what you did. You beat the stuffing out of that little guy, and you stashed him in the dumpster."

"Bullshit," he said. "There was nobody out here. You didn't see a thing."

"He was harmless. The gentlest man I ever met, and you bashed in his head like it was nothing. You killed him, and then you tossed him in the dumpster like a bag of kitchen trash. He only wanted to eat, but you murdered him."

I could see I was getting to him. He wasn't used to people standing up to him, especially homeless derelicts. I was backing him into a corner, which made him dangerous. I had been a New York cop, though. John Delacorte didn't know what real danger was. I was ready if he made any aggressive moves.

"Maybe I'll give you the same," he said. "Nobody would care, you know. People like you infest this city. You're a parasite, just like your buddy last week. Maybe I'll exterminate you, the same way I did him."

He glanced over his shoulder, to make sure nobody was watching, and he turned back to me and lifted the pipe. Two more steps, and he could bury it in my skull.

He never made it. Sean Bayless stepped into the alley from the back door of the restaurant and leveled his service automatic at Delacorte.

"Drop the pipe!" he ordered. "Now!"

Shocked and confused, Delacorte lowered the pipe, but didn't let go of it. As he was distracted, I stepped forward and brought my fist up into his chin in an uppercut that would have made Muhammed Ali proud. Delacorte dropped to the ground, out for the count. I pulled the pocket recorder Sean had given me from my shirt.

"You heard?" I said.

"Every word," Sean said. "Nice punch."

"Think I sprained my wrist," I said, rubbing my hand. "Out of practice."

"You did fine. Take a breather while I cuff this bastard."

Carroll Sampley appeared in the doorway. "I'm sorry I doubted you," he said.

Sean finished securing Delacorte and stepped back to radio for backup. "Thanks for calling me," he said. "Might get my gold shield off this one. You took a big chance, though."

I said, "The best things are worth it."

Sean's involvement got the attention of the Midtown Homicide Squad, in a way I never could have. The forensic team found traces of blood and skin in the threads of the pipe Delacorte had used on Sonny. Without Sonny, though, they couldn't make a match. Luckily, Sonny kept wads of chewed gum in his cigar box. Chuey reluctantly gave it up, and there was enough DNA to put Delacorte away for a long time.

Sweeps Week started five days after I tricked Delacorte into confessing. Chuey was picked up the first day and put on a bus. I have no idea where he landed, but I hope he's somewhere warm, and can pull his life back together without his buddy Sonny.

I avoided the sweep. I spent a few bucks on a nice, nearly new secondhand suit at the thrift store, and I passed the entire convention week hiding in plain sight, hanging out in the bars of the bigger hotels. I slept in the hostel at night, left each morning showered and shaved and looking like a million bucks, and stayed off the streets the rest of the time.

At night, I ate at Carroll Sampley's diner, except now I walked in the front door and he let me sit at a table, where he comped my meals. He kept his bargain, and then some.

A week after sweeps, I sat at the table, reading the newspaper, finishing a fine cup of coffee. Sampley took a break and sat next to me.

"Damned busy lately. Kinda shorthanded. Can you cook?" he asked.

"I can make the microwave go *beep*," I told him.

He sighed and looked out the front window.

"Can you learn?" he asked.

I thought it over. Took me about half a second.

"Yeah," I said. "I can learn."

And, just like that, I became visible again.

About the Author

Retired forensic psychologist and college professor Richard Helms is the author of twenty-three published novels. He has been nominated five times for the Killer Nashville Silver Falchion Award, with one win; eight times for the SMFS Derringer Award, with two wins; eight times for the PWA Shamus Award, winning it in 2021 and 2022; twice for the ITW Thriller Award, with one win in 2011; and twice for the MRI Macavity Award with a win in 2022. He is the former president of the Southeast Chapter of Mystery Writers of America and was the 2017 recipient of that chapter's Magnolia Award for Distinguished Service. He is a past member of the Board of Directors for Mystery Writers of America, in addition to being a member of Private Eye Writers of America, International Thriller Writers, and Sisters in Crime.

His twenty-second novel, ***A Kind and Savage Place***, was published in 2022 by Level Best Books.

Richard Helms and his wife Elaine live in Charlotte, North Carolina

About the Author

www.ingramcontent.com/pod-product-compliance
Lightning Source LLC
Chambersburg PA
CBHW031106030726
47496CB00002BA/401
9780971015999